AT THE OCEAN'S EDGE

HEATHER DIXON

Storm

ALSO BY HEATHER DIXON

Summerville Series

Last Summer at the Lake House

The Summerville Sisters

Burlington

For Andrew.
You're the reason I can write about love so honestly.

ONE

I have an affliction. Although I'm self-aware enough to know that it's my own fault—a self-inflicted affliction. I fall in love way too easily.

Whenever I meet someone new and they check all the boxes for what I consider attractive, I almost instantly develop a deep crush. This can be a problem when you're not a hormonal teenager but are, in fact, a thirty-five-year-old journalist who is supposed to concern herself only with the facts. Still, I allow myself to daydream, turning them into whoever I want them to be in my mind. I let myself feel like I'm back in high school, like it's that perfect but brief moment in your life when your hormones rule everything and your insides churn and your body buzzes whenever you see or speak to the object of your affection. When it's all buildup and not much action. Any time I want that perfect moment in time again—the passion, the tension in the air—I close my eyes and let myself live it, soak in it, feel it vibrate throughout my body because it's fun and exciting. It beats real life any day.

Then I write it all down in my journal, and my new crush

becomes as perfect as I want him to be in my made-up world. In real life, love is messy and complicated, and it often doesn't end well. In my writing, the romance is everything; the guys are heroes, and no hearts get broken. These stories are for my eyes only. I would die if anyone knew I wrote them.

"Do you really think our readers want to read this?" Celine's voice snapped me back to attention.

I was sitting across from my boss in one of the hard-cushioned beige chairs she had decorated her glass-walled office with. It was an oddly boring chair choice, considering Celine usually had impeccable taste. She always looked put together, with well-tailored and perfectly fitting clothes draped across her tall body. Her sleek, pin-straight dark hair was cut and styled well. I had never seen her without a red lip. She stood out at the newspaper's office. Everyone else here wore business casual, or just plain old casual. Today, Celine's sharp collarbones showed through the opening of her crisp white button-down blouse.

"Sorry, read what?"

Celine sighed. She sighed often when she spoke, as if the world around her in general was exhausting.

"This overly flowery article I'm reading right now." She pointed at the screen of her laptop. I watched her for a beat since I knew this was a rhetorical question. "We've talked about this."

"Flowery? Are you sure?" I felt like I had cut back on the over-romanticizing language this time.

"It's a roundup of things to do in the city over the weekend." She paused and then frowned, her lips thinning out. "It doesn't need all these extra descriptive words. Come on, you're better than this. It'll need another edit."

I nodded and shifted in my seat, clasping my hands together. "No problem, I'll get right on it."

"Good. Thanks. Anyway, that's not why I called you in here."

I should have known something else was up. Celine rarely gave feedback on my articles in person so I knew there must have been another reason for her asking me to come in for a quick meeting. I didn't go into the office that much. Not since 2020, when the world had shut down and management realized that most jobs could be done remotely. This was especially true for writers; people like me wanted to stay home, faces free of makeup and pyjama pants on. I lived alone and enjoyed it. I didn't miss going into an office and spending forty-five minutes each morning talking about the weather or listening to stories about Elise's fridge breaking down in the middle of a dinner party, or hearing about the drama among the parents at Ahmad's daughter's soccer game. Actually, the parent drama was pretty interesting, and I got along well with Elise and Ahmad when our paths crossed. I liked all my coworkers. But I also loved being alone. I had a routine going that worked best solo. Each morning, I got up and had a cup of coffee in my favorite giant mug—the one with a huge M painted on it—while writing in my journal. Afterwards, I went for a run, followed by a very long, very hot shower while mentally making the tough decision to put on either a pair of pyjama pants or a pair of leggings. Then I would throw on one of my largest hoodies and sit at my computer with wet hair and no makeup to start work. I loved it.

Today, I was in a pair of dark jeans that cut into my waist, though I couldn't deny they looked nice.

"There's a story idea that just came up," Celine said.

"Oh?" I sat up straighter. "For which section?"

Celine glanced at the screen of her chrome laptop. "Lifestyle."

My back straightened. I loved that section. It was so personal. So intimate. When you wrote for Lifestyle, you could get away with flowery. Most of the time, I was reporting on city hall meeting stories or tips on gardening. It paid the bills, and I was grateful for that. My true love, however, was writing with feeling. My mother called it my "flair". I didn't have much of it in person, but give me a blank page and I could be beautiful.

"It's a feature. A 'day in the life' piece, but more. On Cullen Walsh." Celine settled back into her chair, gripping a pen.

I drew a blank. By the look on Celine's face—her round eyes, the hint of a smile, like she was doing me a huge favor by giving me this piece of information—I could see I should know who he was. I didn't.

This was typical of me. I was generally the last to know anything. I rarely had my finger on the pulse of what was happening, which could be a problem when working for a newspaper—but I didn't worry all that much. I had Sarina to keep me up to date. Sarina and I had been friends since college, and as close as you could get since then. Even though she led a busy life with a five-year-old now, she always managed to send me daily texts to keep me dialed in to what was happening in the world, the latest celebrity gossip, or her life in general. She always took the time to ask me about my life, too. She was as precious to me as water during a drought.

A long pause settled between me and Celine. I needed a moment to think about how to respond. I wanted a chance to flex my creative muscles, and this sounded like a good opportunity to do that. I didn't want her to think I couldn't manage it. On the wall just behind her hung a shiny framed print of her most famous story: the Marshall bus tragedy. My stomach still soured at the thought of it. All those young lives lost at once. It had been so awful, but Celine had treated it with such care and sensitivity. Her story hadn't just stated the facts—those had been covered multiple times by many outlets. No, her account had been so well-written, so detailed and descriptive and human. It was the type of beautiful writing I hoped to be able to achieve one day.

"Meg?" Celine's voice snapped me back to the office. She looked at me expectantly. "The feature. It's a piece on Cullen Walsh's book, of course, but it's more than that. We'd like to know what he's doing, why he ended up in that town, what's next for him."

"His book?" I felt frazzled by my lack of knowledge. Celine must have noticed.

"*The Ninth Village*," she said, a touch of impatience in her tone. "It's everywhere. Tell me you've seen it."

The title flashed through my mind in big, black letters with a gold background—the cover of the book. I had seen it. Everyone had. *That* Cullen? He was huge. Well, as huge as authors can be.

"Right. I know it. But I haven't had a chance to read it yet." I shifted in my seat. "What's the story? Why him?"

"He grew up in Boston. He's a hometown success. You know how readers eat it up whenever there's a story about someone famous who grew up where they live."

I nodded. That was true. A story like that was an easy way to get our paper a bunch of clicks and a lot of readers. I had a gut instinct about which stories would resonate with our audience. It was one of the reasons I was good at my job, despite the flowery prose Celine was trying to beat out of me. A while ago, I'd written some provocative essay-style pieces and a couple had ended up going semi-viral, leading to a lot of attention for the paper. Maybe this was why Celine was giving me the first crack at Lifestyle now.

Celine took a sip of her coffee and placed the tall paper cup in front of her. I tried not to stare at the red-lined imprint her lips had made on it.

"About three months ago Cullen sold his home and moved away to a small town nobody's heard of—he's made it known he's not coming back. We'd like to know why. We want someone to go there and interview him. Follow him around for a couple of days. Get to know him and the town, you know—get to the meat of it. There's got to be some kind of story there."

My head jutted forward an inch, waiting for the rest of Celine's thoughts. She said nothing. My mind was running. Yes, the story could be interesting, and yes, a hometown success was always fun to write, but it wasn't often that I was sent to another town to interview someone for the paper. Something seemed off.

"What?" Celine leaned back in her chair.

I shook my head. "Nothing. I'm sure you're right—there's got to be a story in there."

"It probably has something to do with his family," Celine said. "Or maybe it's something romantic—maybe he went there for the love of his life. I know you're into romance. You'd be able to write it well."

I had to agree with her on that one. It was in my genes. I was born into a family that loved love. Or, it had until my father unceremoniously left my mother when I was fourteen years old. Despite that, ever since I had learned what romance was, I'd been hooked. When I was a kid, my mother used to take me to the movies to see romantic comedies every Friday night—our favorite genre. We would sit in the dark, sharing a bag of popcorn that made our fingers slick with butter, and she would laugh at parts I didn't quite understand. At the end, there was always love. Always a happily ever after. We knew what to expect before the movie had even started, but that was why we went. It was the promise of the premise—the love in the end. My mother would walk out of the theatre and reach for my hand with a half smile still settled on her face and a distant look in her eyes. I adored being with her—just the two of us—especially when she seemed so happy.

My father was a big fan of the theatre, so he took me to shows like *Phantom of the Opera* and *Crazy For You*. When the lights dimmed, I would be on the edge of my seat, caught up in the music and the costumes and the storytelling. It was all so magical, and I simmered and soaked in the experience.

I looked for it in books, too. Love. Tension. Those moments when you hadn't yet put anything into words or acted on your desires. In some ways, it was the perfect moment in time, when the object of your affection could be anyone you wanted them to be. When you could make whatever you wanted to happen in your mind, and there were no consequences because it wasn't real.

That was where I resided for most of my youth. Once hormones kicked in and I started to notice boys, I liked to imagine scenarios with them, like where the meet cute between us would be, and how it would happen. I liked to picture all of it like a movie: the buildup and the attraction. What it would be like to hold a particular boy's hand, or kiss. But I never, ever wanted to act on it. I never wanted to make it real.

That was how I got into writing. It was the way I expressed myself, and it was only for me. It was easier than trying to make it happen in real life. Reality was a letdown. It always had been.

"Can you go tomorrow?" Celine's voice brought me back to the interior of the office. The sun brightened the surface of her desk. Everything was neatly ordered—a jar of pens at the right corner next to a stapler; across from it, an appointment book with several notes written inside, and a to-do list, half-checked off.

"I think so," I said. "Where to?"

Celine flipped through some papers in front of her, searching. "Where was it again? Old Town? Old Place?"

I stiffened in my seat.

"Old—something," Celine continued.

My mouth went dry. I licked my lips. I had a feeling I knew what she was trying to say.

"Old Port?"

"Yes! That's it. Do you know it?"

It took everything I had within me to nod. "I know it."

Celine looked at me as if I were going to continue speaking. I didn't. There wasn't much I was willing to say. Old Port was somewhere I knew well—where I had history. And it was one of the last places I wanted to go.

TWO

Living in Boston came with benefits, and one of the best was my cozy little rectangle of a house. My place was a one-bedroom Victorian brownstone townhome that had been in my family for years. Even though it was tiny, it was in a great location, and I was extremely lucky to have it. My father had decided it needed to be fully renovated just before I took it over and he had splurged on sleek granite countertops and stainless steel appliances. I think he was still attempting to buy my love all these years after leaving my mother. Either way, I adored the way the pale grey walls gave it a crisp and clean feel, while the oversized soft couch and plush chair I'd picked out, along with the scratched-up wooden table and wall of books, made it feel lived-in and warm. It was homey and perfect, situated in a charming neighborhood. It was no wonder I rarely wanted to leave.

That night, I went straight home after work. Elise and Ahmad and a few of my other coworkers liked to stop at a bar close by to grab a quick drink and some snacks on Fridays, especially in the summer, but I preferred to take the twenty-minute walk to my house alone to unwind.

My mother would have liked it if I socialized more often.

She wanted me to get "out there" and meet someone, but I had already tried that. More than once. My past relationships had never worked out well. The men I had dated were nice enough, but something would always cause it to end. Some issue would crop up, and we wouldn't be able to overcome it and they would leave. That was exactly what had happened with Daniel, my most recent ex. We'd met at an industry event called the Digital Publishing Awards only a year ago. He was a photographer for a nature magazine, and he'd stood out to me at first because of his height. He was remarkably tall, with broad shoulders and thick, muscled arms. I was putty whenever he wore a T-shirt. I fell head over heels in the way that I do, and for a while everything was great.

We would spend weeknights together in the city, dining out at intimate restaurants, or getting drinks at some charming bistro. On weekends, we'd spend mornings at a café over coffee and chocolate croissants before heading out to run an errand or two. I liked our days to be quiet and slow, and loved downtime with him, when we had the chance to talk for hours, walking hand in hand through a park. But to my heartache, the togetherness seemed to make him stir crazy. Daniel grew restless. He always wanted to go out with friends, and made constant plans, running from event to event every night. One day he told me we were just too different, we didn't have the same wants and needs. He needed to be with friends and to be busy to "feel alive." I just wanted him. And that was it. He left shortly after and I hadn't talked to him since.

Yet, somehow, I was still in love with love. I still desired romance, and I was still searching for that feeling. I just wasn't willing to have my heart broken again and again anymore to get it.

I couldn't blame my mother for being concerned about me. When you were in your mid-thirties and single, and most of your friends had coupled off and had kids, that was what everyone wanted for you as well. Sarina was an extrovert and always up for nights out with me, but she also had a busy life with her daughter, Chloe. She had her limits on how many Fridays she could ask her partner to stay home with the little one, and I had my limits on how much peopling I could do.

As soon as I walked through the door to my home, I flicked my lights on and dimmed them the way I always did. The warm glow gave the entire room a more romantic, cozy feel. It was how I wanted to view everything in life: slightly darkened, hidden from harsh realities. I went straight to my pale blue bedroom to take off those awful, tight jeans and pull on my most comfortable joggers. Once I had my bra off and my hair up in a loose ponytail, I went to the living room with my laptop and phone in one hand and notebooks in the other. I ordered pizza for dinner, opened a bottle of wine, and sat cross-legged on the couch, ready to settle in for the evening and google the hell out of Cullen Walsh.

The first thing that popped up was an image of his book, *The Ninth Village*, followed by a headshot of him.

The base of my neck tingled. Authors could look like *that*? For one thing, he was young. On the younger side, at least. I guess I'd half expected to see a balding man, or an unkempt-looking person with glasses and grey in his beard. Instead, looking back at me from the screen was someone with thick, shining, sandy-brown hair, swept to one side, a pair of black frames over deep brown eyes, and a half smile, sort of turned up at one side, revealing perfect teeth. He looked like he'd be a hot doctor on a Netflix series.

I clicked over to my local library's website and found *The Ninth Village* available as an e-book loan. When I opened it, I scrolled through the first few pages and stopped on the dedication.

For Jen. Forever. I wish I'd told you I loved you more.

My heart whirled inside my chest for a moment, as if I could somehow understand the love and pain radiating from those words.

I continued to flip until I got to the opening page of the story. Fantasy had never been my favorite genre, but I was instantly drawn in by his first paragraph. His word choice and descriptions were so thoughtful, so precise, it only took a few sentences for me to already know he was an excellent writer. A familiar sensation washed over me—the kind that came whenever I read really good writing. It was a small whiff of jealousy mixed with admiration. I wished I could write that way.

I read and then researched for a while longer, jotting down some key notes about him. He already had a Wikipedia page. Impressive. I learned that this wasn't his first book. Cullen Walsh had written a quiet literary novel several years ago that hadn't seemed to garner much attention. I also learned that he'd been born and raised in Boston—no mention of his move to Old Port, however. Even though I hated myself a bit for it, I did a search to see if he was married. Deep down, there was a tiny part of me that hoped he wouldn't be. It was much easier for me to make up stories for myself about men if they weren't.

I couldn't find much of anything personal about him. Instead, my eye caught a staggering number on the screen in front of me. According to the internet, *The Ninth Village* had sold almost two million copies since it was published. What on earth was he doing in Old Port instead of some flashy house in the expensive part of a big city? I made a note to ask him that when I met him.

I jotted down some more notes and then closed my notebook and my laptop. My plan was to go to Old Port fully prepared with questions written, so I could do a good interview, follow him around a little, and then hopefully get out as fast as I had arrived. It must have been at least five years since I was last there. I thought, very briefly, about calling my mother to tell her

I was going to be in town, but decided against it. She would want me to stay—would never forgive me if I left without visiting. This would be quick, and I could whip a story up from back home later. I could always call him afterwards if I had any further questions.

Celine must have noticed my body language earlier. She'd raised an eyebrow when I'd stiffened at the mention of Old Port.

"Something wrong?" she had asked.

I'd shaken my head. As much as I didn't want to go back to Old Port, I knew there was no way I could turn this story down. I had been asking Celine for more in-depth stories for ages. This was an opportunity to get out of weekend roundups and into more creative writing. So I'd told her it sounded great, that I'd keep track of my mileage and receipts for food and hotel—although there weren't any hotels in Old Port; I'd have to go with something like the Waterfront Suites, which sounded much fancier than it was—and agreed to one night, two days. The chances of finding available rooms for a longer stay in July, the height of tourist season, were slim. Celine thought one night made sense, too. It was easier on the budget. Not to mention, I had booked my summer vacation to start next week. I had no concrete plans, but still. It was my time to be at home and not working. I had decided I'd take an extra-long break—two weeks —so I could completely unwind. I wanted to do things like clean my place from top to bottom, go for long runs, binge my favorite romance movies, visit Sarina. I wanted to disconnect from work and feel like I had truly gotten a break.

Celine had mentioned I could have a few days in lieu if I did the interview over the weekend. Sounded good to me. I had no desire to spend time in Old Port out of the goodness of my heart.

THREE

The next morning, after my coffee and a run, I had a long shower, brushed my teeth and pulled on a pair of loose shorts and a T-shirt. I let my hair air dry, didn't bother with much makeup and put a couple of changes of clothes into a backpack, along with my laptop and notebook. At the last second, I threw my journal into my bag. This was going to be a quick trip, and I wouldn't have time for my daydreams or writing them out, but I brought it anyway, just in case something inspired me. Lately my well of inspiration had dried up. Maybe I did need to get out more.

Once I left my house and was inside my car, my body slumped into my seat as I breathed out. I could do this. I could. Keys in ignition. Pull out of driveway. Drive to Old Port. My chest ached at the thought. The town was nice enough, but I hadn't been back for years.

I didn't bother looking up directions; I didn't need them. I knew how to navigate my way along the highways that would eventually get me to Old Port. And once there, I could find my way around town easily. Most of that place was etched into my memory, as much as I wanted to pretend it wasn't.

If I closed my eyes, I could see the winding road that took you into the main part of town, lined with shops designed for summer tourists. I could picture the calm of the ocean in the morning and imagine the feel of its stark, refreshing cold on my bare skin. I could hear the sharp cry of seagulls, and I could almost smell the bakery—the sweet, yeasty scent of bread they baked daily, or the slightly melted chocolate in their warm cookies. I could identify where the only Italian restaurant was, where to get the best coffee.

I could do all of this because Old Port had once been so familiar to me. But it wasn't any longer.

I arrived at the winding road just before eleven in the morning. My body tensed, as if it thought I needed to brace for impact. I didn't. Of course I didn't. This would be fine. Celine had already arranged a time with Cullen's agent for the interview, so all I had to do was get to the Peach Coffee shop within a few minutes and be the professional that I was.

Ahead of me, right in the middle of the very small town, was the abandoned church, nestled into the bend of the road. Next to it was the town's smaller grocery store. There were only two —one at this end of town and one on the main street. Up ahead, I could see the turn that would take me there. It was weird being back here, in a place I had avoided for so long. I would have thought it might look somewhat different, or feel different, but nothing about it had changed.

I drove past the town's only upscale clothing store, which was busy, despite how expensive the place was, and pulled my car into the back lot of Peach Coffee.

Out front, pots of flowers in bright reds, yellows and purples lined the doorway. Inside, everything looked the same as I remembered. Chalkboard signs with big, loopy handwriting hung on the white walls. Behind the counter, there was only just enough room for a massive, stainless steel coffee and espresso machine that hissed and whirred aggressively. Two large criss-crossed oars were proudly displayed on the wall, as if they were priceless pieces in the Louvre.

I ordered a drip coffee instead of anything special and made my way out the side door to the large patio. Peach Coffee was known for its incredible patio. Big, colorful umbrellas at every table, an exterior wall painted in teal and covered with designs by local artists. It was all so cheery. Now if I could only mask my lack of desire to be here.

I scanned the tables and stopped when I saw someone in the far corner. He had the same sand-colored hair, the same dark-rimmed glasses and defined jaw as in the headshot. It was Cullen Walsh—and he looked even better in person. Heat flashed up my neck and into my cheeks. He was alarmingly handsome. I should have chosen something other than my baggy running shorts and oversized Blondie T-shirt to wear today. Ever since I'd started working from home most of the time, I had taken casual to the next level and now it was creeping into my everyday life.

I walked tall and hoped I looked professional enough as I made my way over to the table and stood over him. He was also dressed casual, thank goodness—a faded grey T-shirt and jeans —but on him it looked trendy. "Cullen Walsh?"

He glanced up, his mouth turned down and the space between his eyebrows creased. "Yes?"

"Hi. I'm Meg Adamson. From the *Globe*."

His face didn't register any understanding at first. A mild panic washed over me. Despite being a journalist, I really didn't enjoy interviewing people. I had never gotten over the shyness I felt as a kid. I took a deep breath. "My editor and your agent set up an interview for us?" I said it like there was some question to it, although I knew Celine would never drop the ball on some-thing like this. She was too professional.

Finally, thankfully, his face changed. His features softened, although he didn't quite smile. I knew from the research I had done that he was a couple of years younger than me, although there was a seriousness about him that made him seem older.

"Oh, hello." He motioned at the chair across from him. "Do you want to sit?"

I did. Suddenly, I very much did want to sit and be here, even though it was Old Port. I removed my crossbody bag over my head and took a seat. I pulled out my notebook and clicked on the recorder app on my phone.

"Nice to meet you. Thanks for taking the time to talk with me. Would you mind if I recorded this?" I asked. "It helps me with my notes later on when I'm writing up the story."

"Sure. Works for me." His voice was bright now. Whatever had preoccupied him right before I showed up was clearly relegated to the back of his mind. He smiled at me—a small smile, but still brilliant. It was one of those smiles that made you feel like there was nowhere he'd rather be but right here, right now, in this very moment. I imagined touching his mouth so I could feel the smoothness of his lips, but then looked down at my notebook, confused by my spontaneous reaction. I didn't even know him.

I chose to start with something easy. People love talking about themselves, but my research had given me the sense that Cullen might be a bit of a tough interviewee. Mentions of his book were everywhere, but he wasn't all over social media, despite his success. "How long have you been in town?" I asked. "You've moved here recently? With your family?"

"Yeah. It's been a few months now, I guess. But no family. It's just me."

I nodded and jotted it down, ignoring the flash of heat in my face. "How are you settling in?" Best to ease into the tougher questions.

"Good, thanks. I like it here. Have you been here before?" His voice was warm, inviting. Already he was very different to the recluse I'd been expecting. And he didn't necessarily seem heartbroken despite what Celine had suggested.

I frowned. "Yeah, a while ago."

His eyebrow lifted, like he was surprised anyone would know this place. Out of all the places in the world you could visit, why come here?

"They've got the best coffee I've ever had," Cullen said. "And the swimming is great."

"Right. You're a big swimmer then?"

"Oh. No, not really. Well, not until recently. I guess I just like the salt water."

"Ah. I'm more of a pool girl." This was going just great. My face flamed at how stilted I sounded. The thing about pools wasn't even true; I didn't know why I'd said it. Maybe it was the surroundings, or maybe it was how alarmingly good-looking Cullen was, but I was off my game. Celine would kill me if she could hear this recording.

He pulled his head back an inch, straightening his body in his seat, like he was confused by my questioning. "Is that going in the article?"

"No, sorry. I've got my notes here." I pulled out my notebook, opening it to flip through the pages and scan my scribbled handwriting. I looked back up again. His tanned and muscled arms were crossed over his chest. A wisp of something circled through my stomach.

"I mean, there will be some detail in the article. I won't know until I write it," I said.

An almost imperceptible frown crossed his face and then disappeared again. He looked to his right, out onto the street. I stilled in my seat. I couldn't be losing him already, could I? I had interviewed enough people to know when it wasn't going well, when it would be a slog to get enough detail to actually write a decent piece. I pushed my shoulders back. I needed to focus.

"This will be for Lifestyle," I said. "It's a human interest piece. People love stories like yours—home-grown success. You sort of came out of nowhere before your success with this book, didn't you? A bit of an underdog story, I'm guessing. Readers will love to get an intimate look at your life now, post-book success, and how you got here." I pushed my hand down on the open pages of my notebook to flatten them out.

He turned back and studied me, like he was deeply interested in everything I said. I squirmed in my seat. I wasn't used to handsome men staring at me like this. Not so much in real life, anyway.

He nudged his glasses up on his nose and let out a small laugh. "I don't know about that."

"About what?" I asked. "Your success?"

He shrugged. "I'm not really comfortable with intimate details. I thought this was going to be about the book."

"It's about both."

He nodded, still watching me with interest, toned arms crossed over his chest.

"Your book has been everywhere—you must have people recognizing you?" I continued. Did that happen for authors? Now that I thought of it, there were dozens of famous authors I'd heard of, but I couldn't tell you what most of them looked like. How great that would be, to have success and fortune, but nobody recognizing you? You could have your privacy and anonymity, but money to live the life you wanted.

"No, not so much," he answered. "But that's okay with me."

I jotted down a note. "It would be for me, too."

He smiled appreciatively, uncrossed his arms. Cullen appeared to be the friendly type, but he played his cards close to his chest. I wasn't sure what story Celine thought there was here. I suspected she wasn't going to be happy without a bit of a hook, though. I needed much more from him.

I opened my mouth to speak again, but a buzzing sound

interrupted me. Cullen pulled his phone from his pocket and glanced at the screen. His jaw tightened.

"Excuse me a minute." He stood and moved away from the table to a corner of the patio.

I nodded at him as he left, feeling a touch deflated. So far, he was a handsome, fairly friendly person who liked oceans and coffee and was uncomfortable with success. Sweet, but I wasn't going to win the Pulitzer with that much.

He came back to the table and stood by his seat. "I'm sorry, but I have to run."

"Oh." I frowned. "Uh, we only just started the interview."

"Can we try again tomorrow? You have my number? I think I have yours somewhere. Sorry."

Before I could answer, he left in a flurry, and I sat alone, kicking myself for not getting off to a better start.

FOUR

After stewing for a while at the interview having been cut short, I finished my coffee and went to the Waterfront Suites to check in. Before I had a chance to go inside, I was stopped by the buzz of my phone. I very fleetingly thought it might be Cullen calling to say he had time for me after all, and the feeling of hope that brewed within me confused me. I'd only just met him.

It wasn't Cullen, but the name on the screen made me smile, nevertheless.

> Where are you? I miss your face

Sarina's texts were often direct like this.
I replied:

> In Old Port

She sent back a series of surprised face emojis and a gif of an interesting-looking man mouthing WTF? I answered with a gif from one of our favorite shows. It was how we communicated after many years of friendship. A familiar language of funny pictures and short, staccato sentences.

> Here for a story

I typed.

> Hope to get out soon. Call you later?

Sarina answered back:

> Yes please. Need details

> Miss you

I sent her a heart emoji and put my phone into my back pocket. We were light-hearted and silly with each other most of the time, but I always ended my chats with her with a heart.

Once I checked in, I planned to set up my laptop, make a few notes to prepare for tomorrow, and convince myself not to dwell on how irritating it was that I'd walked away with no story today. Instead, I would do my best to get settled for the evening. Although getting settled while in Old Port wasn't likely. There was a reason I didn't come here often. It made sense to me, but it wouldn't to most. When you looked around and saw the quaint town right on the ocean, bustling with people in a landscape that vibrated with natural beauty, it was hard to understand how someone couldn't be happy in this place. The salt air. The gentle crashing of waves on the shore. The way the warm summer wind tickled the tiny hairs on your bare arms at night. And the sunsets—every night the sky melted into a sea of corals and pale yellows. There was nothing more beautiful. It should have been everything I could ever want. Instead, it was complicated.

At the check-in desk, an elderly woman wearing a peach-colored T-shirt and dangling macaroni necklaces welcomed me. She caught me eyeing her jewelry.

"Lovely, aren't they?" She spoke loudly and smiled, as if we were in on something together. When I stared back, she tilted her head to one side, a quick, jerky gesture.

A little girl sat behind the desk, set up at her own mini desk with pencil crayons, construction paper, stickers and glue. There were bits of macaroni scattered across her work area. Her head was bent, her hair a curtain across one side of her face.

I caught on. "Oh, those necklaces are gorgeous!" I grinned. "Where did you get them? I would love to have one of my own."

"These are originals. Sorry, not available for sale." The woman glanced over her shoulder and then smiled back at me. "I know the artist though."

At this, the little girl's head snapped up. "Grandma, are you talking about me?"

The woman in peach laughed. "I certainly am. This nice woman likes your necklaces."

The girl approached the desk and looked up at me shyly. She had a smattering of light freckles on her nose, and she grinned with only a hint of the top row of her teeth showing. "Thank you," she said, putting her hands behind her back. "I made them myself."

"You did? They're beautiful. Great work." I smiled at her. "I'm Meg."

"Hi. I'm Emily. This is my grandma. She's watching me today so my mommy can nap."

The elderly woman laughed again, a deep belly laugh. "That's right, Emily. Mommies can use a break every now and again." She turned back to me. "We all can, can't we?"

I nodded, a warmth dropping over me. This woman was happiness and comfort. I liked her immediately.

"I'm Gwen. Nice to meet you. Anyway, are you here to check in? Let me get you sorted."

After Gwen handed me the keys, and after I had said a proper goodbye to Emily, I let myself into my room. The inside was basic but clean, and convenient enough for the night. The beds were draped with outdated floral comforters, and on the wall hung prints of the town from at least fifty years ago. It certainly wasn't anything upscale, but it felt cared-for. Comfortable. I had one of the upper-level suites with a balcony and a view of the ocean, so I put my things down on the bed and went to the sliding door that opened to the balcony.

Outside, the sky was a sharp contrast to the dark of the water, lit up by dusk's unceasing yellows and pinks. I took a seat and watched boats navigate through the gently rocking water, clouds floating across the sky. I could almost be inspired here, in this moment.

I pulled out my notebook and opened it to a blank page. It made sense to jot down a few notes about Cullen while it was still fresh in my mind—what he looked like, my first impressions. There wasn't much, though. I flipped back through the pages before my notes, but didn't find my other research. I had picked up my journal by mistake instead.

The page I had left off on was a story I'd made up about Adam, a man I kept seeing at the coffee shop back home. We showed up to get coffees at the same time every Monday and Friday morning and the barista would call out the flat white for Adam right before my regular drip. He had an affable smile and a handsome face, and I was convinced it was a sign that we kept appearing at the same time on the same two days. It was our meet cute, like in romantic comedies; I was meant to run into him this way. So, the stories began. I imagined what Adam's life was like, where he worked, what kinds of things he did on weekends. It turned into how we would eventually start talking, the way he would suggest we meet up on a weekend afternoon. He had been my most recent muse and at the time I'd seemed to be able to write endlessly about the possibility of him.

And then, one day back in real life, Adam had shown up late. He rushed into the coffee shop, struggling with his bag and barked out his order impatiently. The barista actually flinched. She must have been as surprised as I was to hear him so short and biting, a change from how he usually was. When he got his coffee, he stormed out of the place without thanking anyone.

That was the end for me.

It was hard to imagine romance with someone who yelled at baristas.

Now, sitting back outside on the balcony of my waterfront room, I toyed with the idea of creating a new story. But I was hungry, and my stomach wouldn't let me ignore it for much longer. I closed my journal and tucked it away.

A walk down the main street took me to one of the very few takeout food options in town. I scanned the building names until I saw the familiar fish and chip spot. It used to be my favorite place to get takeout in Old Port. I hadn't been here in so long. I was good at avoiding things and places that made me uncomfortable.

For some reason, it hadn't occurred to me that just about anybody could be here, walking around the streets. I wasn't expecting to hear someone calling my name with a hint of confusion.

"Meg?"

I stopped, arm halfway to grabbing hold of the door handle to the restaurant.

"Meg!" The voice was laced with annoyance now. It was a voice I knew very well.

I turned towards it and attempted to smile.

"Hi, Mom."

FIVE

"What on earth are you doing here and why didn't you tell me you were in town?" My mother's body language gave her away. She had a terrible poker face. In this case, her crossed arms and her narrowed eyes said everything.

"I'm sorry, Mom." I walked towards her and she reluctantly lifted her arms for a hug.

"Come here," she murmured into my hair. "You smell nice. What shampoo is that? Never mind—I'm still mad at you."

"I said I was sorry." I pulled back from her and rested my hands on her forearms. I was sorry. I didn't want to hurt her. She wasn't the reason I had a hard time coming back here. She was only part of it.

"What's going on?" she asked. "You haven't been here in years and now here you are getting takeout? Aren't you on vacation? Did you drive all this way for fish and chips? They're good, but not *that* good."

"I'm working on one more story before my vacation. It's a feature on an author who lives here. It was a last-minute thing."

My mother's forehead creased. "There's an author living here who's famous enough to have a story written about them?"

I nodded.

"And you agreed to write it? To come here?"

Now would be a good time to give her the entire story. Otherwise, I suspected the questions wouldn't stop.

"I couldn't pass up the opportunity. And I'm only staying for one night. At the Waterfront Suites."

Her mouth was a tight line. It was her angry look. Only, as much as she tried to hide it, I saw a flash of hurt cross her expression, too. Mostly in her eyes. I could always read so much in her eyes. I completely understood why she'd be upset, and I felt terrible for causing it.

My mother's face was beautiful, even when angry. She had wide, pale blue eyes, skin softened by time. It was free of makeup; she hadn't worn any for as long as I could remember, and it suited her. She was relaxed and comfortable in her body. She was the type of mother who texted almost daily, who asked about every detail of my life and really wanted to hear it all. She had never missed a single dance performance or soccer game when I was a kid. For some reason that I could no longer fathom, I'd had moments of hating her when I was a teenager, and then in my twenties I'd known I needed her more than even Sarina, and she'd been there. Maybe I should have tried harder to get over my aversion to this place and visited her more often, but she knew it was hard for me, coming back here. We made it work by having her come to see me in Boston instead. I couldn't have known I would run into her now, but I should have been more careful with her feelings. Of course it would hurt her to have me show up in town having not said a word. My throat thickened at what I had done.

"You don't come here for me, but you'll come for a story?"

"I'm sorry. I should have told you I was coming and staying overnight, but I really just wanted to get in, get the interview, and leave. It's not personal, it's work. Honest."

Mom's shoulders were high and tight around her neck and

her arms were back to being crossed over her body. This would take some work.

"I'm really sorry. I am." I took a step closer to her. "How are you doing? What's going on?"

She was silent for a moment, watching me, as if thinking about whether or not to answer. "I'm okay. Do you have time to chat? Maybe grab some dinner?"

I didn't have this in the plan. It would be much easier to get my food, go back to my room and type up a few notes before flicking through some trash on the television and then going to bed early. But I was here, in front of my mother, with her familiar bob of grey hair, gentle creases around her questioning eyes. She didn't deserve this treatment from me.

"Sure."

Her face lit up. It moved me to think that I might be the reason someone else's face could literally light up, and only because I said I had time to spend with them.

We went to the only Italian restaurant in the area, a place called Piatto that was an old favorite of both of ours. The intoxicating scent of garlic and fresh basil lassoed me as soon as we walked inside. This was a place where they brought you soft, doughy bread in a basket and giant meatballs in your spaghetti. A place that was always loud, but never annoyingly so, where it was warm, but not stuffy. Aside from the fish and chips, it was the only good thing about Old Port.

After taking our seats and ordering a pizza and a bottle of wine to share, Mom focused her gaze on me in that way mothers can do. It was her "I'm not going to stop looking at you until you tell me what's going on with you" stare. Finally, I broke and answered her unasked question.

"What? I'm good. Nothing's new with me." I reached forward to pour myself some water.

"It's not like you to come back home," Mom said. "I'm surprised. And I won't lie, it hurts you didn't tell me. Were you planning on telling me?"

Home. That wasn't what Old Port was. It was for my mother, but it hadn't been for me. My parents and I had spent every summer here when I was growing up, in a beach house a few steps away from the ocean. I had loved so much about it: the way the early morning air was crisp and salty, how the sand felt rough on my bare feet, the quaint cottage-like homes with black roofs and bright doors dotting the shore. My mother had moved here full-time for her retirement, so I suppose it should have felt like home in some ways. But it also brought back memories of a time I didn't like to relive. It was a time when I didn't feel right in my skin, when I wasn't certain about anything—in my early teen years, school was tough, my friendships were hard to navigate, my body was changing so much. I felt alone most of the time. And then my parents' marriage had imploded. It was here that I'd found out my dad had cheated, and here that my parents had told me they were separating. My mom seemed to have gotten over it, enough to make a life for herself here. But I couldn't. It was frozen in time for me—forever reminding me of that moment in my life, when my faith in love first got fractured.

I took a deep breath. "I honestly was going to whisk in and out, and that was it. It was meant to be quick. My vacation starts next week and I have a lot to get done around the house."

Mom frowned but didn't say anything. Instead, she reached for a piece of bread and buttered it.

"So you ended up deciding not to go anywhere?"

I shook my head. "I have plans for a staycation." She and I had talked about this. I loved my weeks off at home because it gave me time to do a thorough clean, run errands I'd been meaning to run for weeks, and spend an inordinate amount of time on my couch with a good book. My coworkers often came back from vacation talking about how tired they were, how busy their vacation had been, or how they needed another week off to recover from their week off. I never understood the point of coming back from vacation feeling more exhausted than when you left. Give me slow days, not many plans, and not much to do. That was my idea of relaxation.

"Well, I'm glad you're here now." Her shoulders relaxed again. She paused when the waiter appeared. He poured her a glass of wine and waited for her to sip it. After, she nodded at him appreciatively. "This is lovely, thanks."

He topped up her glass and poured some for me. Mom waited until he'd left before turning to me.

"Have you seen your dad?" Her face was serious, a tightness to her expression.

Dad had had this effect on her ever since the last few years of their marriage. It couldn't have been more of a shock for me to learn as a teenager that the two people I loved the most, the very people who'd introduced me to love and romance, had fallen out of love with one another. Actually, not only that, but had ended their relationship disliking one another intensely. They had told me that love was all you need, but they'd lied. In reality, they hadn't been able to make it work. And since then, they could barely be in the same room.

I didn't fault them for divorcing. It happens. I didn't blame them for any of it now. It was more of a reality check for me. Nothing is sacred or safe in life. Why put yourself out there, hoping for the best and most beautiful life, when nobody seemed to be able to make it last? Not even my parents.

"No, I haven't seen Dad. I told you—I was going to whisk in and out."

Mom frowned again, the lines in her forehead intensifying.

"How's your hiking club going?" I changed the subject and, thankfully, Mom's expression changed, too. She relaxed into her seat and told me about Smokey Hollow, the most scenic spot to hike in the area. She had taken up running at fifty years old, which then turned into brisk walks at sixty, and now in her late sixties, she had started hiking several times a week with a group of people.

I smiled and nodded while she spoke. I admired and loved my mother. Very much. And I had to admit that this was enjoyable. It was just that Old Port reminded me of the terrible time —when our life had felt cold and nobody spoke to one another, let alone smiled or hugged each other. My stomach still dropped when I thought about how I'd felt in that home in the summers. So chilled and isolated, my skin would tingle. I'd barely talked. I'd been completely alone.

I never wanted to go back to that feeling again.

"Oh my God," my mother whispered. Her eyes flicked over my shoulder to the corner of the room. Her face had gone white-grey. Goosebumps sprang up on the backs of my arms.

"What?"

"It's her," she said. "It's *Susan*." The name came out like a hiss.

I turned and saw a bouncy head of grey hair, smartly cut short to frame her face. It was a pretty face, made up of soft lines. A face I hated, because it was the face of my father's third wife.

"Shoot. I don't think she saw us. Do you?" I turned back around and hunched over, as if that could hide me from sight. I hoped my father wasn't with her. I didn't particularly want to see him either. Our relationship had been strained for so long now. It took work, and I didn't have the energy for it.

"It's okay. She's getting takeout. She's leaving." My mother's voice was low. "She's gone." Her shoulders lowered.

My father had remarried twice after my mother. I'd quickly realized he was in love with the idea of love, but not enough to stick through the tough times, or the icky times, when the romance was hard to come by. When my mother had started to go through "the change", when her face had broken out in perimenopausal acne and she was tired all the time, it was as if my father hadn't remembered that love wasn't meant to be only for the pretty and the easy moments.

I would never subject myself to that kind of love. My poor mother had done everything right, and when she was her most real, he'd left her. There was no way I wanted to be looking over my shoulder, white-faced and sick to my stomach at sixty-eight years old.

After the pizza was finished and the wine was gone, after Mom's last sip of cappuccino, we left Piatto and hugged goodbye.

"I love you, Meg. Please don't keep me on the outside of everything," Mom said, hoisting her purse over her shoulder.

"I love you, too. Are you walking home?" It wasn't even dark yet, but still. She was alone at night. There was so much aloneness in her life, and I could tell she didn't like the solitude in the way that I did. Anger at my father still stabbed at me after all these years. I kept waiting for it to completely subside, but it hadn't yet.

"I'm fine. Go back to your room and get some rest. Call me later, okay?" She smiled and then turned on her heel.

"Love you," I called after her again. She waved a thin arm in the air and kept walking.

My phone vibrated in my hand. I glanced at the screen, expecting to see another text from Sarina. Instead, it was Cullen.

> Hi. So sorry about earlier. Does 10 am tomorrow work for you?

Something about his text caused a humming in my limbs.

> Sure

> Great

He picked out a place. This time we were meeting on the beach. I slid my phone into my pocket and began heading back to the Waterfront Suites.

I pictured his face, his faded grey T-shirt, the way the muscles in his arms flexed when he moved. I forced myself to stop thinking before I pictured anything else. Tomorrow was about getting details. I needed to go deeper and really get to know the man behind the good looks so I could write a piece with depth the way I knew I could. There was a story there. I just had to find it.

SIX

The next morning, I stood at the edge of the ocean watching frothy white waves somersault onto the shore. The clouds stretching across the sky made it hard to see through to the bottom of the murky water, even though it was relatively shallow here. I had my overnight bag in the car, having already checked out from Waterfront Suites, and my notebook in my hand. My phone was in my back pocket. And now, I waited.

Conducting an interview on a beach next to the water wasn't ideal. I'd likely struggle with making notes properly without a seat and table, but I was all set to record our conversation and determined to get enough material for the story this time. Cullen had suggested the location. He'd said it was calming. I wondered why that was important to him.

I had shared that feeling for the beach once. I used to swim in this water as a kid. I used to dive under and let the coolness glide over my eyelids, around my body. I'd do handstands underwater, my fingers digging deep into the soft, squishy ground, having asked my mom and dad to watch me. I'd swim far out on a dare to prove that I was brave to the boy I had a crush on. Other times I would just float on my back and let the lull of the moving water soothe me. My skin tingled and my heart warmed at the few good memories I could recall, but I pushed them away. I wasn't here to reminisce.

"Hey. You're here already," Cullen's voice called from behind me.

I turned to face him. He had on a black T-shirt and jeans. Very casual and regular, except for the way his clothes fit him—his shirt a little loose, but fitted enough to see his frame, the sleeves short and tight around his muscular upper arms, his jeans low on his hips. There was a relaxed handsomeness to him, like it came easy.

I noticed all of this—I couldn't help but notice—but I wasn't about to make notes. Celine would kill me if I tried to include clothing details in a story. She liked specifics, but she hated anything that could make a piece sound like it should be in a popular magazine or a blog rather than a newspaper. And that was what I was here for. A job.

"Hi. How are you?" I asked.

Cullen approached and stood in front of me, a small smile turning one side of his mouth up again. The way his mouth did that was dangerous. I'd have to be careful.

"I'm good," he said. "Thank you for doing this. Sorry about yesterday."

"No problem at all." I held up my phone, the recorder app open. "I'll be recording this, and I'll just make some notes while we speak if you don't mind." I pulled out my notebook and opened it to the last page I had scribbled on.

The words scrawled across the page were about Adam. This was my journal, not my notebook. I flipped forward a couple of pages hastily and cleared my throat. "So. We were talking about when you moved here when we last spoke."

"Right. I've been here for a few months. I like it. Very peaceful. You said you'd been here before?"

I nodded. "A long time ago, yes. What made you decide to

move here?" I glanced at my journal again. It would have to do for now. I clicked my pen.

"I was looking for some space. And for a quiet life, I guess," he said.

"Because of all the success with the book? Were you being hounded?"

Cullen's eyes widened for a second and he let out a loud laugh. It wasn't unkind. It was joyful. "No. Not hounded at all. I don't think that would ever be the case for me. As an author, anyway."

"You never know."

He shrugged and then smiled. His head inclined slightly forward so he could look down at me from where he stood. He was tall, and I had always liked that. Not to mention the smile. It was just like in his headshot. Half of his mouth turned up, almost lazily. The surface of my skin hummed. Damn it. This was inconvenient.

All of this was as familiar to me as my own reflection. My hand was itching to write about his defined jaw and his wavy hair in my journal. I wanted to disappear into a world of love and possibility—all imagined, all safe. Cullen fit the description of the perfect hero I liked to write about, only with him, something felt different. Something felt slightly more real. I shook my head, and he might have noticed because he gave me a questioning look.

"Can you tell me about the book?" I asked. "What made you want to write it?"

Cullen crossed an arm over his torso and I noticed a tattoo drawn up his forearm. How had I missed that earlier? Forearms were a weakness of mine. Forearms covered in tattoos—forget it. I'm done.

"I've always been a writer. I just didn't pursue it properly until a few years ago. I had the idea from when I was a teenager,

I think. I had to become an adult before I took myself seriously enough to do it."

I wrote point form notes as quickly as he spoke. This was good, but I was a long way from finding the real story yet.

"What was your childhood like? Were you close with your family? Do you have siblings?" A series of personal questions would usually stir something up. Sometimes I asked them because I genuinely wanted to know. Other times I asked them to throw the interviewee off a little. When they were vulnerable, they might tell you the good stuff.

Cullen's jaw tightened. "I, uh... I don't usually talk about my family."

There was something there. I caught it in his reaction. "I thought I'd try to get more of the real you in the story. If you don't mind."

His eyes flicked to mine. "I don't. But I thought this was about my novel?"

"It is—partly. But readers like to know about the person. I write for the *Globe*, you grew up in Boston, which is why we're doing a feature on you."

His mouth tensed. So far, most of the interview had seemed unpleasant for him, but I had barely asked any questions with much depth.

"Do you mind if we continue this later?" he said. "I'm really sorry, but I keep feeling my phone buzz with texts." He patted the back pocket of his jeans and then pulled his phone out to stare at it.

My mouth fell open an inch. He couldn't be bailing on me again. I had one day left to do this interview, and I hadn't even had a chance to follow him around yet, like Celine had asked. I didn't have enough to write a story. What would I tell her?

"I need all the time we've got," I said.

He looked up from his phone. "Do you think you might have enough to go on?"

My eyebrows shot up. He was a writer—how could he think I had enough to write a story on him?

"No. We haven't covered anything that I couldn't have googled about you." Speaking so directly to him likely wasn't going to help with trying to get Cullen to open up, but I couldn't help myself. I needed more time.

"I'm sorry," he said. His mouth twisted. "Could we just do this by phone? You could call me tomorrow? I promise I'll make time."

I sighed and gave a small nod to be polite, but inside, I felt furious.

"Great." He turned and left, and I found myself alone, once again.

"That's not the kind of interview we were hoping for." Celine's voice was thick with disappointment.

I'd called her from the car, ready to head back home, but my stomach dropped at her response.

"I know. He bailed on me both times we met. I couldn't get beyond the basics to even begin to interview him." I let my head fall back and closed my eyes. All of this had been so irritating. I was good at what I did, but Cullen was making me look bad.

"That's your job. To pin people down and get the story."

"I know," I repeated, trying to hide the edge from my voice. "I'm going to have to call him and get more out of him."

"I thought we went over this. A phone call won't cut it. It's a more involved piece for the Lifestyle section. It needs depth. It can't be just another story about a writer and where he got his inspiration from. We want to know about the person. What is going on in his life? What makes him unique? Where's the story?"

I gripped the steering wheel. "I agree it needs depth. I've tried, but he's been impossible so far. I'm not even sure there *is* a story. He seems like a regular guy who wrote a book that a lot of people like. He lives in a boring small town, probably to write more books."

It struck me as odd that Celine was pushing this. I wondered if it was due to budget issues or advertisers—I wasn't sure. I knew there was pressure on Celine to increase our readers. It always came back to advertising dollars. But I didn't see how this story was going to make that much of a difference.

"There's a story there," Celine said. "And I would like you to get to it. I told you, people eat it up when there's someone from their hometown who follows their dreams and has big success. It's inspirational and heartwarming. I see this as having potential, Meg. But you have to do the storytelling part."

I took a deep breath. I could do the storytelling part, but I needed a subject. This was close to impossible. "He couldn't meet with me long enough," I protested. "He's the one who suggested we do it by phone."

"This requires time. In person. I thought you'd spend the entire day with him at the very least. See his place. Get to know what he does each day."

I shifted in my seat. I tried to think about other articles we'd done that had required this level of time and commitment. I hadn't written one. Celine's piece on the Marshall bus tragedy flashed through my mind. She had devoted so much to it. It was so beautiful, but that was a piece about a tragic loss, the devastation of a community when a bus carrying a hockey team crashed, killing twenty people. This was about one guy who wrote a book. The two pieces were in no way comparable.

I considered my options. I could tell Celine this was all I could do and write an article that disappointed her and would probably limit my future in writing more creative pieces. Or I could insist on more time with Cullen and find an angle that Celine seemed certain was there, so I could write a piece that showed off my talent and skill.

"I'll try again," I said. "But there's one issue. I'm supposed to be on vacation, starting tomorrow."

"You can have a few days in lieu."

My shoulders tightened. This wasn't the way I'd seen things going with the interview. I thought it would be relatively easy, and I would be done by now. But I wasn't, and I could tell Celine didn't think it was a big deal to interrupt my vacation. Nobody thought it was a big deal when you were single and without kids. True, I hadn't booked a flight or made any specific plans. But my time was still my time.

"Okay," I agreed. What else could I say? I was stuck.

The air in the car had gone swampy, causing a dull throb at the back of my skull. I rolled down the window so I could breathe. Then I turned the key in the ignition to drive it back into the parking lot because I knew, as much as I wanted to, I couldn't avoid this. I had to get hold of Cullen again and find out what his deal was.

Back at the Waterfront Suites, Gwen looked at me from behind the desk with an apologetic smile.

"I'm so sorry, but we're fully booked."

"There's nothing?" I asked.

She shook her head. "I wish I could help you, but it's tourist season."

I closed my eyes and felt my body deflate. Now what?

"Thanks." I tried to smile. It wasn't her fault Cullen kept cancelling on me. It wasn't my fault, either, but I had to somehow make it all work out.

Outside the office, the air was as hot as before, only now it felt even more oppressive. I put a hand up to my forehead as if my touch could heal the throbbing. There was only one good option I could think of in the moment.

. . .

"Meg?" My mother's voice came through the phone with an edge of confusion.

I explained to her what was happening. "I need to stay here in town, but everything is booked."

"Do you want to come and stay with me?" she asked.

"If that's okay?"

"Of course it is. I would love that. But what about your vacation?"

"I know." I rested my hip on the side of my car. "I have to push it out."

I heard her mouth make a smacking noise in disapproval on the other end. "That's not fair to you, but it would be great to have you stay with me. For as long as you like."

I breathed out. This wasn't ideal, but thank goodness for Mom. She had always been there for me, in her understated way, always exactly what I needed. Shame flickered through me again when I thought of my original plan to come here and leave without seeing her.

"Are you coming right over, or are you going back home for more of your things?"

I hadn't thought of that. I only had a couple changes of clothes. Who knew how much more I would need? But the drive home was a four-hour round trip. Too long and exhausting.

"I'll pick up some T-shirts in town. I should only be a couple more days."

"Okay. Well, come over when you're ready, then. I'll make up the spare bed right now."

I thanked her and clicked off the phone. I didn't want to be here for longer, but I was an adult, and adulthood seemed to involve doing things you didn't want to, over and over again, because you had to. At least I got to choose what I wanted for dinner each day. Anyway, the least I could do now was be grateful to my mother.

When I checked my phone for any missed texts, Cullen and his plush lips and tanned, tattooed forearms flashed through my mind. I shook the thought away, irritated at how difficult he had been. This was the problem with reality. Cullen could have been perfect in my journal, but now I knew he wasn't respectful of time—a small detail, but it was there in the back of my mind. I pushed myself off the edge of the car. I didn't need the distraction of writing in my journal anyway. I had a job to do.

When I arrived at my mother's house on the water, my senses were overwhelmed with familiarity. The gentle, rhythmic sound of the ocean lapping on the shore, the smell of salt air laced with freshly mown grass, the sight of treetops in the distance blowing in the wind. These were some of the best parts of my childhood summers. My mother and father had bought this beach home before I was born, and my mother kept it after the divorce. She said she had built a life here and just because it was taking a turn didn't mean she should give it all up. My father had been fine with it. He'd wanted to move on. That seemed to be the problem in our family. Everyone wanted to move on, except for Mom.

She appeared in the doorway, her short hair falling around her face, framing it softly.

"I'm glad you're here," she said. "Want me to make us something to eat?"

"Hi." I reached for her and wrapped an arm around her neck. She smelled fresh, like soap and clean laundry. "Sure, I could eat." I wasn't sure I was hungry, but I knew I would accept whatever my mother offered. It was her way of comforting me—to take care of me, to make sure I had everything I needed.

"Good. I can always eat." She turned and started to walk down the short hallway towards the kitchen. "Come in."

"I've got to grab my things," I called after her. My laptop and notebooks were loose in the front seat of my car.

Outside on the gravel-filled driveway, I heard a screen door slap shut next door. I swivelled round, prepared to say hi to Mom's neighbor. That was how it was done in Old Port—it didn't matter if you knew them well or not, everyone waved. Everyone nodded and smiled and asked how you were. It was one of those unnervingly sweet things about small town life. If I was honest with myself, I missed that when I was in the city.

"Hi," I called before I could tell who I was talking to.

"Oh. Hello." Cullen stopped dead in his tracks and looked back at me, his face registering surprise. "I didn't know you knew where I lived."

The air around me seemed to have changed. I froze, mid-step.

"I don't. I didn't. I—I'm visiting my mother."

Cullen put both his hands into the front pockets of his jeans, his shoulders raised. He glanced behind me at my mom's house. "Your mother?"

My confusion was overwhelming. Cullen lived here? But the neighbor's cottage had always belonged to Mrs. Brown—a sweet older woman who kept to herself, but liked our family, so always made time to talk. I suppose she could have moved away at any time. I hadn't been back in ages, and I'd never thought to ask Mom about her.

"You live here?" I asked instead of answering him. "This is the place you moved into when you came to Old Port?"

He nodded, pushing his glasses up on his nose.

"What happened to Mrs. Brown?"

He took a step closer to me. "She moved into a retirement home closer to her son."

I opened my mouth to say something, but he shook his head. "Wait. You had no idea I lived here? This isn't about the story?"

"No, I honestly had no idea—but I guess I am here because

of the story. My editor asked me to stay in town longer so I can talk to you some more. She told me a phone call won't cut it. I'm staying with my mother."

He nodded again, slowly this time, as if he were processing my words. "Are you from here? And—what kind of a story are you doing that a phone call won't cut it?"

I looked up at the trees, as if an answer would appear out of mid-air. I didn't know what kind of a story this was, or why Celine had insisted I stay. I didn't know what she thought I would find out about Cullen, but I could tell her expectations for the story were high, and I wanted to do a good job. I wanted to show her I could write the way she did. It was the only way up for me.

When I brought my gaze back down, Cullen had moved closer. Close enough for me to notice the lines furrowed in the middle of his forehead, the way his eyes were deep brown and stormy. He had a rugged, brooding look to him. I rolled my shoulders and spoke as confidently as I could muster.

"I told you, you're a hometown success. It'll be a great story, I promise."

He shifted weight from one leg to the other. "Okay. I guess that sounds alright. I'm sure it'll be great—especially if it's as good as that piece you wrote on the inside lives and finances of Boston influencers."

My eyes snapped to his, my pulse speeding up. "My influencer piece? You read it?" I had never been recognized in public before because of my writing. This was weird, and also extremely satisfying.

"Oh. Well, yes." He stumbled. "I googled you." His cheeks flushed and I felt my own face warm up in response. I looked away. When I opened my mouth to speak, my throat thickened. I didn't want to move.

"Do you need to interview me now?" Cullen asked. He had a hand cupped over his brow to shade his eyes from the sun. His gaze moved from my eyes to my lips and then back again. He removed his hand from his brow and cleared his throat.

I did want to interview him now. The truth was, I found myself wanting to stay here, to find an excuse to keep talking to him.

"I thought you were busy." I had no idea why I chose to say that instead.

"I was. I'm really sorry about that. I have some time, if you're free?" He put his hands back in his pockets and he did that thing with his mouth again—the half smile.

My chest thrummed. I could only imagine how mad Celine would be at me right now if she knew that I was thinking I might be in trouble. It might be hard to interview and write a story about someone I couldn't deny I was attracted to. Maybe I did want to write about him in my journal.

"Meg?" My mother's voice called across the drive. She was in the doorway, glancing from me to Cullen. "I've got the food ready." She raised a hand to wave at him.

He waved back.

"Can I text you about a time? Maybe tomorrow?" I asked. I couldn't ditch my mother as soon as I arrived. Not after she had made us something to eat. "I just got here."

"Of course."

As I walked away, I couldn't ignore the odd feeling, almost a lightness, circling in my stomach, tumbling and crashing outward like a wave and washing over the surface of my skin.

SEVEN

The next morning, the aromatic, earthy scent of fresh coffee reached me before I even made it out of bed.

When I got to the kitchen, I went to the edge of the sink and looked through the window, down to the dock where my mother was sitting. It was where she'd always spent the early morning and dusk, when the heat of the sun no longer threatened to burn her. She watched the water, as if she were studying it.

I filled a mug and went down to join her, settling into the seat next to hers.

"How was your sleep?" She turned and glanced over at me, a hint of a smile lighting up her face.

"Good, thanks." It had been. I'd slept soundly and deeply for most of the night, lulled by the gentle crashing and receding of the rhythmic waves.

"Like old times," Mom said.

Solid night's sleep aside, I considered how long it had been since I'd felt good and settled in this house. I couldn't remember, but I didn't say that to Mom.

"I guess I've got to shower and get started on this interview again. It's been a hard one." I didn't know why I hadn't told her the interview was with her neighbor, but I hadn't. Instead, I'd let her think we were just introducing ourselves yesterday. Maybe I wanted to keep Cullen to myself for a bit. After a moment, I stood, even though part of me would have liked to sit there and watch the water with Mom for longer. The quiet of the early morning reminded me of the more peaceful moments I'd had in Old Port. I had almost forgotten them completely.

"How come it's been difficult? You don't usually have issues with writing, do you? You're always scribbling in that journal." Mom tilted her head up to me.

"I don't know. He's not telling me much yet. I don't know who he is." I couldn't understand Cullen. I had to get closer to him to get to know him better.

"You're so good at what you do, you'll be able to get what you need." Mom sipped her coffee and directed her gaze back at the ocean. At least she had confidence in me.

"Thanks." I leaned over to give her a quick kiss on the cheek. "See you later?"

She nodded at me, so I left and went upstairs to grab my phone. After a few texts back and forth, I nailed down a new plan to meet up with Cullen. This time, I took control and chose the place. So far, the coffee shop hadn't worked and down by the water hadn't either, even though they both should have been perfectly fine for an interview location. I could see I would need to go somewhere he couldn't be distracted by his phone.

When I arrived at the spot we had agreed upon, Cullen was already there.

"Hey. So... this?" he called to me, pointing at the building behind him as I pulled into the parking lot.

I stopped the car and got out. "What?"

"We're renting bikes?"

"Don't tell me you don't know how to ride a bike." I put my

keys into my fanny pack and pulled it over my head and one of my shoulders, resting it across my chest.

"No, I do. Bikes are great, but I don't think I've ever done an interview while riding one." He glanced from the building back to me again. His dark eyes sparkled. "How will you take notes?"

I tapped the side of my head. "I'm going to keep it all up here."

He laughed, his eyes creasing at the edges. I liked how it made him look, soft and comfortable, like your favorite hoodie.

"I'll also be recording it. You okay with that?" I asked.

"Sure."

After we got our bike rentals, we walked them over to the start of a long pathway that led into downtown. Cullen looked at the stretch of road ahead of us.

"Where are we going?"

There was a route I used to take as a kid that wound all the way through town. It was a good mix of gorgeous scenery and places to stop off when you needed a break. You could be beside the water one minute and then at the town's pub for lunch the next. I knew the route by heart, which was why I'd chosen it. I wouldn't need to concentrate on where we were going and instead could focus on asking all the right questions.

"Follow me. I'll show you." I got onto the bike and stood with one leg on the ground like a kick stand, my other foot on top of the pedal.

"Okay." He shrugged, but also grinned and held my eye. "Lead the way. I'm all yours."

My chest flickered. If I didn't know better, I'd think he was flirting with me. Or maybe I just wanted to believe that was what was happening. But this wasn't a made-up romantic scenario from my journal.

The first place I planned to go was the pier. I had spent so much time there as a kid, watching the boats go by in the distance. I settled into a groove at an even pace on my bike and Cullen matched my speed.

"So," I asked, after we had been biking for a few minutes, "why'd you move here?"

"I was looking for something different."

"You mentioned quieter?" I asked, fumbling with my phone in one hand and clicking on the recorder app.

He shook his head. "Actually, I wouldn't say quieter. Just... different. I guess I wanted to feel more freedom."

I tipped my head but kept my eyes on the road in front of us. "Freedom? This is the last place I would describe as freeing."

It was Cullen's turn to tilt his head. I could feel his gaze on me. "What do you mean?"

"What did *you* mean?" I asked, changing the focus. This was supposed to be about him. "About needing to feel more freedom?"

He smiled at me and adjusted his hands on the handlebars. "Nice dodge of my question there."

I laughed.

After a moment, he spoke again. "I felt confined where I was. A little trapped, I guess."

He didn't expand on it and I wanted to push, but was wary about him shutting down again. I decided to change tack.

"Did you have a happy childhood?"

"Wow. You're going right for the deeply personal questions, hey? Is this payback because I've been difficult for you?" His mouth twisted into another smile.

"Maybe." I winked at him. *Winked at him.* What was I *doing?* I was flirting without even being conscious of it. This was the effect he had on me.

He laughed, but then the smile slowly fell from his face. "My childhood was good." He focused on the road ahead again. "It was really good."

I pursed my lips to suppress a sigh. I could see this was going to be tough. I didn't usually have this much trouble getting information out of someone. Those Boston influencers had been more than happy to give me details, but they were also used to splashing their private lives all over social media. Cullen was different.

"And now? What's your life like now that you've moved here?"

"It's been peaceful. This place is so relaxing. I mean, I'm sure you know. Did you used to live here? Or do you only visit your mother?"

"We came here in the summers when I was growing up. Every summer of my childhood." My voice sounded flatter than I'd meant it to, giving away more than I'd intended. "It's been a long time since I've been back."

"Why's that? You don't like it here?"

I considered the question. It was hard to come back to a place you didn't think of as home because of the way it made you feel. I associated it with painful memories and with loss.

"It's been too long. I don't have any attachment to it. That's all," I said. "We're here." I got off my bike and walked it to the top of a hill overlooking the pier. Cullen followed.

"What are we doing here?"

"I thought we could watch the boats for a bit."

He turned and studied me.

"What?" I asked.

"Nothing. I just didn't take you for a boat enthusiast." He lay his bike down on its side and took a seat on top of the grassy hill. I sat next to him.

"I'm not. But I do like the beauty of it all."

"The beauty of what?"

I gestured around me. "The sound of the ocean rolling in, the way the warm breeze feels on my bare skin, the rumbling of the boats. The joy this place brings to the kids. You should see the way they wave their little arms madly in the air and then jump up and down when a boat passes or its horn sounds."

Cullen's dark eyes were squarely focused on my face. I felt heat rush to my cheeks again.

"What?" I shifted and intentionally turned to glance away from him, down to the other end of the pier, even though I liked the way he was looking at me.

"You're a romantic," he said.

"A what?" I looked back.

"A romantic. I can tell by the way you see the world. The way you just described the things you see here—a place you claim you don't like all that much."

How was he able to read me so well? There was no point denying it. "I guess. I'm not sure who I am. What about you?"

"What about me?"

"Are you a romantic, too?" I gave him a sidelong glance. He sat cross-legged, his hands fiddling with the grass in front of him. His head was tipped down, a small smile settled on his face.

"I think I'm a bit of a realist. Can you be a realist and a romantic at the same time?"

"Maybe," I answered.

"Anyway, I think it's nice to see the world romantically. It certainly helps with writing," he said. "You're really good at what you do. I've been reading more of your stuff."

A tingling swept up the back of my neck and across my face. Even though my work was out there and meant for public consumption, knowing someone had read it caused such a deep vulnerability at my very core. It was like I was walking around naked in public. *Oh, God.* Now I was thinking about being naked in front of Cullen. I needed to get a grip, and get the interview back on track.

"So... how did you come up with the idea for your book?" *Seriously?* I was disappointed in myself almost as soon as the words were out of my mouth. It was such a predictable question —one I was sure Cullen had been asked by many people. He brought his head back up now, one eyebrow raised.

"I took part of it from real life. The story of the boy, the coming-of-age part, I adapted a lot of that from my life growing up." His face brightened and a genuine smile appeared. "I used my parents as inspiration. I wanted to show that the main character was truly loved, had a solid foundation before his life was rocked. I think that part flowed naturally for me because I thought of my mom and dad when I wrote about the protagonist's parents. They made it easy to give a true depiction of what love is. I don't think I've ever been able to authentically write a bad parent character. I can't, because I always think of them."

"That's sweet," I said, turning toward him to get a better look. I liked the joy I saw in his expression. It was an infectious happiness. "So your book is somewhat of a love letter to them?"

"Yes and no. I obviously wanted to tell an exciting story with a plot full of adventure, about courage and bravery, but I also knew I wanted something deeper. I wanted to tell a story about love, and how the many forms of it can help you survive. How it makes you who you are. Without love, what have we got?" He took a breath and looked down shyly.

"I like that," I said. I felt an urge to tell him how inspiring it was to hear his backstory, how I wanted to know more, how I loved to talk about love. Instead, I awkwardly said, "I look forward to reading more of it."

His body straightened where he sat. "Oh. Yeah, thank you. I hope you enjoy it."

A lightheaded rush went through me. Why had I just admitted to him that I hadn't even read all of his book yet? I had gotten through a lot of it but wasn't quite finished.

"If you don't like it, don't tell me though." He smiled faintly.

"I wouldn't do that," I said. "Anyway, I really like what I've read so far. I'm sure the rest of it is just as great. Everyone loves it. You're a huge success."

"Am I?"

I twisted to face him. "How can you not know that?"

"I don't know. I don't read my reviews, and I'm not on social media."

"Nothing?" I asked.

He shrugged.

"Not even TikTok? That's where all the books have been taking off."

"What's a TikTok?" he asked.

I laughed and nudged his arm a little. "Well, you're big time. Trust me."

"I don't know about big time, but thank you." He bowed his head and looked like he was seriously studying the grass in front of him. After a minute, he glanced back up, his eyes sparkling again. There was a tiny scar over his left eyebrow. I found myself wanting to touch it, to run my finger over the top of his skin.

"Hey. Can I take you somewhere I love going?" he asked.

"You mean here in town?"

"Yeah." He stood and brushed the grass off the backs of his legs. "This place is so great." He smiled and held out a hand.

"Sure." I took his hand, and a jolt went through me at how warm and strong it was. When I stood and we were up close, I couldn't help but notice how good he smelled—like hints of salt water and fresh rain. Like an early morning in the ocean.

"Lead the way," I said, taking my hand out of his.

He held my gaze and then laughed. Electricity flickered through my limbs.

Fifteen minutes later, we were on the other side of town. You could get anywhere within mere minutes around here. I had always found it so suffocating. Cullen, on the other hand, kept talking about how convenient it was, how nice it was to get where you needed to go without traffic or crowds. I mostly nodded silently, but I liked how optimistic and positive he was. It was refreshing to be around someone so content.

"We're here." Cullen got off his bike in front of the local farmer's market. He turned to me, already smiling, like he was in on a joke, but my expression must have given away what I was feeling. He looked at me and said, "You're disappointed."

"No," I protested. Did I seem annoyed?

"You get that look when you're slightly irritated. I've seen it twice before." He smiled when he said it.

I touched my face, embarrassed. "When?"

"Both times I cut the interview short. Anyway, I don't know if you've been here before, but I do know how this place looks," he said, gesturing to the building behind him. It was a tall, red-brick structure that seemed a bit shabby.

"Like a regular old farmer's market?" I asked.

"Yes, but it's magical inside. Trust me. The food, the smells, the colors. And the fresh coffee. Can't forget the coffee." He spoke excitedly, his voice speeding up and then slowing again. "I love it here. And besides—it's perfect for a romantic." He held my eye.

I felt a rush of warmth to my face yet again. It was beginning to bother me how often this was happening.

The truth was, I had been here before. I used to come here as a kid with my dad. He liked to pick out fresh vegetables for our dinners. And even though it had changed since my youth, it was familiar enough to bring back memories. Dad would hold onto my hand and point out all the things Cullen had just mentioned—the vibrant colors of the fresh produce, the smells of coffee brewing and cinnamon buns coming out of the ovens, the low hum of conversation around us as we wandered up and down the rows.

Yet, whenever I was reminded of nostalgic moments like this, it instantly brought back the cold feeling, too. I couldn't help but associate this place with the stiff, stilted conversations my parents had had in front of me, or the grief etched into their faces, the fights I'd heard them having late at night when they thought I was asleep. I had long gotten over the fact that their marriage had ended, but I didn't think I'd ever be able to feel good about Old Port anymore. It wasn't home. It was a place where the romance had died, and the reality of life had smacked me in the face.

"Let's go then," I said, hoping I hid the reluctance from my voice. I followed Cullen into the market and walked alongside him as I took in the sights and smells once again. The silence between us felt easy, even though we didn't know one another very well yet. He made it this way. My shoulders loosened when I was around him; my body felt weightless. At one point, my forearm brushed against his and the feel of his smooth skin skimming over mine was fantastic.

"So, when are you going to tell me some real details about your life?" I decided to be bold with my questioning. "What about with respect to your book? Aside from your lovely-sounding parents, is there a specific real-life experience you've had that you used in the story?"

He slipped his hands into his pockets. "You know, I already feel oddly close to you."

"Oddly?" I smiled.

"Well, we just met, and I know you're writing a story about me, but I feel like I can be honest with you."

I nodded, but kept quiet. It also felt oddly good for me to hear him say that.

"Several years ago, my sister died."

A shock of cold rushed over me at the pained expression on his face. "I'm so sorry," I said. This was deeply personal, and he had already told me he wasn't comfortable with sharing a lot. I wanted so much to be sensitive and respectful.

"Thanks. It was awful. She was in a terrible accident." His forehead tensed, and he was quiet for a moment. "It's been horrible for my parents. Losing your child has to be the worst thing that can happen. They've had a really hard time dealing with it, so they sold their house and moved to escape the memories of it, and I ended up deciding I needed a change, too. I moved here to start over."

"I can't imagine. Do you see your parents often?"

His jaw flexed. "Not as often as I should."

I allowed a silence to fall between us as we wandered slowly past booths and stalls with gourmet cheeses and spices and oils, wanting him to feel able to keep talking if he needed to. After a moment, he spoke again.

"They want to try and protect me from the pain. They encouraged me to move here. I think they knew a place like this would make me happy again."

I let it all sink in. "Was she older or younger than you?"

He turned to me and his eyes had an inner glow to them. "She was older."

"What was she like?"

"She was quiet, but she somehow always lit up the room." His voice thickened with emotion. "And she was patient. Like, incredibly patient. I was a bit of an annoying little brother. She was also funny and easy to like. She had so many friends. Everyone at work loved her."

"What did she do?"

"She was an athletic therapist."

I nodded. I could see the pain etched onto his face and I felt for him; I wanted to say something that might help take it away.

"Anyway, I used that pain and grief and put it into my book. In every description of sadness and gut-wrenching loss, I placed my own loss. It was how I was able to make sense of it in real life

—like my own therapy. But I never talk about her or my family in interviews. I like to keep them private." He glanced sideways at me. "You won't use what I've said in the article, will you?"

I shook my head without thinking, answering on instinct. "Of course not. I'm so sorry. I can't imagine what it must be like for you." This was beyond human interest material. This was obviously deeply personal to Cullen. "From what I've read, you write about grief and loss beautifully."

Cullen shrugged. "I don't know. But thanks for listening," he said. "It feels really good to talk about her." He smiled at me earnestly, like I was light and levity, and a gentle pulse went through my limbs.

We continued on through the rest of the farmer's market, chatting about Cullen's house in Old Port, about his book, even a little more about his family. He seemed more comfortable now that he'd talked about his sister, and he opened up more about his writing. I was starting to understand him better, to realize where his inspiration and motivation came from, and I was getting a stronger picture of the man behind the writing. In turn, I grew more confident I'd be able to get that sense of the real Cullen Walsh down on paper in a way that would make readers feel connected, even without going deeply into his personal family history. I already, unexpectedly, felt connected to him, too.

"I like how honest you are about your pain." I turned my head. He looked pensive, but didn't respond to me. Instead, he quickly rolled his shoulders, straightening up while he gestured toward a coffee stand. He gave me a cheerful look.

"You have to try this coffee. It'll change your life."

"That's a pretty bold statement," I said. He guided me over to the coffee stand and stopped to buy us both a cup. When he took his first sip, he made a quiet, throaty sound, like a groan. My knees almost buckled.

After the coffee, we got back on our bikes and I took him

down the rest of the route, past the bakery (he had already been several times), the Port Dairy with the best ice cream for miles around, and through the buzz of the main street before we got back to the bike rental spot.

"Thank you for doing this," I said after returning my bike. We were standing next to my car. I didn't want this to end. I had some of it recorded, but the rest I wanted to memorize for later. Like how close our bodies had been to one another when we'd walked through the market, the ease of our conversation, the way he'd kept smiling at me. I wanted to write about those kinds of details in my journal. But first, I would need to type up the notes I'd kept in my head and start getting a draft down of the article before the detail got away from me.

He stood next to me, his forearms crossed over his chest. "This might have been my most favorite interview ever."

I tried to hide my smile, but could sense it breaking across the entirety of my face.

"Do you think you've got enough?" he asked, his brow slightly furrowed.

"I'm not sure." I might have enough material now to write a draft of the article, but I couldn't rule out needing to ask more, to get more detail and go deeper. And I was one hundred per cent certain I didn't want whatever this was with Cullen to end. It felt like more than an interview. "I'll start writing it, and maybe I could let you know if I have more questions?"

"That sounds great," he said. He watched me with serious eyes under dark lashes, and there was a shift in energy, like the air around us was charged. "I'd love to see you again."

EIGHT

The sunrise in Old Port had almost been wiped from my mind. I'd forgotten the beauty of the silence, the feel of the cool air before it warmed for the day, the sound of the odd fish jumping or a bird landing on the surface of the water—until I was in front of it once again, sitting on my mother's porch, coffee in hand. It was a Tuesday in mid-July. Soon the beach would be busy with kids playing, boats rushing by. It would smell more like coconut sunscreen than the saltiness of the ocean as droves of people showed up for a day at the beach. But for now, it was serene and peaceful.

I sipped my coffee, thinking about what to do next, aside from getting myself some breakfast. I didn't know if I should start writing the story on Cullen while I was here, or pack my few things and head home. It made sense to leave and get my vacation started back at home the way I had intended to, but I was here, with vacation days ahead of me, and my mother wanted me to stay. I could feel my old resistance to this place starting to yield as the real sights and sounds began to slowly wash away the old, painful memories of years ago. Besides, I didn't have much waiting for me back at my empty house in Boston.

I turned my head almost subconsciously, only slightly aware of what I was looking for. A glimpse of the house next to my mother's. Cullen's house was quiet, the dock empty and still. I would have taken him for an early riser—it was the best time to write after all—but maybe he didn't like to have coffee by the water first thing the way I did. I couldn't imagine staying inside when your backyard looked like this.

"What are you looking at?" My mother's voice came from behind me.

I sat upright, squaring my shoulders. "Me? Nothing. Just looking around. The ocean's so beautiful at this time in the morning."

My mother took a seat next to me, her hands wrapped around a coffee mug. "So, are you going to take pity on me and stay for a couple of days?"

"I should probably get back." My answer was only half-hearted, but my mother's face fell in response. "Mom—" I started to protest.

"No, it's fine. I know you have a busy life. And you've got your vacation." She shifted in her seat, took a sip of her coffee. I could tell she was trying to show me she was unfazed.

"I don't really have any plans for my vacation." Maybe I could stay. I couldn't deny I loved the slow days in Old Port, walking around barefoot, not making many decisions other than what to eat. It had been so long since I had done this. I had almost forgotten the good parts. And if I stayed, it meant I might get to spend more time with Cullen. If I needed more material, I could ask him in person rather than calling and chatting on the phone.

"I'm lucky to have you for as long as I get."

I tilted my head at her. It was such a "Mom" thing to say.

"Morning," a deep voice called, carrying from across the

water. Cullen. He was standing at the edge of his dock, coffee cup in one hand, his other stretched up into the air.

My mother lifted an arm and waved back. "Morning!" she called. And then, quietly to me, "That's my new-ish neighbor. You met him the other day, didn't you? He's handsome as heck."

"Mom." I nudged her with my elbow.

"What? He is." She turned in Cullen's direction and waved him over. "Come sit!"

I tucked my hair behind my ear. This was interesting. Cullen had to have better things to do than sit with me and my mother and watch the water. I didn't particularly want him to come over and see my makeup-free face first thing in the morning. Or my pyjamas from Walmart with the little hearts on the pants. But he was already on his way.

"Thanks," he said when he arrived. He took the seat on the other side of my mother. Thank goodness for space.

"This is my daughter, Meg." My mother gestured to me. "I think you two met the other day?"

"We did," Cullen said. His eyes flicked to mine. "Hi."

"Hi." As if I had zero control, my cheeks flushed yet again.

My mother glanced from me to Cullen and then back to me again. I knew her looks. She didn't have to say anything, even though I could tell she was about to. I jumped in.

"Actually, Cullen is the author I'm doing the story on. His book is a huge success."

Cullen winced and rubbed at the back of his neck. "You keep saying that. Your daughter is good at flattering me."

One of my mother's eyebrows shot up. She smiled. She was enjoying this.

"Really?" She leaned forward in her seat. "How did I not know this about you? What's it called? Maybe I've read it."

"*The Ninth Village*," I said. I googled it quickly on my phone and showed her a picture of the cover.

"I've seen that!" She turned in her seat towards him. "I can't believe I have a famous author living next to me and you didn't tell me!"

Cullen's ears appeared to be going red. Maybe he was shy. Or maybe his success made him uncomfortable. I had a hard time understanding that, though. If I could write a story for the paper that was beautiful and captivating enough to have many, many people love it, I think I would really enjoy that—and the fact that it could lead to so much more.

"Anyway, I'm writing a human interest story on him and it'll be great. You'll have to read it," I said, to somewhat take the attention away from him.

"Of course I will. It'll be fantastic." My mother was good at hyping me up. "She's an excellent writer." She smiled at Cullen and patted my knee when she said it.

"I know. I've read her work." He caught my eye and held it.

I stiffened a little in my seat. All of this was awkward. Me, barefoot and in my PJs, sitting with Cullen and my mother on her dock. It was somehow too intimate.

"I should get changed." I stood. "See you later?" It was something I always said, a casual goodbye I used all the time, but it was loaded with meaning this time. I went upstairs and got into the shower, my mind working it over as I shampooed my hair.

I do want to see him later.

Maybe I would stay for a while.

Later, the sound of a knock on my bedroom door yanked me from my daydreaming.

"Meg?" It was my mother's voice.

I had been sitting at my desk writing in my journal. This time it had been about Cullen. It had been impossible not to. He was in every thought I had lately. I snapped my journal shut, a little lightheaded, and slid it into my bag beside the desk. I pulled out my work notebook instead. "Yes?"

"Can I come in?"

"Sure." I opened my notebook to make it look like I had been working, not writing out my fantasies again. It sounded so embarrassing when I put it that way.

"Can I make you some lunch?" Mom leaned against the edge of the doorframe.

"Sure, that sounds great, thanks."

After she left, I threw on a hoodie and went to the kitchen where my mother was busy making her signature picnic lunch. I smiled. When I was little, I considered this a huge treat. My mother would roll up slices of turkey and cut up some cheese and apple and I'd think I had the best meal that had ever been created. Now, it was called "charcuterie", but when I was a kid, it was just my most favorite meal. I took the plate she handed me and went out to the porch to sit.

The ocean was calm today; an immense blanket of deep azure, gently rolling and rocking while the sun sparkled on top of the surface like dewdrops on a spider web. The water was one of the few positive memories I had of this place. I had once heard lakes and oceans referred to as "blue space". I liked that term. The water was where I felt my most alive and good in my skin and the ocean was where I would go as a kid when the house was thick with tension. I felt free when I was in it. I wondered if I would still feel that way.

"What's your plan for the rest of the day?" my mother asked.

"Not much. How about you?"

"Actually, I was thinking we could go to the market and the grocery store to pick up some food for tonight."

"What's tonight?"

"I'm making a nice dinner." Her eyes twinkled with what I could only consider a hint of mischief.

"Why?" I asked.

"I've invited a guest over," she said. Before I could open my mouth to ask who, she continued, "It's Cullen. I've invited Cullen over. He's just so handsome and he's so accomplished. Talk about an interesting dinner guest!"

My arms and legs tingled. I looked away from my mother for a moment so she couldn't see whatever my face was doing. She would know as soon as she saw it what I was feeling. Mothers were like that. I turned back to her when she spoke again.

"I also thought it might be good for you to get to know him better. For your story." A hint of a smile tugged at the corner of her mouth.

"Thanks," I said. I looked down at my bare feet and wriggled my toes. I wanted to talk to her more about him, but I was sure my voice would betray me. Besides, even I didn't know what was happening or what I was feeling. I was writing about Cullen in my journal, so there was obviously something there, but I was also responsible for writing an unbiased piece on him for the paper. Not to mention, I would be leaving soon to go back to my regular life. This all had to be temporary, the way all my daydreams and journal stories were.

After lunch, I reluctantly put on shoes and went into town. I'd told my mother I'd pick up the extra food she needed at the grocery store so she could stay home and prep, and I decided to take my time meandering through the shops. It was nice not having to do much of anything.

Getting to the other end of town took no time. I parked in one of the strips of parking spots along the side of a pathway that led through town and walked across the street to the sidewalk. It was busy, as usual for summer, filled with people and dogs and strollers. Happy families on vacation, meandering while snacking on ice cream. It was what Old Port was known for in the summer months—the lively crowd of people. I remembered it being busy, and even right now it was hard to navigate, but I guessed after all these years my mother must have got used to it. Ahead of me on the right was one of the only things I had never stopped loving about this place: the bookstore. Everafter Books was set up in a little old house that had creaking floors and winding steps that took you to the upstairs level. It was lined with floor-to-ceiling bookshelves that held every kind of book you'd ever want or need.

The smell of fresh paper and smoky inks came to me as soon as I stepped through the doorway, instantly recalling my teen years. Any time I'd wanted to get away from the stiff, cold feeling circling through our home, I came here or to the ocean. I could spend hours browsing through the aisles in this shop and nobody had ever made me leave because I wasn't buying anything.

I went to the fiction section and ran my hand over a row of books. Rows and rows of places I had never been, characters I had yet to meet. There was something so hopeful about books. There was so much possibility in those pages. When reality was dull and couldn't meet your expectations, a story could open you up to so much more.

After several minutes browsing, I picked up a book with a summery cover, one that I hadn't heard of before, and went to the front to pay. A familiar face smiled back at me when I placed it on the countertop.

"Gwen?" I said. It was the woman from Waterfront Suites.

"That's me," she answered. "How are you— I'm sorry, I'm terrible with names. It has to be old age."

"Meg," I said and smiled. "You work here, too?"

She shrugged and grinned. "Only as a favor. My friend Derek owns this place and needs a hand every now and again."

"That's nice. I love it here."

Gwen put a hand on the book and slid it across the counter toward her. "You know it? I love it, too. So many great books." She eyed mine. "Like this one. I read it last month. You'll enjoy it, I'm sure." She rang it up and bagged it for me.

"Thank you."

"So you found another place to stay?" Gwen asked.

"I did. I'll probably be here for a while."

"That's great. You should come by Waterfront Suites again. We're having a summer barbecue Friday night. Food and drinks and good company. It'll be fun." Her smile was radiant. I could feel myself warming to the idea of this town even more than I had already.

"Sure. Thank you." I left the shop, new book in hand.

Outside, I took my time walking toward the grocery store. Maybe I had been wrong to write off Old Port without giving it another chance. I'd avoided coming back here, but maybe I needed to reframe how I thought about it. Yes, the past had been bad, and when I thought about the fighting and the unhappy times, I associated most of it with this town. But could there possibly be more good to it than I'd been open to seeing?

I crossed the street with one of the grocery stores in my line of sight. What had Mom said she needed again? Cheese, I thought. Something else, too. I should have made a list. I glanced up, as if the answer would come from the vibrant blue sky stretching atop of me, when I bumped into someone.

"I'm sorry. I didn't mean to—" I looked down and saw who it was. Susan. My father's third wife. She wore linen pants and a neat blouse, an outfit that felt a bit too polished for a retiree in the middle of summer. Dark-rimmed glasses accentuated her wide, surprised eyes.

"Meg?"

"Susan. Hello." I shuffled on the spot. How awkward. She was one of the last people I wanted to run into. Susan was exactly the type of unkind, ungracious woman I most disliked.

It wasn't enough that my mother was her husband's ex; whenever I'd talked to Susan in the past, she'd had to make it clear that my mother was "less than" because she was alone. It was the way Susan saw things, but it was a ridiculously outdated view of the world.

"What are you doing here?" she asked.

"I'm staying in town."

"Oh. Well. For how long?"

It seemed a direct question, and not one she needed to know the answer to, to be honest. "I don't know. A while, I guess. I'm staying with my mother."

Her fake smile faltered, and a shadow crossed her expression. She ran a hand over her smooth grey bob. "That's nice, dear. It's good to see you." Her words oozed insincerity.

I hated that she called me "dear". I was not dear to her; we weren't familiar enough for that. And also, she wasn't eighty-nine years old.

"Do you plan to visit your father?"

She remained very still as she waited for my response, and when I shook my head, I could have sworn she breathed out.

"I don't think I'll have time."

"A daughter should always make time for her father. It's the right thing to do. Our Lisa always makes time for us, but I understand you're busy with your big job in the city."

"Lisa isn't my father's daughter," I pointed out.

The fake smile dropped from her face completely. "We consider her ours. We're a family."

It was one of the things I couldn't understand about my father. He and Susan both referred to Lisa as their daughter, even though he'd only met Lisa when she was in her early twenties. She was a grown woman, not living with her mother any longer, but Susan had insisted he refer to Lisa as his child.

The air was thick and damp with humidity now. I mumbled something about how I really needed to get going and nodded at

Susan, hoping it was polite but direct enough. When she nodded back at me, I left and crossed the street, as if I were dismissed. I went as quickly as I could while still looking natural until I reached the grocery store.

Susan had been and always would be a physical reminder of the fact that to my father, my mother hadn't been enough. Our old life hadn't been enough. I supposed it never stopped hurting to have been rejected and replaced by your father, no matter how old you were.

Inside the store, I grabbed a basket and glanced around at where I wanted to go first. The air conditioning cooled my flustered skin.

I had started to think that Old Port might be okay, that I could exist here and see it as something other than what it had been for me in the past, but I was wrong. I couldn't.

This place wasn't for me.

NINE

Back at my mom's house, I found her puttering around the kitchen, whisking up homemade sauces and prepping steak and shrimp for barbecuing that evening. I had forgotten she was so good at barbecuing, but she reminded me she'd had to be after my father left. There was a lot she'd had to figure out and fine-tune after he was gone. It made my heart swell for her.

To busy myself before dinner, I pulled out my laptop and worked on more of my notes on Cullen. I knew how I wanted the hook to go. I would draw readers in with an unexpected line about him, something about how he was equal parts reclusive and open and honest.

Cullen Walsh has never been on social media. He doesn't know what TikTok is. Yet he's comfortable and inviting with his words, as if being social comes easy to him. Imagine dark and brooding, mixed with brown-eyed warmth.

It needed massaging before I moved on to describe more of him, but it would get there. I wanted to include who he was, where we met to talk—I felt a need for the readers to immediately warm to him the way I had.

After a few hours, I saved my work, satisfied with how it had turned out so far. I considered what Celine might think, or whether it was up to her standards. I opened a tab and googled her name plus Marshall so I could read her article again. *Damn.* It was so good. She had expertly treated a horrific accident with such responsibility and care. What was it about the way she worded each sentence? She made her story seem like art—a mix of both beautiful storytelling and compelling subjects. I felt everything when I read her work.

This was a very different piece, and I wasn't able to tell if my writing was anywhere near as good as Celine's, but I suspected it wasn't, so I closed my laptop to get dressed for dinner.

The only clean items of clothing I had left were a loose black T-shirt and a pair of black leggings. They were fine for around the house, and I had even convinced myself that they were somewhat dressier than normal because they were all black, but they weren't right for tonight. Instead, I asked my mother if I could borrow something. When she told me to go right ahead, I went straight to her closet where I found several cute little sundresses that I suspected she hadn't worn in at least a decade that were just coming back in style. I picked a pale pink one that complemented my coloring and put it on before going out to the kitchen.

"Wow." My mother paused, mid-whisking, and smiled at me. "You look beautiful."

"Thank you. Can I help?" I moved toward her, but she shooed me away.

"I've got it, thank you. Why don't you pour yourself a glass of wine? Go out back."

I took her up on the offer. With a glass of cold, crisp pinot grigio in hand, I went out to her porch so I could sit and watch the water. The whisperings of the trees as their branches and leaves rustled was better than any drug I could take. As a kid, when the warm wind blew, I used to close my eyes and listen to that sound. I did it again now. My body relaxed into the chair. I could stay like this forever.

"I hope I'm not intruding." Cullen's deep voice floated into my consciousness. I opened my eyes. He stood above me, a glass of wine also in hand, his shoulders rounded. "Your mother sent me out here, but I didn't want to bother you. You look so relaxed."

I put a hand out to gesture to the chair next to me. "Please. Sit." I liked that he was here. I found myself thinking about him so often.

"Thanks. It smells fantastic in there." He breathed in appreciatively.

"She's a great cook."

"I believe it," he said. "But she wouldn't let me help at all."

I laughed. "Me neither. That's why I'm out here. Not that I'm complaining." I held up my glass. "Cheers."

Cullen finally took the seat next to me and leaned forward, clinking his glass against mine. "What are we cheersing to?"

Maybe it was the wine already working its way into my bloodstream—it didn't take much for me to feel it--but my body was buzzing, so I said it. "To you. And me. And us being here together."

Cullen's eyebrows shot up high on his forehead—only for a second, but I caught it.

"Here in front of the ocean," I added, as if it would help distract from me having admitted out loud that I was picturing us together.

"Cheers to you. And your story. I hope it turns out romantic." Cullen gazed at me and did the half-smile I could see was his signature. It went straight to my head, making me dizzy. I looked away, out at the water, so he couldn't see my face. I could sense with my peripheral vision that he had also turned to face the horizon.

"I suppose it's easy to find the romance and beauty when you're here." He nodded at the water.

"I don't know about that," I said. "The ocean is mesmerizing, but I think you've got quite a different view of this place than I have."

He turned to me. "Old Port? I don't get it."

I shrugged.

"It's so serene here." He looked around and then back at me again. "There's so much to enjoy about it, and we've established that you're a romantic. And yet—you don't like it here all that much. It doesn't make sense."

"I'm not a big fan, I guess. I used to love it, but... It's a tiny town where there's not much to do, and everyone knows everyone else's business."

Cullen eyed me. He was silent for a while and then he sat up straighter. "I have an idea."

"An idea?"

"Yeah. How long are you here for?" he asked.

I hadn't thought all of that through. At least for the next few days, I supposed, but I hadn't made a solid plan, which wasn't like me. "A couple of days. Maybe longer."

"I'll take what I can get. In the next few days, I'd like to show you Old Port the way I see it."

I'll take what I can get.

"Why?" I asked.

"Because I bet I can get you to love this place again."

I didn't think it was possible for me to love Old Port, and I didn't understand why Cullen wanted me to either. He must have sensed my trepidation because he leaned toward me and touched my arm. A jolt went through me at the way his hand felt on my bare skin. It was electric, and I wanted him to keep it there.

"I know it probably seems silly," he said, "but I've really become a new person since moving here. I feel so free and good in my skin. I've had my eyes opened to the simplicity and beauty of a lot of things in life. I think it's something everyone should get a chance to experience." He watched me for a moment, presumably waiting for an answer.

I considered what he'd said. At the very least, I would get more time to get to know him. I told myself that would make for a better article, which would make Celine happy, and would mean more opportunity for me in my career going forward.

"All I have to do is go with you around town?"

He nodded. "That's all."

I shrugged. "Okay, I'm in."

This would be interesting. But there was no way I would be falling in love with anything remotely related to this town.

After I agreed to Cullen's plan, we didn't speak about it again. Instead, we sat with my mother around her candlelit table out on the back deck as the sun began to lower in the early evening sky, talking about work and life, and books and movies we'd loved. We passed around thick slices of sourdough bread and a bottle of pinot grigio. I let the wine warm my stomach and bring a flush to my cheeks as I watched Cullen chatting easily with my mom, complimenting her on the way she seared and cooked the steaks. It *was* impressive how good she was at cooking. She was a great hostess and it felt good to see her in her home setting. The entire evening was close to perfect.

After we had eaten, I made my mother sit and enjoy the sunset while I picked up the dishes to bring them inside.

"This is the best part of the day though—you can't miss it." She pointed to the bright pinks and oranges taking over the skies as the sun dipped below the horizon.

I motioned for her and Cullen to both stay where they were while I balanced three plates in my arms. "I can see it tomorrow."

My mother glanced up at me from her seat, a little gleam in her eyes. Her face had gone pink from the wine and the fresh air, and her hair was still wild from the heat of cooking. She looked beautiful and happy.

"I'm glad you're staying," she said.

"Me too." I smiled at her.

Cullen stood. "Please. Let me help." He took the plates from my hands, even while I protested, and went to the kitchen.

My mother settled back into her chair, apparently unbothered by this.

"He's our guest," I loud-whispered to her.

"He's also a man who offered to clean up without being asked." She laughed.

I laughed, too, and when Cullen came back outside he stopped in front of me. "What's funny?"

"Nothing. I'm just happy," I said.

This made him grin, and an oddly satisfying wave of giddiness came over me.

Later, after cups of coffee and more conversation, Cullen stretched in his seat and thanked my mother for a lovely night.

"Meg, do you mind seeing him out? I need to get up to bed. I'm exhausted now." She stood and then yawned and stretched in a showy kind of manner. I tried to catch her eye to see what she was up to.

"Thank you again for everything." Cullen stood and tucked his chair in. "This was so nice."

"Anytime. It's great to have you here." She patted his arm and then went inside and up the stairs, which left me standing next to Cullen, alone on the back deck, something my mother seemed to have carefully planned.

"Well," I said, although I had no follow-up.

"Well." Cullen put his hands in his pockets. He took a step closer to me. I breathed in and then seemed to stop taking in air. "I should get home. I have plans to make for you and I." His eyes sparkled. He was so close and he smelled so good. Fresh, like the outdoors.

I nodded at him. "Sounds good."

"Keep your day free, please."

"The entire day?" I asked.

"Yeah. We'll need a lot of time." He smiled at me—a warm, gentle smile.

I wasn't expecting what it did to my stomach, or the rest of my body. A fizz radiated through me. My heart pounded as I realized I wanted him to reach out and touch me again. Instead, I smiled up at him.

"See you tomorrow."

TEN

I tried not to overthink what to wear the next morning, but failed. I had no idea what to expect, so I texted Cullen.

> What should I dress for today? Adventure? Sightseeing? Lots of eating?

The thought bubble appeared on my phone almost instantly. I liked his promptness.

> Wear anything you want

I frowned. That didn't help.

> But what kinds of things are we going to do?

> No hints

> You'll have to wait and see

This time I smiled, even though I preferred to be prepared. The bubbles appeared again. I waited.

You looked great in that dress last night

My heart sped up. I stared at my phone, trying to think of the right reply. This would be a good time to text Sarina and get her help. She was quick and smart with her words, and she never failed to make me laugh. She would know the perfect thing to say right now. But it was early, and she was likely knee-deep in the morning routine of cleaning up cereal and trying to convince a five-year-old to wear clothes. When I couldn't come up with a reply myself, I answered with a simple:

Thanks

and a smiling face, then tossed my phone down on my bed. I wasn't about to wear a dress. That would be much too obvious. But I decided against my loose shorts and a baggy T-shirt.

I went to the pile of clean laundry I had put in the washer and dryer late last night and pulled out my most flattering tank top—a cropped, loose and surprisingly hip tank, the only one I owned that I would call fashionable—and a pair of tight shorts. It was a good mix of casual and a little bit trendy.

At the front door, I fiddled with my hair and tried not to keep looking at myself in the mirror in the hallway. I was fine. This was fine.

"On your way out?" Mom called from the tiny living room.

"Yeah. Probably for a few hours."

She got up and walked to the hallway, about to turn into the kitchen, and stopped. "Who with?" There was a hint of a smile on her face already.

"Mom." I shook my head.

"What? I'm just asking my daughter a question."

"I'm going out with Cullen. It's strictly research." I was trying to convince myself of this as much as I was my mother. A knock at the door saved me from any further explanation. "There he is. I should go. See you later."

When I pulled open the door, I stepped outside immediately to prevent Cullen and my mother from striking up a conversation, but this meant I moved in too close too quick.

"Hi," Cullen said, tilting his head down at me. "Are you ready for this?" He had on a grey T-shirt and long black shorts, relaxed and casual. I had picked the right outfit for whatever we were going to do.

I took a deep breath. "I think so."

The truth was, I wasn't so sure. I didn't like having no idea what was happening, I preferred a bit of a plan or an outline. I took a deep breath and told myself to just go with it, in the name of research.

"Come with me." He turned and walked toward the road, hands in pockets. No car in sight.

"Are we taking bikes again?"

"No," he called over his shoulder. "We're walking."

It was hot out today. I already knew my way around Old Port, and now it was clear we weren't going to go much further than the middle of town. I'd thought maybe we'd drive around, see some pretty scenery, he'd talk about how great it all was and then we'd grab a bite to eat somewhere. I'd imagined myself asking him more questions and getting to know him better for my story. This wasn't turning out to be what I'd thought it would. But it was a day with Cullen. The idea of that alone excited me.

"Lead the way," I said.

Cullen glanced at me, his eyes roaming up and down. "You chose well. You look great."

His text about my dress flashed through my mind and I felt my cheeks burn. It had been a while since I'd had this feeling in real life. I had been avoiding serious relationships after Daniel because they were always a let-down in some way or other. I liked to date, sure. But whenever I had gotten close to someone, it just hadn't lived up to what I'd wanted or expected. Now I was trying not to overthink whatever this was with Cullen because I didn't want it to end in disappointment, the way it always did. I already liked him a little too much for that. Clearly, I wasn't doing a great job of keeping this professional.

"So, are you working on anything new?" I asked as we walked. I kept my eyes on the road ahead of us. It was long and flat, and eventually wound into town. There wasn't much to see here except for one edge of the ocean.

"No, not really. I haven't had any ideas."

"Really?"

He turned to me. "That surprises you?"

"Well, your book is so epic. You built entire worlds and also created this beautiful, believable love story. Your brain must be full of cool ideas."

He laughed lightly, a low chuckle. "Wait. Did you finish it?"

I brushed a hair out of my face. "I did." And it was good. Really, really good. I didn't expect to love it because it wasn't my typical genre. I was much more of a contemporary girl, but Cullen's book was fantasy and also a love story, and so well-written. After he'd left last night I'd stayed up later than I'd meant to, reading it. I'd settled into one of my mother's plush, oversized chairs and allowed myself to be captivated and carried away by Cullen's storytelling and writing. Once I'd read the final words, goosebumps had sprung up on my arms and tears had pricked at my eyes. I'd brushed my cheeks with my fingertips and sniffed, adjusting myself on the chair, relieved that my mother hadn't been there to see my reaction. To most, it would be only a book. To me, it was a beautiful, moving peek into who Cullen was.

"And?"

"I'm very impressed," I said.

Cullen held my gaze. "Thank you."

I smiled up at him and wondered how long he would keep looking at me. I turned away, energy humming through my body.

"We're almost at our first stop."

I wasn't quite sure how that was possible. We hadn't gone very far yet. We were only on the main street in the middle of all the shops. I'd been here a million times, there was nothing new Cullen could show me. I was about to tell him so, but he had this wide-eyed excited look of anticipation on his handsome face.

"Where is it?" I asked.

He pointed at the bakery. The Old Port Bakery, where I had gone so many times as a kid I couldn't even count.

"I know it well."

"Ah, but have you been there lately?"

I tilted my head. "No, but I'm not sure how that makes a difference." Nothing around here ever changed. People from the town were almost proud of the fact.

"It does. You'll see." He jerked his head to the side to indicate I should follow him.

Inside, the familiar fresh bakery air immediately surrounded me. It was sweet and yeasty, like warm bread, just like I'd remembered when I was first driving here. There were rows of cookies and tarts and tiny cakes, and behind that were scones and rolls and every type of bread you could imagine.

"Amazing, isn't it?" Cullen stood next to me, his shoulder brushing against mine.

"Yes, but I've been here before. This isn't new to me."

"I know that. I didn't say I was going to show you things you'd never seen before. I said I was going to try to get you to fall in love with this town again. I'm starting with food. Specifically, fresh baked food. Because you can't get much better than that."

He had a point. Still. I wasn't convinced a bakery—no

matter how good it was—could negate all the bad associations I had with this town.

"Okay, don't look." He gestured for me to turn around.

"Don't look? At what?"

"I'm going to get a few things for you to try, but I don't want you to see what they are."

I rolled my eyes but also smiled at the same time to show Cullen I was being a good sport, even if this sounded slightly ridiculous.

"Why don't I wait outside?" I suggested.

"Okay, but can you come back in when I'm ready? You need to try them in here, surrounded by the smells." His eyes were bright, like he was thrilled by his idea, and I couldn't help but laugh at his enthusiasm. I found it kind of charming.

I went out to the front of the shop and stood with my back to the window so I couldn't see inside. Families walked by on the sidewalk in front of me—kids with melting ice creams, toddlers on their parents' shoulders. Most of the people strolled at a slow pace, soaking in the sun and the best the summer had to offer. As much as I'd wanted to forget it, Old Port in summer had a pull for me. It was the way people looked so relaxed and happy all the time, the way my skin tingled from the sun and salt water, the way I would sleep so deeply at night with the windows open to let in the delicate warm air.

When I heard a knock on the window behind me, I turned to see Cullen motioning for me to come in. He had one arm behind his back—holding the baked goods, I gathered. I went back inside.

"Alright, now close your eyes and when I say so, open your mouth."

I raised an eyebrow.

Cullen tipped his head to one side. "Meg. Come on. Can you give it a go?"

"I feel silly. There are people around." A few of the workers behind the counter glanced at us and then smiled to themselves, but for the most part, none of the locals noticed. They were coming in and out, busy purchasing butter tarts and loaves of bread and cherry pies.

"I promise this will be worth it."

He was certainly sure of himself. I sighed. "Fine. This is weird, though."

"I know." He laughed.

I folded my arms across my chest first and closed my eyes. I decided to wait until he was ready before I opened my mouth. There was no way was I going to stand here with my mouth hanging open in the middle of the town bakery.

"Okay," he said. "Open."

I did, and even though I knew it was coming, it took me by surprise when I felt the brush of his fingers across my lips. His touch sent a warm thrill down my spine. And then, before I had any time to consider my reaction, my taste buds were overwhelmed by flavors. Savory, rich butter. A hint of sweet tanginess that settled at the tip of my tongue. There was a soft flakiness to whatever it was I was tasting. I chewed and then ran my tongue around my mouth. They must have added something new to the bakery's menu. I couldn't remember anything being this good in the past.

"That was delicious," I said. "Can I open my eyes?"

"Hang on. I've got something else for you."

This time, it was rich chocolate, a thick but soft texture with a hint of salty crunch. It had to be a brownie, but again, I couldn't remember tasting anything quite like this before. The flavors were all so balanced and perfect.

"Wow."

"I know," Cullen said. "One more."

This one was a fluffy bread. There was a hint of sourness to it, but the tanginess was balanced by sweetness. It was airy and light and incredible.

"You can open your eyes now," Cullen said. I did, and found him studying me. "What did you think?"

"Those were all delicious. What were they?"

"A scone, a brownie and sourdough bread with butter." He had a small brown box in his hand with a little wooden knife and the remainder of each thing I had tasted, along with a few cookies, a couple of muffins and some croissants. "I thought you could take this home and share the other ones with your mother."

"That's kind of you, thank you. But why did you have me taste them with my eyes closed while standing in the bakery?" This was a very strange thing to do, albeit delicious and kind of fun. I didn't see a direct connection to loving the town again.

"I thought it was the best way for you to really taste it and smell it," he said. "Was everything the way you remembered it, or was it like new again?"

If I was being honest, it was all new to me. I didn't remember the bakery this way. "It was better than I remembered."

He nodded. "I know this might sound hokey, but when you really focus on something, it's easier to notice the good things about it."

"That does sound hokey." I let out a small laugh. His chin dipped and he gave me a playful look of annoyance. I held up a hand to stop him before he had a chance to protest. "But you're right, it makes sense. I'm glad I got to taste these things, and I'm even happier that I can take home the leftovers."

His deep brown eyes focused on me while he stood close, not moving, as if he was zeroed in and interested in everything I had to say, every little detail about me. I imagined reaching out to him, brushing a piece of hair off his forehead. The space between us felt like nothing at all.

"I spend a lot of time thinking about the small, simple good things in life," he said.

"Oh?"

"Sometimes I even make a list on my notes app." He grinned and held up his phone. "I write down daily activities that make me happy. Like, having a coffee while I work on my book early in the morning. Or going for a swim in the ocean to start my day. Having a long, hot shower. Reading. Eating something from this bakery. Simple things."

I tried not to picture him showering. "All good things. But why do you write them down?"

"As little reminders. And then I try to fit one in each day. It helps make me happy, you know? I think in the long run, it helps me to have a more satisfying life when I do something that makes me happy every day."

I liked that. It was so easy.

"What little things do you love to do?" he asked.

I immediately thought of my journal, but "I make up epic romantic love stories starring me" was the last thing I was going to say.

"I don't know. I'd have to think about it," I said. "Coffee is up there."

He let out a laugh, and it was warm and rich.

"Thanks for this," I said, pointing to the bakery box, although I meant much more than the food.

"You're welcome. But we're not done yet. Follow me." His hand brushed my wrist as he went to the door of the bakery, sending a shiver through me. Cullen stopped at the entrance to make sure I was behind. He pushed his glasses up onto the bridge of his nose just as one half of his mouth went up. My entire system of senses felt as if they were on high alert now. I realized in that moment that I was going to follow him. Anywhere.

ELEVEN

After the bakery, we walked around town some more. Cullen asked me to follow him down a hidden, off the beaten path to get to our next stop. I thought I knew Old Port like the back of my hand, but I was thrown for a loop by the spot in front of me. We went through some patchy grass that led to a narrow pathway of trees and brush, until we came to a clearing—and I finally recognized where we were. Up ahead, there were dunes and just beyond that, the beach.

I knew the beach, of course. I'd loved it as a kid. I used to come here to watch the waves roll in. Another place I was already familiar with.

"You're not going to get me to close my eyes again, are you?" I teased.

"Ha. Maybe."

Cullen walked ahead and then stopped suddenly to take his shoes off. The sun overhead hadn't reached its height of heat yet, so the sand wouldn't be too hot for bare feet.

"Want to go down there for a walk?" He pointed to the edge of the water. Right where the surf met the sand.

"For a long walk on the beach?" I put a hand on my hip. I

knew I sounded like a cynic, but I couldn't help it. I'd thought this would be an experience that was new to me. Something unexpected. So far, we'd been to the bakery and the beach.

"Will you trust me already? It'll be fun." Cullen made his way down to the edge of water, so I took my shoes off and placed them, along with the box from the bakery, next to Cullen's on the seat of a picnic table nearby, before heading down there myself.

There was a breeze coming off the water. That gorgeous, fresh, salty air that cooled my skin and whipped my hair around my face. How long had it been since I had been back to the water? It must have been ages, but my shoulders instantly loosened and my body relaxed, as if from muscle memory.

"There's a spot up ahead in a bit that I love to go to. It's my thinking spot." Cullen's head was bowed, his hands in his pockets as he walked.

"About your books?"

"Book. I still only have the one in this genre."

"A hugely successful one," I said. "Everyone must be dying for your next."

A pained expression flashed across his face. "That's the problem. The buildup. People are expecting me to recreate whatever it was that I did, and they loved, with *The Ninth Village*."

I didn't quite understand. "That shouldn't be too complicated, should it? You did it once already."

A short bark of a laugh. "It sounds easy. But the expectations are so high. I feel completely blocked because I'm so worried about messing it up and having people hate it."

That sounded awful. I could sort of relate. I had been writing in my journal for so long about personal things, and I could never in a million years imagine having someone else read my words. To also have people critique them on top of that? I shuddered.

"I'm sorry. That sounds hard," I said.

"It'll be alright. I have to wait for my mojo to reappear, I guess."

I laughed at this. "I'd like to see your mojo in action."

His gaze met mine. "You would?"

My face went hot. Why had I said that? Words often came out of my mouth without me thinking them through first.

"Let's hope it shows up when you need it," I said, instead of answering.

We approached the edge of the beach, where a rock face appeared. I followed Cullen off the beach and up a sandy dune to a grass-covered area. There was a house just beyond.

"Are we leaving? We left our shoes back at the other end of the beach."

"No, not leaving yet. I want to show you this one spot though." Cullen gestured for me to follow him through another patch of grass. We went past the house and came to the edge of a small cliff. Below us was a protected cove, an area enclosed by a semicircle of huge rock faces facing the water.

"Isn't this private property?" I glanced back at the house behind us. It felt like we were in their backyard.

"I know the owners. They won't mind." Cullen pointed to an almost-hidden stairway at the edge of the cliff. "Let's go down there."

I glanced behind me again and then turned back to see Cullen descending the somewhat rickety wood stairs. I followed. The ocean crashed against the rocks underneath us, creating monumental splashes and waves. The sound instantly brought me back to my childhood: summer nights spent falling asleep listening to the sound of the tide. That had always been a special kind of memory. One that couldn't be erased by my family's past.

"There's a specific spot I like to sit in," Cullen called over his shoulder.

"You like to sit here?" I must have misheard him. Waves were crashing all over the rocks in a frenzy. This didn't seem like a calm area to relax.

"Yeah. Right here." He hiked up his shorts a bit and sat on the edge of one of the rocks down close to the water. His legs dangled down the side. "Only your legs should get wet."

"Should?" I repeated. He glanced up over his shoulder at me and smiled.

"It depends on the size of the waves. Are you willing to risk it?"

I considered the waves and the spot where Cullen was seated. It seemed safe. I moved closer to him and took a seat. My toes skimmed the water below me, barely touching.

"Now what?" I asked.

"Now we sit and enjoy the sound and the feel of the water." He had to raise his voice over the echoing of the surf in the cove. It was loud, but somehow also calming.

I looked out in front of us. There were no slow waves rolling in like the ones by my mother's place. Instead, the water was wild and rough, splashing white and frothy below us. I studied the way the waves moved, in a rhythmic manner, as if they knew exactly which way to go. The crashing nearly blocked out all other sounds around me. There were no birds squawking up in the sky, no kids yelling to one another in the water. There was only me and Cullen and the ocean.

"They're getting bigger," Cullen said. Just as he pointed to the water, I noticed a huge wave rolling in.

"That one's not going to get much smaller before it gets to us." I went to move, to stand to get away from the water, but Cullen put his hand over mine. The hairs at the back of my neck stood up.

"Wait."

Every part of my body felt him touch me.

"Wait for what?" I asked. The wave rolled in and crashed

on the rocks underneath us. Water splashed up and onto my legs, a little on my arms and torso. I yelped with surprise, even though I had seen it coming, and then I laughed.

"Whenever I get near the water, I feel like I'm a kid again," Cullen said. His eyes sparkled when he grinned. Droplets of water glistened on his tanned skin. His head snapped back to the water in front of us. "Here comes another one."

This time, it was even bigger. The bottom of my shorts got wet. My head fell back when I laughed this time. Cullen moved his hand away from mine. I wanted him to put it back immediately. I wanted to reach out and touch his jaw, feel his rough stubble under my fingers.

We stayed on the rocks for a while, in this secret paradise, in some kind of dreamlike existence. I couldn't say how long we were there, because I was so caught up in it. Alone in the cove, sitting under the warm sun, listening to the sound of the water, anticipating the size of the waves. Both a surge of energy and a sense of calmness flowed through me.

I didn't want the spell to break.

Later, part-soaked, we walked back to get our shoes and left the beach. I had to admit to myself that I had been having fun. The bakery, the cove and the ocean—it had been impossible not to get caught up in the enchantment of it.

"Thanks for this." I bent over to pick up my shoes.

"You're welcome. Have you had fun so far?"

"So far?" I straightened up and eyed him.

"What? You think I only planned out two stops on our tour of Old Port? Was it that easy? Have I convinced you to fall in love already?"

My eyes darted away from him, over his shoulder. *Don't answer that question.*

"I don't know..." I began.

"There's a lot more coming. But later," he said, and then looked away before returning his gaze back to me.

"Sounds good," I said. I liked the idea of there being more to come. I was inspired by being here. The sounds and smells. I should get back to writing the article while I was feeling it.

"Great." He nodded.

A swirl of anticipation moved through my stomach. What was Cullen doing to me? He was handsome and interesting, and he seemed like maybe he was interested in me a little. We were having a good time. It sucked to think it wouldn't last. I gave my head a small shake. I wasn't sure why I was thinking long-term at all. Long-term didn't work for me. It hadn't in the past; it hadn't for my parents. There was no point in hoping for something I already knew was too hard.

TWELVE

At home, I wrote about Cullen. I started in my journal, even though I knew I should work on the article. I wanted to capture details from today before they were hard to remember. Surprisingly, instead of making up a wildly romantic scenario like I usually would, I found that I had instead written an account of the day as it had happened.

I bit the end of my pen and frowned at my journal. I was too old for this. But then again, when I wrote, I could be anyone. Anything could happen. It was a nice reprieve from normal life. I sighed and slid my journal under the pillow of my old bed. I had to write more of my article, not this. I tapped away on my laptop, deleting words as quickly as I was writing them. They weren't flowing today. It didn't make sense. I had almost all I needed, and had just spent the whole day exploring with Cullen. I should be able to close my eyes and focus and then write, but it wasn't working.

My phone buzzed.

How'd it go in Old Port?

It was Sarina.

Hey! Good, thanks. Staying here a little longer

Really? Thought you couldn't stand going back

She was right. But that was before. Now it felt different, and I knew why, but wasn't willing to admit it out loud to anyone. Not yet.

Things changed this week. We need to catch up! You should come visit me here sometime

How are you?

I'm good. I'd love that… fill me in when we meet! Gotta run

I sent her a heart emoji and put my phone down so I could turn back to my article. Then on impulse I snapped my laptop shut. It could wait.

In the kitchen, my mother pulled things out of the fridge and cupboards. She moved swiftly; it was clear she knew the layout of this room, knew these walls and this furniture, like the back of her hand. I studied her. When my father had first left, I'd thought she was going to come apart. She had relied on him and the pattern of their lives the way most partners do. One person always takes the garbage out or is the one to always put the laundry away. When one person is always cooking and the other is cleaning, or one handles the mortgage and the other pays the utility bills, it's natural to fall into a rhythm, or into a dependence on each other. For some reason I'd thought she would struggle with the weight of it all, but she hadn't.

"Let me make dinner tonight," I said.

She kept moving through the motions, grabbing a bottle of olive oil, placing a tomato onto a cutting board. "It's okay. I don't mind."

"No, really. Let me do it."

She finally stopped moving and turned to me. "Oh. Okay, sure. Thank you. But why?"

"I want to do something nice for you," I said. "You're letting me stay here, and you're taking care of me. I want to thank you. Why don't you take a glass of wine and sit outside and relax? I'll be out as soon as I get something in the oven."

"I had salmon ready—"

I gave her a gentle push toward the sliding back door. "I know. I've got it. Go."

She smiled and took the bottle of wine I handed her before heading out to the back deck to sit and watch the sun lower in the sky.

I went to work. I searched for what kind of spice to put on the salmon; I found the right ingredients in the fridge to make a chopped salad. I tried to go the extra mile because my mother deserved it. She had always done things for me without me asking. I wanted to return the favor now that I could.

Once the salad was made and the salmon was in the oven, I placed some cheddar and crackers on a plate, grabbed a knife and went out to sit with her. This time of day hadn't always been my favorite as a kid growing up, but I could appreciate it now that I was older. Sitting out on the deck, listening to the sound of the town going quiet, before it got dark, but after the heat of the sun had started to dim. My body loosened, as if it had been waiting for this.

"I brought snacks," I said, placing the plate on the table in front of us.

"Perfect. Thank you." My mother handed me the bottle of wine. "Want some?"

I poured a glass and enjoyed the sharpness on my tongue.

"How was your day today?" she asked.

"It was good." I smiled to myself at the memory of the cove, being in the bakery.

"You spent it with Cullen? For the story?" There was a hint of a smile on her face.

"Yes. For the story."

It was the truth, although I could sense my mother had already detected there might be something more there. Being with Cullen was surprising. We did small, simple things, and yet it felt like there was a strong pull between us. I couldn't help but want to steal looks at him whenever I was near him. I liked the way the corners of his eyes crinkled when he smiled. I liked listening to him speak. I hadn't felt this way in real life for as long as I could remember. It worried me.

"What happened?" my mother asked.

I turned to her. "What do you mean?"

"Your face changed. You were smiling, and you looked so calm, and then it changed so quickly, like you had remembered something."

"No. It's nothing. I'm fine."

I could sense her studying me the way mothers do.

"Have you been out much lately? Have you been trying to see anyone?"

My eyes darted to the ocean around me. I didn't want to have this kind of chat again. I knew she had the best of intentions, but I didn't want to talk about how single I was, how alone my life was. We had been over this.

"No, not really. But I'm fine. You know that. Look at me." I held my arms out and waved them up and down my body in exaggeration, to show her I was perfectly okay and she had nothing to worry about. I tried to make light of the situation, because otherwise it had the potential to ruin the pleasantness of the moment.

"I know you're great as you are. I worry about you. That's all."

"Why? I've got a good job and I'm doing well for myself. I

don't need to date to be complete. Look at you. You've been single for years and you're happy."

"That's true," she said. "It doesn't have to do with dating so much. It's more that all you do is write for work or write in that notebook of yours. You spend so much time writing, and not as much time living your life. You don't go out a lot or see friends." She put a hand out and rested it on my arm. I let it sit for a moment before I pulled my arm away. It was embarrassing that she'd picked up on my journal writing, but she didn't know what I was writing at least. And I didn't think that what she was saying was necessarily true.

"I see friends," I said. "I've been making plans with Sarina to come visit."

"That's nice!" My mother's voice went up. She loved Sarina. "When? How long are you planning on staying here?"

"I don't know." I bounced my foot in place, my leg overcome with restlessness. "Why? Do you have plans? I didn't even ask how long would be okay. I'm sorry."

She shook her head. "Don't be sorry, and stay as long as you like. Please. I don't get a lot of time with you, so when I do, I'm happy to soak it up. Even if I had plans, it wouldn't mean you had to leave."

"Okay. If you're sure," I said, placing a square of cheese onto a cracker. "But please be honest with me and just tell me if I'm overstaying."

She laughed. "I could never get enough of you. You're my favorite person on the planet."

It sounded like an exaggeration, but I knew it wasn't. I gave her an appreciative smile. When I glanced out at the ocean and watched the waves roll in, when I took a sip of my crisp white wine, when I looked at my mother, I thought of how lucky I was. And when thoughts of Cullen crept into my head, I thought of how good things could potentially be, too.

THIRTEEN

The next day I sat down by the water with my laptop, working on my story for Celine. It was starting to take shape, and I was actually quite proud of it. I was lost in my words when I heard the familiar sound of Cullen's voice calling my name, low and husky. Sexy. I shook my head. I couldn't be thinking of how sexy his voice was while trying to write an unbiased story on him.

"Meg!"

He was at the end of his dock, calling to me and waving. He had on a pair of long, checkered grey and black board shorts and a white T-shirt.

I waved back at him.

"Can I come over?" He gestured to where I was sitting.

"Sure," I called back. The rest of the story could wait—and I didn't mind. It was unnerving, but I liked the low humming in my body, like it reacted when I knew he was near. And it was nice that he felt comfortable enough to drop by and sit and chat, as if we were old friends. What were we? I hadn't really thought about it. I hadn't wanted to put a label on it, because then I might have to admit to myself that we were nothing more than writer and subject. I felt something between us, but I couldn't tell if I did something exciting and weird to his insides the way he did to mine.

"What are you writing? Is it about me?" He peered at my computer screen and smiled as he took the seat next to me.

"It *is* about you, actually," I answered. Normally, I would shut my screen, embarrassed to have anyone other than Celine look at my work before it was finished. "Do you want to see some of it?" This was so uncharacteristic of me. I liked the way I was around him.

"Sure."

I pointed my laptop in his direction. "You can read the intro. But that's all."

He moved closer, his eyes scanning the screen. I looked away. After a few minutes, he straightened up.

"Wow. That's really good."

"You don't have to say that." I tried to keep my voice light. I didn't want him to see how awkward I felt.

"I'm not just saying it. I mean it. It's really engaging." His eyes went to my face and stayed there. "You're a talented writer."

I looked away and then glanced back. He looked down briefly before his eyes went to mine again. Back and forth, back and forth, trying not to be obvious.

"Thank you," I said.

"It feels a little weird to read about myself," he said. "Especially when you're saying such nice things."

"Really?" That surprised me. Even without any social media, he had to be used to the attention by now. All the requests for interviews and appearances at conferences.

"Can I read a little more?" There was a slight gleam in his eye as he moved closer. His arm brushed my thigh. He grinned at me, clearly oblivious to the fact that I had sucked in and was holding my breath.

"Sure." I leaned in closer and pointed the screen at him. "Only a tiny bit."

He turned to the screen and his eyes went back and forth as he read. I tried not to stare. At one point, he went to touch the keyboard, but paused.

"Can I scroll down a bit more?"

"Sure." I studied his face, looking for any type of reaction.

After a brief moment, his face changed. The lightness left. His mouth made a tight line across his face and he scratched at his chin.

"Oh. Is everything okay?" I sat upright and swivelled the laptop around back to me. How bad was my story? I had a moment of fear flood my veins as I imagined every possible scenario. Maybe I had written something awful about him? Or worse—had I accidentally typed out some of my innermost desires onto my screen instead of capturing them in my journal? No. I couldn't have.

"I think I may have touched something. On your keyboard," he said.

I glanced at my screen and found that it wasn't the story I was writing reflecting back at me. He must have clicked on one of the dozens of tabs I'd left open. It took me a second, but I realized what I was looking at. It was Celine's story. The Marshall bus piece. I had been reading it for inspiration earlier.

"That's, uh—that's a really sad story," he said, his voice low and heavy. "Why are you reading it?"

"I didn't realize it was still open. It's just something from our paper from a while ago." I closed the tab and then eyed him. His reaction was so... physical. I wanted to reach out and touch his arm, or run a hand down his back, but that would be much too familiar.

"Oh." He was still quiet when he gestured at my laptop. "Hope I didn't mess anything up on there."

I studied him, this subdued version of Cullen. I wasn't used to it. "No, I'm sure it's fine."

I gave the story a quick scan. It *was* fine, nothing accidentally added by fumbling fingers. Now I wanted to put my laptop away and change the subject, or distract him to get back to the usual Cullen.

"Hey, I heard there's going to be a barbecue tomorrow night at the Waterfront Suites. The woman who works there—"

"Gwen?" Cullen interjected.

"You know her?"

He nodded. "She's great." His signature smile returned faintly.

"She said it's a community thing. Everyone goes. Want to check it out with me?"

Cullen leaned forward and scratched at his ankle. "With you? I'd love to." He straightened up again and looked out toward the ocean.

I nodded, even though I knew he wasn't looking at me, and my body melted into my seat in relief.

FOURTEEN

The following day was Friday, and I spent most of it on the couch with a book. I hadn't experienced this for so many years, but I remembered now how my body had relaxed when I was here at the beach house. It was like muscle memory from child-hood. I'd wind down and take every day slow back then. Today was no different. I spent at least four hours reading before I even considered getting showered.

My mother did her thing—coffee and the crossword in the morning, followed by some gardening in the back where she had planted the most gorgeous dahlias and hydrangeas. We ate lunch outside, then she ran a few errands in town. Before she left, I asked her if she wanted to join me at the barbecue that evening. Otherwise, she'd be here alone. Again. She seemed to enjoy her quiet life—I'd witnessed it with my own eyes—but I couldn't help but wonder how much aloneness was too much for her.

"Aren't you going with Cullen?" she asked.

"Yes, but that doesn't matter. It's not a date."

"It's not?" She slid the strap of her purse over her shoulder and eyed me.

"No. I'm interviewing him for work. That's all."

We both knew that was a lie. As much as I tried to deny it, I liked him. I enjoyed his company, I wanted to be around him as much as I could.

"You go. I might pop by at some point to see what it's all about, but I'll see how I feel later."

"You're sure?"

"Yes, I'm fine. This is what I'm used to, and I like it." It sounded like she was trying to convince me, or maybe herself. She gave me a pointed look when I didn't respond right away.

"Okay. Okay, I'll go with Cullen. But if you change your mind, please just say so?"

"I will." She gave me a quick hug, patted my back three times and then left the house.

In the bathroom, I planned to do my "everything shower". It was a bit of a luxury; the type of shower where I would take my time, deep condition my hair, exfoliate with a fruity scrub, shave my legs. I told myself it had nothing to do with seeing Cullen this evening.

After the shower, I moisturized my entire body, blow-dried my hair for the first time since I'd got to Old Port and then borrowed another sundress from my mother. I looked for some tinted lip gloss that I knew had been sitting in my purse for at least three months, but decided against it. There was a fine line between looking nice and looking like I was trying a little too hard.

Cullen and I had agreed to meet and walk to the barbecue together. It was close enough to do so, and the afternoon sunshine was at the perfect spot in the clear sky—not at its oppressively hot height, and not completely vanished behind clouds. Outside, when I heard the faint sound of gravel underfoot, my heart quickened before I even looked up.

"Hey," Cullen said.

I was right. "Hey, you."

"You look—really great." He did this thing with his lip—kind of bit it a little—and then put his hands in his pockets.

I wasn't able to stop the smile from widening across my face. Daniel hadn't been the type to openly compliment me. He'd once told me he thought it was a given that I knew he thought I looked nice. I think it's good to actually hear it from time to time.

"Should we go?" I asked.

Cullen put a hand out as if to say "you first". I liked this polite, chivalrous side to him. I wanted to brush my hand over his, but I opted for walking close to him instead. He smelled good, like his usual tangy, fresh soap. It embarrassed me that I already knew his smell.

We didn't even have to reach the Waterfront Suites before I could hear the hum of conversation. Out front and on a patch of grassy land just to the right of the entrance, near the water, people milled about, talking, laughing. Kids chased one another. A barbecue was set up and smoking, burgers and sausages and hot dogs on the grill. Faint music played in the background.

"I didn't know it was going to be such a party," I said to Cullen.

"It's a Friday evening in July in a seaside town. This is when we party. Are you up for getting wild?"

"Ha. I don't think I know how to do wild," I said.

He grinned and shook his head. "I bet that's not true. You seem like you've got a side to you not many see."

I swallowed, trying to think of a response, but coming up short. I liked this, it felt like flirting, but for some reason it wasn't coming easy to me. "Maybe," I said, and smiled. There. That might sound mysterious or teasing. Or a little bit pathetic.

Just ahead of us, Gwen stood at a large table next to the barbecue, pouring kids plastic glasses of pink lemonade. Emily was beside her, helping Gwen pass the drinks out, a giant grin on her face. The simplicity of childhood and the joy you could get from pink lemonade was sweet. There was an outdoor seating area set up in the shade. I gestured to it.

"Should we sit?"

"I'll grab us drinks."

While Cullen went in search of something a little stronger than pink lemonade, I surveyed the crowd. There was laughter and smiling and loud conversation. I didn't remember Old Port being like this. I couldn't recall Friday evenings in July being joyous.

After a moment, Gwen came to my side.

"Meg! I'm so glad you made it." She leaned in and hugged me. We were hugging now. I liked it. "Did I see you here with Cullen?"

"I'm writing a story on him," I said.

"Lucky you." She nudged me with an elbow, one eyebrow raised, and I couldn't help but laugh. "Listen, please enjoy yourself. Have something to eat. Have some drinks. I have to make sure everyone is taken care of, but if you need anything let me know."

I nodded and thanked her. She barely knew me, yet she was so welcoming. It sent a warm glow through me.

Cullen came back holding two cans of beer and handed me one. "Did you want a plastic glass for that? Sorry, we don't really do fancy around here. You probably remember that though."

I shrugged. "I don't remember anything very fancy about Old Port, no. But this is good, thanks." I took a sip. The beer was refreshing and bold, and it went down easy. I'd have to be careful.

"I'm sure your life in Boston is much more *big city*. All wine bars and fine cuisine." His voice was light when he spoke, as if he didn't mean anything by it.

"That kind of scene is great sometimes, but it's not really me."

"No?"

I shook my head. "I'm more of a homebody."

"I'm the same." He nodded. "I think authors get used to being recluses. We don't get out much, since we spend a lot of time alone, typing away." He looked at me. "I'm sure you know."

"I'm not an author."

He seemed to consider what I said, and then nudged his glasses up on his face. "You write. You're a writer. It's all very similar."

I didn't think it was exactly the same. My type of writing couldn't be compared to Cullen's and all his success, but I appreciated the nod to my work. It was nice to be taken seriously.

"Maybe you don't spend a lot of time alone," he said. "You must be out with friends or on dates a lot."

I smiled. "I don't get out much, no. I really don't mind being alone, but I guess there's a limit to everything." I thought of my mother. I hoped she would come by.

"You're thinking about something?" Cullen studied me now, his eyebrows drawn in.

"No, I'm good." I gave my head a small shake and smiled. I wanted to be present. Maybe I'd get more detail for my article. Although, that wasn't why I was happy to be here.

"How about you?" I asked. "Do you date much?"

He seemed to think about the question. "Nothing really serious."

I wondered what that meant. "So you do date?" I shouldn't pry, but I could pretend it was all in the name of research.

"Here and there."

There was no reason for the pang of jealousy I felt. I was writing an article about him, looking for answers. And of course he dated. He was an adult. This was all very irrational of me, and I had no right to feel it, but things with Cullen seemed different somehow.

"Nobody has really interested me all that much," he said. "Well, not yet, anyway." He held my eye when he spoke. I had to look away. My fingers tingled with anticipation, but any smart response I could think of got stuck in my throat.

After a few hours, a couple of delicious burgers and some of Gwen's pink lemonade, Cullen and I decided to head back. It wasn't late, but Cullen kept yawning.

"Busy week," he explained. "I've been staying up way too late writing most nights."

We thanked and hugged Gwen, and then started to make the walk back. The night air was warm, and the sky was lit up by a brilliant moon.

My phone vibrated with a text from my mother.

> Not going to make it to the barbecue. But I'm
> going to play cards with some friends. Be back
> later. Love you xoxo

"Everything okay?" Cullen asked.

"It's great."

When we got to the patch of land in front of the two cottages, we stopped and stood facing one another. I surprised myself by looking away, rather than directly up at Cullen. The moment felt too charged. I didn't know what to do with my eyes, or with any part of me.

"What are you up to now?" Cullen asked.

"Nothing really. I was going to read. Or have a glass of wine and listen to the water for a bit. Boring stuff."

"It sounds perfect." He didn't move.

Don't read into this. Don't read into it.

"Want to join me?" I asked. I nearly squinted, but didn't want him to see me visibly cringing.

"Yes."

The melting sensation came over me again. Somehow, my jelly limbs carried me inside, where I opened a bottle of wine and poured two glasses, intensely aware all the time of Cullen leaning against the counter as I got our drinks, walking behind me as I led the way out to the porch, sitting beside me as we watched the sky and listened to the lull of the waves, his arm so close to mine we were almost touching.

After two glasses of wine, maybe a little more, my face was flushed and my body buzzed. I was in the little sweet spot—if I had even another sip of wine, I would feel terrible and regret it the next day, but if I stopped now, I'd feel good for the rest of the evening.

We had talked about everything and nothing in particular. Cullen had shown an interest in my writing. He'd asked questions and looked so interested in me when I spoke. The way I was feeling about him was something unique. He was both sweet and sexy.

"I think I'll probably make some tea," I said as I placed my wine glass on the small table between us on the porch. "Would you like some?"

"I don't know."

"Oh. You don't?" My shoulders dropped. He must be ready to get back home.

He looked right into my eyes. "I was hoping we could go inside."

Every inch of my body flashed with heat. I nodded.

Inside, I fumbled with the light switch and then the things on the counter in front of me: a pad of paper, a pen, my set of keys. I couldn't stand still. Cullen came closer until he was standing just in front of me.

"Meg."

"Yes?" I couldn't look directly at him. My body wouldn't allow me to lift my head and maintain eye contact for a second longer. Why did I have to be so awkward?

"Meg," he repeated. This time, after a pause, I looked up. His eyes were serious and focused, his mouth in a straight line and his jaw flexed. His skin was a perfect blend of smooth along his forehead and cheeks, but rough and rugged with stubble by his jawline. He reached out and put his hands on my upper arms.

My knees almost buckled. Jolts of electricity radiated from my stomach downward. His touch was so warm. I wanted this. I hadn't known how much I'd wanted his hands on me until they were there. He moved them slowly, lightly, up and down, and I almost gasped.

When he leaned in, I closed my eyes. It felt like forever until I could sense his face close, the space between us disappearing until his mouth was on mine. His soft, full lips kissed me in a way that was both hungry and tender, his stubble brushing my skin. My body relaxed into his and he pulled my arms closer, my head tilting back. He tasted like a hint of wine. His kiss grew more urgent.

I had been telling myself I hadn't been waiting for this, but I had. I had been waiting for Cullen for so long. I'd been writing fantasies about love and quiet passion because it was exciting and fun, but they were nothing compared to this. The real thing —and with someone as interesting and kind and handsome as Cullen, who was incredible at kissing and doing things with his hands that made my body ignite.

I ran my hands up his broad back and into his hair. I placed a hand on the side of his face and ran my fingers over his light stubble. He let out a tiny sound, almost a moan.

Oh god.

The sound of a car on gravel came from out front, through

the window. I pulled back. Cullen ran a hand through his hair and leaned back on the counter, letting out a breath.

"Damn it," I said. My voice was hoarse.

"Yeah." He looked at me and smiled, wide and slow.

My stomach flipped. I might never recover from this.

"I better go." He hesitated for a moment, but then brushed past me, toward the back door, dragging his hand lightly over my stomach and the small of my back as he went. I closed my eyes.

"Hey! Hello," my mother called from the front door. I opened my eyes again and Cullen was gone.

"In the kitchen," I answered.

She came into the room and placed her bag on the counter. "Did you have a good night?"

"I did." I smiled, turning towards the kettle to hide the flush in my cheeks. "I'm making tea. Do you want some?"

"Sure. Let's go drink it on the porch. It's beautiful tonight."

It was.

FIFTEEN

Celine emailed me early the next day. I was still in bed when I reached for my phone. There were a few social media notifications, a text with a funny dog meme from Sarina and the email from Celine. I didn't want to open it. I was still trying to relive last night over and over again. Cullen's lips. His hands. I didn't want the dream to break and reality to set in.

But the truth was, reality paid the bills. I rolled over in bed and opened the email anyway. Celine said she knew I was on vacation, so no rush to respond, but at the same time, she wanted to check in and see if I was still on track to deliver the article as soon as I was back, by her new—now somewhat firm—due date. I sighed at my phone.

I tapped back a quick response and told her I would have it to her on time, things were good, and also could I get my lieu days into the schedule? I didn't want her to forget that I was essentially working on my time off. She didn't need to know that I didn't mind because it meant I could be with Cullen.

I shifted in bed and clicked off my phone, placing it on the nightstand. My notebook was sitting there, with my journal just underneath it. I didn't feel like writing in either. Instead, I got up and glanced at myself in a mirror. I had on an oversized, loose v-neck with a pair of shorts, and my hair was big and wild from sleep, but I thought it gave me a sexy kind of vibe. I went downstairs and filled a cup of coffee before heading out to the porch. Mom was already out there.

"Morning. Is there any particular reason you're smiling to yourself?" she greeted me.

"What? I'm not," I said. "Am I?" I took a seat next to her.

"You are."

I would have to try harder to hide my feelings, but I was still glowing from last night, and I really didn't want to push any of that feeling down or away. Then again, I had no idea what it all meant. I was hoping to see Cullen soon to find out if there would be more of it.

"Have you decided how much longer you're going to stay for?" Mom sipped from her flower-printed coffee cup. "No rush to get going. I like you here."

I liked me here, too. For now. But I couldn't deny the small part of me that longed for my city life again—back in my house, walking the busy streets, ordering anything I wanted for dinner because there was so much to choose from. Old Port felt good right here and now, but I hadn't lost sight of the fact that it wasn't my reality.

"I'm not sure." It had already been a week, much longer than I had expected to stay. Since I had booked a longer-than-usual break from work, I still had another week off, and I had been ready to go back home. But then—Cullen.

"You're doing it again. Smiling."

"I am not," I said.

"This wouldn't have anything to do with my neighbor, would it?"

"No, it has nothing to do with him." I wasn't sure if I was a good enough liar to pull that off. I tried anyway. "It's just a story for work."

"Okay, then. So, you won't care at all that he's coming over here right now?"

I froze. My eyes darted in the direction of his house. She was right. He was walking over here, a mug in his hand. He had on a faded blue T-shirt with "Quiksilver" printed across it in big white letters and a pair of board shorts again. I'd felt sexy earlier, but now I doubted myself. I ran a hand through my wild hair to try and tame it, or fluff it. Whatever would make me look like I hadn't just rolled out of bed.

"You look fine," Mom said to me. Then she raised her voice and called to him. "Good morning! Come join us."

"Hello." Cullen gazed directly at me when he approached.

"Hi." My face instantly heated. I observed his body language—searching for signs of something. Nothing different from the usual Cullen. That was both good and bad. Good because my mother didn't need any more signs to convince her I had a thing for my interviewee. And bad because I had a thing for my interviewee, and I couldn't tell if it was reciprocated. Maybe he casually kissed women all the time. We hadn't actually gotten very in-depth last night before we were interrupted.

"It's gorgeous out today, isn't it?" My mother pointed out at the horizon. The waves were calm and there was only a delicate breeze. "It's going to be nice all week."

"Is it?" Cullen asked. "That's perfect. We need good weather for our next outing, hey, Meg?"

I turned to him. "We have another outing?"

"I thought we could go somewhere together."

My stomach flipped. "Sure. When?"

My mother took a sip of her coffee to hide her smile. I wanted to nudge her, but I also didn't want Cullen to notice.

"How about tomorrow, if you'll still be here? I have some book things I have to get done today."

"Sounds good. I'll be here." I took a sip of my coffee to hide my own smile.

. . .

Later, when I was in my old bedroom, my clothes on the bed in front of me, I could see I was in desperate need of more of my things. I had been wearing the same two pairs of shorts and borrowing shirts and dresses from my mother for days now. It wasn't going to work for much longer. It didn't escape me that I wanted to stay for a while. It also didn't escape me why. I thought of Cullen's mouth again, of his lips. I wasn't clear where we stood with all of that, but I hoped I'd get a chance to discover tomorrow.

For now, I'd have to make the drive back home. I might as well do it when I had nothing much planned. The hours in the car wouldn't be great, but at least I had a wide-open day in front of me.

I grabbed my bag and told my mother the plan.

"I'll be back by dinnertime." I leaned in to kiss her on the cheek. "Want me to pick us up something to eat in town on my way back?"

"That's perfect. I'll be cleaning all day, so I won't have much time for cooking."

"Cleaning?"

"It's Rosie, Helen and Nancy Time tomorrow." Her smile lit up her entire face.

This was an annual get together with three of her oldest and best friends. They came to visit for a few days and played cards, consumed endless snacks and drinks, and caught up on what had been going on in their lives. They would almost always go for a swim in the ocean in the mornings, stay up late talking, and take things slow in between. They had been doing it for as long as I could remember, and my mother looked forward to it every year.

I smiled at the thought of my mother's friends. I adored them. They filled up the room with their conversation and personalities. When I was around when I was younger, they'd offer to make me something to eat while telling me to sit and rest and also asking me about my life without prying. They were experts at making you feel important and cared for. And they had been there for my mother when she'd desperately needed someone. I think I loved them the most because of that.

"I completely forgot," I said. "I'm going to be in the way."

"Nonsense." My mother shook her head. "They love you. You know that."

"And I love them, but I'll keep myself busy as much as I can, anyway."

My plans with Cullen would keep me occupied. Even though I didn't know what we were doing, I couldn't wait. I hoped I wasn't getting ahead of myself.

"I'm sure you will." My mother lightly hip-checked me.

I laughed and gave her a quick squeeze before telling her to behave and making my way to my car. As much as I didn't want to leave Cullen behind, it would be good to check on my house and get some of my clothes. I could pop into my favorite coffee shop, too. Mom's coffee was great, but it wasn't the same as in the city.

After a relatively uneventful drive home, I unlocked my front door and went inside to a stuffy room filled with stale air. I opened the windows in the kitchen and living room; it wasn't too hot out today and the breeze would be nice. Sounds of cars whisking down the main road came into the room. Not as relaxing as the whooshing of the ocean, obviously, but it was home. I spent time sorting through the mail, emptying out my fridge of anything that had gone bad and taking my garbage out. Then I gathered up a few of my most flattering tops and shorts and put them on my bed to pack later.

My phone dinged. I pulled it from my back pocket and looked at the screen. It was Cullen.

Hope you don't stay away too long

How come?

I was flirting with him. Not typical of me—I generally saved that for the journal—but Cullen brought it out in me. I was a little different after that kiss.

I'm looking forward to seeing you again

The three bubbles indicated he was still typing.

Alone

My breath quickened and my body seemed to liquefy. I felt those words in every inch of me.

SIXTEEN

I needed a coffee before I could do anything else, so I left my home and went for a walk. It was actually pretty good to be back. The streets in my neighborhood vibrated with energy in the best way, even for late July when most cities quietened down.

I turned onto the street for my favorite coffee shop and stopped abruptly. My stomach dropped at what I saw. Up a few feet ahead, walking in my direction, was my ex, Daniel.

He straightened and took his hands out of his pockets when he saw me. "Oh. Meg, hi."

I supposed I would have to stop. He slowed down in front of me and stood with his arms dangling at his sides awkwardly. This wasn't at all what I wanted to do, but at least he was alone and not with a new girlfriend—which I was sure he must have by now.

"Hi," I said. "How are you?"

"Good, thanks. And you?"

I nodded in response.

This was the worst part about running into an ex—the polite small talk. It was almost worse than seeing him with a new partner. At least that would be painful but quick. I wondered how long we would have to stand here, pretending.

"How's work been going?" he asked.

A little while longer, obviously.

"It's pretty good. I'm working on a story about an author. I've actually been out of town interviewing him, but just popped back home to get some things."

I had no idea why I told him all of this. He likely wasn't interested. I could tell by the way his eyes had a glazed look when I spoke. It was a stark reminder of how things had ended for us. One moment, I was all in, invested in our relationship and certain Daniel was going to work out. The next thing I knew, he was out. I hadn't been enough for him. I wasn't interesting enough, or exciting enough. I'd thought the initial love we'd had for one another would have meant that we could withstand the differences. But it didn't and we couldn't.

It was embarrassing to think about how into us I had been. I would have gotten married if he'd wanted. I would have been happy to join our homes and our bank accounts. Maybe I'd have spent more time going out than I had wanted, but it would have been for the good of us. I'd written in my journal about Daniel, before we'd started dating. I'd had fantasies about getting married and how romantic he would be. I'd waited for Daniel to realize how perfect things could be. I'd waited for him to whisk me off my feet. I'd waited for him to fall in love with me like I had with him.

And then it had ended. I wasn't enough. Love wasn't, either.

"How about you?" I asked to be polite, although I wanted to get out of there. This was too awkward and painful.

"I've been busy with work, and other stuff." He shifted a bit and looked over my shoulder. He wanted out of here, too.

"Other stuff?" I couldn't help myself.

Daniel fiddled with his watch, casting his gaze around us,

refusing to look right at me. "Uh, wedding plans, actually. I'm getting married."

I froze, but attempted to plaster a smile onto my face. "Oh. Congratulations." It was all I could choke out, and my voice sounded weird. I hoped he hadn't noticed.

His face softened when he looked at me, like he was relieved I hadn't started crying or made a scene. Of course I wouldn't. Not for him. Although it was awful, standing here in front of him. The problem wasn't Daniel. It was me.

"I should get going," I said.

"Right. Of course. Good to see you." Daniel reached out for me. Before I could stop myself, I backed up a step, as if by instinct, out of reach.

He raised his eyebrows, and then his expression changed, his mouth a firm line across his face. He nodded. "See you," he said.

"See you."

While I walked away, I pulled out my phone and texted Sarina with a shaking hand.

> He's getting married

I didn't need to explain; she would know who I was talking about. And, when I needed her most, my phone rang.

"He's what??" Sarina's voice on the other end was loud, bordering on shrill, as if she was outraged on my behalf. She likely was. God, I loved her.

"Getting married," I said. "Just ran into him."

"In Old Port?"

"No, I came home to grab a few things before I head back."

"Well, good luck to whoever has to listen to him drone on about himself for the rest of their lives."

I laughed dryly. He hadn't been that bad, had he? "I should have expected it."

"Why?" Sarina asked.

"Because people our age are getting married. They're finding their people." *Just not me.*

"And you will, too," Sarina said, as if she heard my inner thoughts. "You have to wait until you find someone who makes you feel as wonderful as you are. You can't settle for less, you're too good for that."

I thanked her for the talk, a surge of fondness powering through me at the way she was always there for me.

"I better run. I have to grab some clothes and head back." My voice threatened to break, and I was disappointed in myself for it. Daniel wasn't worth it, Sarina was right.

"Call me back if you need me. Remember, you dodged a bullet by not getting tied down to him."

I laughed again, only I wasn't quite convinced. Not because of Daniel in particular, but because he was a reminder that there was something wrong with me. Something about me that wasn't loveable enough. I said goodbye to Sarina and hurried the rest of the way home.

After closing windows again and doing a quick tidy of my bedroom, living room and kitchen, I stood by the front door, bag slung over my shoulder, and took a last look around. Everything was neat and clean and emptied out. I hadn't noticed before, but my house was a bit sterile. A far cry from the way my mother's place was filled with books on the table in the living room, with food always out on the counter, sweaters hung over the back of chairs in the kitchen. Her home had a comfortable, lived-in feel. I had always remembered it as the cold, stiff place where our family had fallen apart, but Mom had moved on.

Maybe I needed to do the same. Alone, standing in the middle of my empty townhouse, the tears came. It felt irrational to cry over Daniel. He meant nothing to me anymore, I knew that. My heart knew it. But my brain had other thoughts, whirling around, whispering to me that it was my fault, I was the issue, I was the one who couldn't make things work. Before I knew it, I was spiralling into other thoughts—memories of times when I'd caused a fight with a friend when I was younger, or when my coworkers had asked everyone to lunch except for me, pieces of my past coming back to me. The bad pieces, when my parents had fought, when I'd tried to distract them, or when I'd hoped my hugs would help clear up the issues and we could all go back to being who we were supposed to be: a happy family who loved each other. It was as if I was trying to gather every shred of evidence I could find to prove my dark thoughts about myself. I had once heard a social worker on social media saying that you shouldn't go looking for confirmation that you don't belong, or that you're not enough, because you'll always find it. She said that the truth about who we are lives in our hearts. It was a good reminder, but hard to follow in the moment. Especially because my heart felt shattered.

My phone rang. I gave myself a moment and then I wiped at my tears with the back of my hand.

"Hello?" I couldn't hide the hoarse *I've just been crying* sound that came from the back of my throat.

"Meg?" It was Cullen, his voice laced with confusion and concern. "What's going on? Are you okay?"

"I'm fine," I lied and then sniffled. "What's up?"

"I was calling to see when you thought you might be back in town. Are you sure you're alright?"

I thought about carrying on with the pretense that all was well, but I also wanted to be honest with him. Things felt different after that kiss. At least, they did for me.

"I ran into my ex. He's getting married."

"Oh," he said quietly. "I'm sorry."

I immediately regretted telling him. We weren't there yet with sharing these kinds of details, and he probably had no idea what this meant, or why I was so upset over my ex. Why *was* I so upset?

"It's nothing. It's not a big deal. He doesn't matter to me anymore. I guess it's just that feeling of being—" I paused, not sure how to finish my sentence.

"What?" Cullen's voice was gentle.

"Not the one," I said. I cleared my throat, embarrassed at how pathetic I probably sounded to him. "Anyway, I'm fine, and I was just about to leave. See you soon?"

"Yeah. Sure. Meg... take care. Drive carefully."

I thanked him, said goodbye, and hung up. All I wanted to do was leave the house and get out of the city so I could rid myself of the feelings Daniel had brought back, and be back in Old Port with a fresh outlook. Even though it wasn't clear what was going to happen between me and Cullen, being there had to be better than here right now.

As I drove, I tried my best not to let the thoughts floating around the back of my mind—the ones that made connections between what happened with Daniel and what might happen with Cullen—ruin this for me.

I arrived in town and went straight to Piatto, where I ordered myself and my mother a pizza and a plate of their house meatballs—our favorite—and made my way back home to her.

Inside her house, I was greeted with the fresh, sharp smell of pine. Mom had been cleaning all day and the place sparkled, yet somehow still maintained the comfortable, cozy feeling I had come to love this past week.

"Mom?" I placed the pizza on the counter and pulled a couple of plates and wine glasses from the cupboard.

"You're back." My mother appeared in the doorway of the kitchen, her face flushed and pieces of her hair at her temple escaping her ponytail. She leaned against the frame. "I'm wiped."

"Good thing I made us dinner, then."

She laughed. "Let's go outside to eat."

We sat at the small table to the right of the porch and watched the sky transform into a wash of color while we ate. I tried not to glance at Cullen's house over and over again, but I mustn't have done a very good job.

"I haven't seen him all day," my mother said.

I could sense a prickly feeling in my chest. Cullen and I had kissed, and he'd shown interest afterwards—the flirty text, the phone call—but then I'd potentially ruined the vibe by admitting how sad my personal life was. I didn't know where we stood or what we were. All I knew was that I wanted to hear from him again. I wanted more of him: his words, his hands, the way he made me feel. It was much more intense than it had been with Daniel, and I was starting to realize nobody had ever had this effect on me before. I hadn't realized it could feel like this.

"Let's eat," I said. I didn't want to overanalyze him, or what I was feeling just yet with anyone. If I spoke it out loud, I would be releasing my hopes and wishes into the universe, which would make it all the more painful if things went the way they had with Daniel. Instead, I kept everything bottled up, where it was safe.

SEVENTEEN

The next morning, I got up and showered, dressed in the best casual clothes I'd brought with me—and then frowned when I glanced around my bedroom. Something had changed. Mom had cleaned in here, too, and everything was sparkling, but that wasn't it. It took a while until I noticed it. My nightstand was clear. I had brought my laptop with me when I went back home, but left my notebook and journal beside my bed. Neither one of them was still there. Panic cascaded over me. I'd left my journal behind because I thought nobody would come into this room, but the possibility of anyone else touching it or reading it, even my mother, caused an intense mix of embarrassment and fear.

"Mom?" I called as I went into the hallway. "Have you seen my notebooks? They moved from my nightstand."

She appeared at the doorway of the kitchen. "I can't remember, but I'm sure they're around somewhere. I wouldn't have moved them far."

"Did you read them?"

"Of course not. Why?" she asked.

I shook my head. "I just need them back."

"I'll keep an eye out. I'm sure they'll turn up."

I nodded, and decided that would have to be good enough. She wouldn't read them. They were safe for now.

I left the bedroom, putting my phone in my pocket in an attempt to stop staring at it. Cullen hadn't messaged yet. I didn't want to seem needy, so I didn't want to send the first text, but then I was mad at myself for even having the thought that sending a text made a woman needy. In this day and age, the last thing I needed to worry about was how a text message made me seem to a man I didn't even know all that well yet.

Although, I couldn't deny that I wanted to know him better. I wondered what he'd been thinking about last night, wondered what the day held for us. He had said today was the day he wanted to get together again. I hoped that was the case, but for now, I planned to have coffee on the porch, the way I had most mornings for the last week, and wait to see what unfolded. Only, the moment I entered the kitchen, I was met with the sound of unbridled excitement.

"Meg!" As soon as Rosie saw me, her arms shot straight up in the air and her round eyes widened, like I was the best thing that had ever happened to her. "Your mother said you were here. I'm so glad! I'm so happy to see you." She came toward me and wrapped her arms around me, pulling me into her. The softness of her body was comforting, like a threadbare blanket, worn with time.

"Hi," I said and kissed her cheek. "You're here early."

"We couldn't wait for this day to begin." She let me go, but held onto my forearms as she studied me. "God, you look fantastic. What are you putting on your skin? It's perfection."

I touched the side of my face. It was quite smooth today, actually. "We? Are Helen and Nancy here already, too?"

As if on cue, they came through the doorway, bags in hand. Helen placed hers down when she saw me and came over for a hug.

"Meg. How are you?" She squeezed me in a motherly way.

"I'm good, how are you?" I turned to Nancy, who was also by my side now. "So good to see you again." These women were comfort and love and everything that was right with the world.

When my mother's life had first imploded and her world had fallen apart, it was Rosie and Nancy and Helen who were by her side, bringing food wrapped in foil, doing her laundry when she fell behind, keeping her company at night after I had gone to bed. It was like a death had occurred and these women were not going to let my mother endure any of it alone. They helped her through one of the roughest times in her life so she could eventually see the positive in her new situation—starting over in her forties with a daughter to take care of, a job to be successful at and a house to keep running. And she'd done it. She'd managed it all without my father, in large part because of her friends. I'd never forget that.

They moved around the kitchen now, taking groceries from bags and placing them in the fridge or the cupboards. Helen got herself a mug and filled it with coffee. They were comfortable here; they knew where everything was and helped themselves.

"Need a cup?" Helen asked me, gesturing to the coffee.

"Yes, please."

She filled a mug up and placed it in my hands. "Your mother says you like to have it out on the porch. You should go out there now." One of her eyebrows raised as she spoke and she tried to hide a smile.

I tilted my head at her. Mom had obviously told her about Cullen. I bet they were hoping he'd come over, so they could get a good look at him. My mother laughed, so I spun around to face her. "What is going on?"

"Nothing," she said. "Just go enjoy your coffee. We're going to catch up in here." She shooed me towards the door. I left the kitchen with my cup, certain they were up to something.

Out on the porch, I stopped in my tracks when I saw Cullen's lean silhouette. He was seated on one side, sipping from a mug. He turned when the screen door slapped loudly against the frame and straightened in his seat.

"I was invited over by your mother and her friends."

It took everything I had not to stare at his perfect mouth. "They're funny." I sat next to him.

"They seem it," he said. "They're nice."

I liked the way his voice softened when he said that.

"So, it's a full house?" He glanced behind us and into the kitchen window, then leaned toward me an inch.

"Only for a couple of days."

"You could always come over. You know, if you need some space."

I didn't look at him, even though I wanted to search for signs of what he meant. He put a hand out and touched my arm briefly before pulling away again. It was enough for me to understand.

"I'd love to," I said.

"How about now?"

Yes. Now. Now was perfect.

Inside Cullen's house were white and taupe wood-paneled walls that gave off a beachy, bright vibe. The ceilings were high and the huge windows let sunlight into every room. We stood in the kitchen, which was small, with the same wood paneling, only painted in a green that complemented the grey flooring. It was both modern and seaside. There were canisters set out on the countertop and a small table in the corner, right under a window with a view of the ocean. It was stunning and yet homey at the same time. Although, the last thing on my mind at the moment was Cullen's sense of style in home decor.

I tried my hardest not to look directly at him. It felt too intimate. It was funny how I could daydream of a moment like this, and write about it over and over in my journal, only to find myself in the situation in real life and be immobilized by shyness. I didn't want to move or get too close or look right at him.

"I've missed you," he said.

"It's only been a day." I tried to laugh.

"I know. But I have." He gestured to the living room. "Want to sit?"

I nodded and followed him, taking a seat on the couch. He sat next to me. It felt like I was in slow-motion, and I had no idea what to do with my head or my neck, so I studied the things he had in his living room: the book on the table in front of me, the coffee mug that looked like it had been used just recently. Our hands were by our sides, flat on the couch between us, and eventually, the edge of his fingers found mine. Just a whisper of a touch, but a weightlessness, a floating sensation went through me. I almost closed my eyes. I wanted to sigh. It felt so good when he touched me.

I finally turned to look at him and he turned, too. His face was so close, I could smell him: fresh, clean skin, like he had recently showered. I wanted to touch his face again, to run my hands over him and hear him make that quiet moan once more. Instead, I blurted out, "What?"

I don't know why I said awkward things like that. It was so far from sexy or flirty. Our fingers were still touching. I didn't move.

"I don't know."

He didn't know? What did that mean? I stiffened. Cullen shifted in his seat and started rambling.

"No, I mean. I know. I know. I know that I really like you. And I know that your ex must be an idiot to have let you go." He paused and ran a hand through his hair. "What I don't know is if it's okay for me to do this." He gestured to his hand. "To touch you. To kiss you."

It was hard for me to speak, but I managed to get a few words out. "It's okay. It's very okay."

His eyes went to mine, then crinkled when he smiled. He gently pulled me to standing and placed one of his hands on my arm and the other on my lower back. It felt foreign to have someone touch me like this. This was different from Daniel. So much better. I was temporarily breathless. I stared up at him, saying nothing, not moving.

He looked down at me, his face serious as he studied my mouth. And then he was kissing me. His hands were on my back, his face pressed into mine. His lips parted and he kissed me long and soft at first, slowly getting more urgent. My legs were limp.

We moved together, touching and kissing, into another room, somehow up the stairs and into his bedroom. He went to the bed first and sat. Something bold ignited in me and I approached him, straddling his lap. I took his face in my hands. My god. His eyes were so deep and dark. So gorgeous. He put his hand on the outside of my thigh, gripping just below my hip. When he touched me, I couldn't think in any rational kind of way, so I didn't try any longer. I let myself go. I let the moment take me away.

Afterwards, we stayed in bed, our hands entwined in one another's, my legs over his under the covers. We talked about all the things we had already covered so far, but this time with more depth. Cullen told me about his family, his writing. I told him about how I loved my job, but wasn't sure what I wanted from life yet. He hugged me close to him, whispered into my hair. His skin was so warm and smooth, it felt like it belonged against mine. Eventually we had to get up. We both threw our clothes back on and went outside to sit on his porch.

"Are you still up for an outing?" he asked.

I was up for anything as long as it meant I could spend more time with him. It muddled things, being completely engrossed with the person I was writing an article about, but I didn't care. I was good enough at my job that I could find a way to separate the two.

"I'd love that."

He squinted into the sun, and I loved the way his face looked in that moment, as if the day were full of possibility and there was nowhere else he'd rather be. My limbs tingled and the weightlessness I'd felt in my body earlier returned. I had no idea reality could be this good.

EIGHTEEN

That afternoon, we wandered around town again, only this time, we did it hand in hand. I was self-conscious at first; it had been so long since I'd shown affection to someone in public in Old Port. In Boston, you were nearly erased in the sea of people wandering the busy city streets. Here, It felt as though everyone had their eyes on you and knew your business. I was unsettled, but only briefly. Spending the day with Cullen was like being in a dreamlike state, and he more than made up for any momentary awkwardness I felt.

"What are you thinking?" Cullen asked. He ran his thumb up and down over mine slowly as we walked down the main strip of town, past clothing shops selling T-shirts in every color imaginable, "Old Port" printed across them.

"Nothing much. I'm content. I like being this happy."

He squeezed my hand and then released it. "Me too."

We were two people, but it felt like we were connected, like we were one. I couldn't explain this feeling, so I only tried to savor it. We stopped in at Peach to get iced coffee but took it to go so we could continue walking. It was the kind of gorgeous day where you wanted to be outside as much as possible—the type of day where the sun lit up the blue sky and warmed everything underneath it.

"What's a typical day look like for you?" I asked.

"Is this an interview question? Are we back to business?" His eyes sparked.

"No." I gave him a light nudge with my elbow. "I'm curious. Is this what your days are like? I can't imagine this kind of freedom with my schedule every day."

"Pretty much. After I quit my job to write full-time, a whole world of flexibility opened up for me."

That sounded incredible. Imagine having slow mornings every day, or time to take a walk through town when you wanted it, not only on your lunch hour.

"Why doesn't everyone do that?" I joked.

"I'm lucky. I don't deny that. I worked hard and I think I wrote a great book, but I was also in the right place at the right time and my book took off. Without that luck, I'd never be able to afford this kind of flexibility."

I took a sip of my iced coffee while I thought about it. "What else would you do if you couldn't make a living out of your writing?"

"I was a teacher before." He shrugged. "I'd probably do that again."

"You were? What grade?" I loved the thought of Cullen as a teacher.

"Fifth. It's a cute age. They're old enough to have these great conversations with, and they'll really engage in class, but they haven't developed the dreaded hormones yet that you get with pre-teens and teens."

I smiled at the thought of Cullen and a class full of kids sitting around him, eager to hear him speak. He had a way about him that would make him a fantastic teacher.

"What about you? Have you always wanted to be a journalist?" he asked.

"I don't think I've ever known what kind of job I wanted. All I knew was that I loved writing. English was the only class I truly enjoyed in high school, so my mother encouraged me to take a degree in my favorite subject and figure out the job thing after college."

"Smart mom," Cullen said.

I nodded.

"What about now? Do you enjoy your job?"

I thought about this. What would I do if I wasn't writing for a paper? I would write even if I could only do it as a hobby, but you can't support yourself on journaling about romantic encounters. My face warmed at the thought of my journal and the types of stories I wrote for myself. It was one thing to do this as a teen, but as an adult, it was another.

"I like writing, but there's not a lot of creative freedom in the kind of stories I write for the paper. It's mostly news that people need, but doesn't make for exciting writing assignments."

"Am I exciting?" He turned to look at me, a half smile on his face and that spark back in his eyes.

"Yes," I said. "You're very exciting to write about. I'm enjoying the research." I leaned into him.

He laughed and then squeezed my hand again. "So am I."

We spent the rest of the day together, outside, in the sun, down at the beach, stopping for ice cream and then back at his place once again. He made dinner and we drank wine and then took each other's clothes off. I could have stayed in his bed with him forever. I didn't dare to think about the logistics of all of this. What the future held if we wanted to be together. That would mean staying in Old Port, where Cullen's life was and mine wasn't. I had a job and a place back in the city, and I'd sworn I would never come back here again for any significant amount of time. Anyway, I was getting way ahead of myself. This was fun right now, and it felt incredible to be with him, but

I had no idea what it meant to Cullen, and it was too soon to ask.

Instead of going home to an already busy house with my mother and her friends, I texted her to tell her I planned to spend the night at Cullen's. She sent back a few emojis that I wouldn't have guessed she knew the meaning of, and then told me to take my time. After that, I fell asleep with Cullen's arms around me.

When I woke the next morning, the sun was just beginning to rise. It must have been five thirty or six in the morning. I was always an early riser, but I could see that Cullen had no desire to get up. I went silently out of the room and down to his kitchen where I eyed the fancy espresso machine. I had no idea how to work that. I scanned the countertop and spotted a regular old drip coffee machine. Thank goodness. I made coffee as quietly as I could and turned to lean on the counter while I waited for it to brew.

Out through the window, the ocean was in full view, lit up by the early morning sun and sparkling like sea glass. It was no wonder Cullen was so taken with Old Port. It was stunning here. Of course, I always thought people romanticized this kind of place in summer. Cullen and my mother lived here permanently, and it had to be awful in the winter.

I gave my head a small shake. I had to stop thinking long-term. I had no idea what we had the start of and I didn't want to jump to conclusions. I always ended up being disappointed when I did that.

Once the coffee was brewed, I poured a cup, pulled on a hoodie that was draped over a chair and went out to Cullen's porch to sit. It wasn't long before I spotted someone walking down by the beach, their long hair flowing behind them. I could tell even from this distance that it was Rosie. When she glanced up at the houses, I raised my arm in the air and waved at her. She waved back and headed in my direction.

"Good morning," she said as she approached. "I'm going to wager a bet that you had a good night."

I couldn't stop the smile from spreading across my face even if I had wanted to. "I did."

"Where is this guy? I'm not interrupting post-sex coffee, am I?"

This time, my face flushed. I had almost forgotten how blunt Rosie could be. It was funny, if slightly embarrassing. "He's still asleep. So how was your evening? Did you ladies stay up late?"

She gestured to the seat next to me. "Mind if I sit down? I've already been for a long walk."

"Please."

She settled into the seat and looked out at the ocean. "We had a really lovely night. I'm so lucky to be friends with those women."

I murmured my agreement. "How many years has it been now?"

She looked up into the air. "Oh, I'd say about thirty, maybe thirty-five years."

It was hard to imagine having someone in your life for that long. Rosie *was* lucky. They all were.

"I couldn't live without my friends, that's for sure. But sometimes it's also nice to have someone special. The extra-benefits kind of person in your life." She directed her eyes behind us at Cullen's house. "Especially when you're so young, like you."

"Has my mother been working on you? I know she wants me to settle down, but I keep telling her I'm happy with my life." I wasn't upset. Rosie couldn't ever upset me, and my mother only meant well.

"I know that. Your mother knows you're happy, too. You

don't need a partner to complete you, you're so successful already. But it's a nice thing to share your life with someone special and I think she wants that for you."

"It didn't work out so well for her," I said stiffly. "And look at her now, she doesn't have anyone and she's just fine."

Rosie reached over and touched my knee. "You're just fine. We know that. What happened between your parents is something that can happen to anyone. Heck, it happens all the time. But it's no reason to avoid sharing your life with someone, Meg. There's a lot of good that comes out of opening yourself up to a relationship. A meaningful one. Even your mother would tell you that."

I sipped my coffee and didn't say anything. I didn't want to explain how I had tried, but that people like Daniel would come and go. Who knew if I could make it work with Cullen? History told me I couldn't.

"Anyway, I hope you're having fun. You deserve it." She glanced behind us again.

"I am," I said. Cullen made my body respond and react in ways it hadn't before. I was enjoying the high of it, but that didn't mean it would last. The chances of it turning into a long-term thing that worked out for both of us for the rest of our lives was slim.

"I'd better get back. The girls will wonder where I am." Rosie stood and smiled down at me. She leaned in and gave me a kiss on the cheek. "Don't rush home. Take your time over here." She winked.

"Okay, okay. I get the hint." I grinned at her.

"Who's hinting? I'm flat-out telling you to sow your wild oats while you're young, and see where it takes you. That guy is handsome as hell—I wouldn't let him go."

I laughed and waved as Rosie descended the few steps down the porch and made her way back to my mother's house.

NINETEEN

For the most part, I took my mother and Rosie's advice. I didn't think about where things might be going and spent as much time with Cullen as I could for the next several days. I allowed myself to be whisked up by the feelings he churned inside of me. I was riding a wave of something incredible when we walked through town, went to the beach, when he held my hand as we sat in the cove he had taken me to on our tour of Old Port. We went out for dinner, took long drives. He made me elaborate breakfasts of homemade waffles and bacon and fruit. We explored one another's bodies slowly, gently, as if we wanted to make it last forever. It could have been the sun and the salt air, or it could have been getting caught up in the early part of a romance, but when I had a quiet moment to myself, I realized I was unbelievably happy. I hadn't thought that could happen here.

I was so happy, I hadn't felt any need to write in my journal in days, which was a good thing because I hadn't been able to find it yet. I wasn't looking very hard, and that wasn't like me, but I supposed I had turned over a new leaf. I liked the new me.

One evening, Cullen and I went to the front porch of his

house to listen to the quiet sigh of the waves. He poured two glasses of crisp, cold white wine and handed me one. When he sat down, he made a happy sighing sound, like he was relaxed.

"That good, hey?"

He glanced over at me. His face was serious. "Spending time with you has been that good."

"I'm glad."

"I mean it, Meg. I haven't had someone meaningful in my life in a long time."

Outside of my embarrassing moment on the phone, we hadn't spoken about exes. I sometimes wondered how it was possible Cullen was single. I assumed he'd chosen to be.

"Why not?" We had reached the point where I felt like we could have deeper conversations. I could ask these kinds of questions and not worry that he was thinking I would put it into the story.

"I had some serious relationships in the past, but they fizzled out. Nothing dramatic. We were never the right fit. I haven't yet met someone who feels right."

I hoped I felt right. "I'm surprised by that," I said instead. "But I'm glad."

He turned to me and smiled. "I am, too." He took a sip of his wine then looked out at the water. "What about you? How on earth have you not found the right one yet? You're the kind of girl who so many people would want to have in their life."

It warmed me to hear him say that, but I didn't quite believe it, so I only shrugged in response. "I guess it's the same story. I had partners, but nobody felt right." I thought of Daniel. Before Cullen, the truth was that nobody had been able to live up to my expectations. I knew this about myself, but I couldn't help it. When I wrote in my journal about men and who I thought they were or how they would act, it wasn't because I was delusional. It was because I thought I deserved something that good. That perfect. But that guy hadn't shown up. And when I thought I might have it, like with Daniel, he'd left. I hadn't been willing to admit that the perfect one might never show up.

"When did you stop coming to Old Port?"

The change in conversation surprised me. "A long time ago. I moved out when I went to university and wanted a good job and a big life in the city. I wanted to be independent and put the past behind me, so I eventually stopped coming back here. My mom seemed to get it and said she liked her trips to the city to visit me. We never really talked about it. It's been years now."

"Have you missed it?"

I shrugged. "No."

He was silent for a moment.

Now that we were here, side by side in a quiet moment, watching the sun kiss the horizon before it gave way to twilight, I didn't feel the need to keep everything so close to my chest.

"I stopped coming because I had bad memories of this place. My parents had always raised me to believe that love was enough. They didn't have a lot of money when they first met, they didn't have fancy jobs or have lots of family close by, but they had each other. They had this beautiful kind of mutual love for one another. And then it all fell apart."

"What happened?"

I must have looked uncomfortable because Cullen reached for my hand.

"Only if you want to talk about it."

"It's fine." I shifted in my seat. "When I was fourteen years old, my father fell out of love with my mother. That's the only way I can describe it. She didn't do anything, except grow older. I think he wasn't prepared for the reality of life—women get older, life gets more mundane. Sometimes you go through stretches where you can't find time to be alone or have meaningful conversations, or you're too tired to do more than just get by. I saw Mom tired a lot of the time because she had a lot to do. She had work, a house to clean because my father didn't do much of that, she had me to take care of—even as I was getting older, I needed her, just in a different way. She had a lot on her shoulders and she was trying to do it all, so I think sometimes the last thing that was a priority for her was putting on her face and making sure her man was happy."

I couldn't help the anger that crept into my voice. It still hurt so much to think about, even after all this time. I wanted to forget it all and forgive him, but my relationship with him was still strained. I felt a protectiveness over my mother.

"Sounds like he had some old-fashioned expectations."

I shrugged. "I'm not sure. The only thing I know is that he wanted his life to constantly be some kind of dream-like, happy existence where things were always good. He had a vision of what he wanted, and when it wasn't working out, he fell out of love with my mother and their life together and cheated on her. Then he left her. And me. He left the both of us. He remarried and then left that woman, too. He's onto his third wife now." I shook my head. "I don't know if he'll ever be satisfied."

Cullen squeezed my hand. "That must have been really hard."

"It was." My throat ached. I felt a prickling behind my eyes, and I was angry at myself. My father didn't deserve this kind of emotion from me.

"Does he live in town?" Cullen asked.

"Yes. He loved Old Port as much as my mother, so he got another place in town. My mom was fine with it. They don't run into one another too often. I don't see him much at all."

"I'm sorry."

"Thanks." I went quiet. I had never shared this much with someone before now. I didn't know what to say next.

Cullen spoke instead. "All families are psychotic."

I twisted around to face him. That seemed like a harsh assessment. "What?"

He let out a soft laugh. "It's the title of a book I read once."

"Authors." I rolled my eyes.

"What I mean is, all families are complicated and have their problems. Mine do, too. Why else would I run away to a small coastal town to live alone?" He laughed again. "I guess we have to figure out if we can forgive, forget and learn to accept our family in our lives as they are."

"That's hard."

"I know. But that's life, isn't it? It's very far from perfect most of the time."

He was right, I knew it, but I wasn't sure how to have my father in my life. He served as a constant reminder that reality was a let-down and it was almost impossible to be good enough.

"Let's talk about something else." I didn't want to dwell on the imperfections of life. It was too depressing.

"How about we don't talk at all?" Cullen lifted an eyebrow at me and I laughed. We put our wine glasses down and went inside.

TWENTY

It was Friday, and the end of my second week in Old Port. My vacation would be over in two days. I didn't want to think about it. Not only did I not want to imagine leaving Cullen behind, I didn't want to finish writing the article either. It was as if by putting it off, I could delay time and I wouldn't have to think of Cullen as a job, but as a new part of my life. I turned to texting with Sarina for distraction.

Miss you

Same. Is Old Port a permanent thing?? Are you relocating for love??

I laughed.

No, I'll be back home soon

I had a story to write and a life to get back to, but it pained me to think about it.

Give me details

I smiled at my phone.

> Not like this. When I see you next. Which is when??

> I hope soon

I was leaving in two days to return to go back home and back to work, so I could see her then, but part of me wanted to show her the Old Port I'd discovered. My mother loved Sarina and always welcomed company anyway.

> Want to come visit??

The bubble that indicated she was still typing disappeared. It reappeared and then disappeared one more time before she sent another message.

> I can come for a day trip! Can't stay overnight because of the ankle biter tho. How about tomorrow?

I grinned and replied:

> YES!!

> Send me the address and I'll see you tomorrow

Sarina typed back and added a few x's and o's.

I texted her a link to Peach Coffee because we would need a good hour to catch up on each other's lives over lattes first. Then we could wander around town, drop into the bakery, see the beach. I wasn't sure yet if I'd let Cullen meet her. That seemed like a big step. It would have to be a game time decision.

. . .

The next morning, I arrived at Peach Coffee to find Sarina already there. She waved at me from the table she was sitting at. She had a massive ceramic mug in front of her, filled with frothy, milky coffee.

"Uh, excuse me, miss? I believe I ordered the large coffee," Sarina said as I approached. She gestured at her mug.

I laughed at the movie reference: *So I Married An Axe Murderer*. We'd come across it when we were younger and it had quickly become one of our favorites. We used to spend lazy Sundays together, lounging on the couch, eating takeout and watching it.

Sarina and I had first met in college and hadn't warmed to one another immediately. Sarina was loud and blunt and, for the most part, told you exactly what she was thinking. It was one of the things I now loved most about her, but at one point, I'd not known what to do with her straight-talking attitude. Later, she told me that she'd mistaken my shyness for snobbery. But we'd overcome our differences and bonded over our love of being silly. Sarina could laugh louder and harder than anyone I had ever met, and she had the same effect on me. My cheeks often hurt after spending a few hours together.

Now she lived in a suburb about thirty minutes away from my place in the city, so we didn't see each other as often as we would like. We were both busy—me with work and Sarina with both work and her daughter.

Sarina and her husband, Jeff, had had Chloe with no issues whatsoever, but when they'd tried to have another child, it hadn't happened. They'd spent three years going through fertility treatments before agreeing that they had tried enough. Sarina had told me it had stung in ways she couldn't explain when people had tried to make them feel better by saying things like, "But you already have Chloe. At least you have one." I had held her hand, helping her through it on so many occasions, my heart breaking for her. Over time, she had grown to quietly accept their situation.

"Life goes on," Sarina said to me one afternoon. She kissed Chloe's head and watched her with a sad smile. I knew she had accepted it, but it was hard.

I grabbed my own giant latte and took the seat across from Sarina. Her shiny, sand-colored bob brushed against my cheek as she leaned forward for a hug. It had been in a coffee shop like this that Sarina had told me about her first miscarriage. We'd cried together, hugged, and eventually, after talking and talking, sat in an easy silence. We had been through a lot together.

"So. Tell me," she said, "what is going on with you and the author?"

I shifted in my seat. "He's wonderful. He's smart and fun and I love being around him. But I don't know where it's going."

Sarina leaned forward. "And?"

"What do you mean?"

"You love being around him, so why can't you just enjoy that and let things happen instead of overanalyzing?" She sipped her latte and watched me.

"I know. Anyway, once my vacation is over, I'm going back to Boston and he'll stay here. So I guess that's that."

"Why would that be that?"

I shrugged. "It's far. We wouldn't be together most of the time."

"Maybe you don't need to be in the same city to make it work," Sarina said.

I wasn't convinced. My mother and father hadn't been able to survive the harsh realities of life—and they'd lived together. I assumed that if we put an obstacle in our way on top of all the other things life throws at you, there was no way Cullen and I would make it.

"I don't know." I took a sip of my coffee.

"I think you'll find you're fine. You just have to be willing to try it out. Sometimes things aren't perfect, or they don't work out the way you always imagined they would—but you get used to the new reality and even find you love it." Sarina glanced down at her phone as the screen lit up with a photo of Chloe. "See? It's like the universe is proving my point." She smiled at the image of her daughter and then held up the phone to me. Jeff had sent her a text.

> Chloe made us a drawing

I waited while she clicked on the phone and opened her text messages. She burst into laughter, her head flung back and eyes closed.

"What?" I asked.

She raised her eyes back to mine and wiped at a tear. "Chloe made us a picture for Jeff's birthday." She had trouble getting the words out between her laughs. "She labeled it, too. It's an 'enormous cake'."

I grinned, anticipating what she was looking at. Then Sarina pointed her phone at me again. On it was a colorful drawing of a three-tiered birthday cake and Chloe's messy, five-year-old scrawl. She had labeled it 'enormos cack'.

A peal of laughter burst from me. We both doubled over and shook, me until my sides hurt, and Sarina until her eyes were wet and red. Eventually, we regained composure.

"I'm saving that forever and ever. Chloe's going to hate me for it."

"You're terrible. But you're right, you can't ever delete that."

Sarina asked more about Cullen. I told her what had happened over the last couple of weeks, laughing when Sarina's eyes widened and her smile grew bigger the more I told her about him. We spent a while longer chatting about Chloe, and also about Jeff and Sarina's work. We talked about my article, how my mother was, and how it surprised me that I had already ended up here so long. Sarina grinned at me in a knowing manner.

"Love can do funny things to you," she said.

I shrugged again because I didn't know what else to say.

"Do you think you're there yet?" Sarina asked.

"Where?"

"In looooove," Sarina said, drawing out the word.

I took a sip of my latte and placed it down in front of me, my hands wrapped around the large mug.

"It's only been a couple of weeks but... I'm head over heels." It took a lot to admit that.

"That's great! You haven't found someone good enough in so long, Meg. This is a good thing. Don't overthink it, okay? Go with it."

I tried to let her words really sink in. *Go with it.* I could do that.

Couldn't I?

No, there was no way I could *not* overthink. Overthinking was my thing. After the coffee shop, Sarina and I wandered through town, popping in and out of the shops that lined the main strip. She was fascinated by the sheer amount of stuff you could find and buy at some of the stores.

"Do people really buy dish towels with kooky phrases on them when they're on vacation?" She held up a towel with "Beach, please" printed on it.

I snorted. "I guess?"

We went to the water next and walked up and down the shoreline, still talking. We could talk for hours and never run out of something to say, or we could enjoy the silence and not feel a need to fill it. It was one of the things I loved most about Sarina. Spending time with her was always so easy.

After the beach, we visited my mother, who was thrilled to see Sarina again. We had lunch on her porch.

"Is that his place?" Sarina gestured toward Cullen's cottage.

I nodded, directing my eyes down at my sliced turkey sandwich. I wasn't ready for Sarina to meet Cullen. Sarina knew me better than anyone; she was as close to me as family. She was my comfort and safety. I couldn't pinpoint why, but I didn't want to combine my two worlds. It was as if I wanted to be sure I knew what I had with Cullen first. It felt real and perfect to me, but I had been wrong in the past.

We stayed on the porch until Sarina had to eventually make the drive back home. It had only been a short visit, but I understood that she had to get back in time for Chloe's bedtime, and I appreciated her making the drive for me.

"I don't want to go. It's so calming here," Sarina said. She sighed and looked out at the horizon, resting back into her chair.

"I don't want you to go either." I reached out and squeezed her hand. "But I'll take any amount of time I can get with you. And I have to leave tomorrow anyway." The thought weighed heavy on my mind. What was next for me and Cullen after I was gone?

As if she could read my mind, Sarina stood and leaned in to hug me. She whispered, "Don't overthink this. Just enjoy. You deserve that."

I hugged her back, wishing there was some way we could both stay here for longer.

Only, the reality was, I had a job to do. I *had* to focus on work. Cullen was a job. Of course, I hadn't thought of him that way after these past couple of weeks. It had been like a dream here—one where I could never have imagined so much happiness. Now it was all ending, and I had a story to write. I wanted so badly to know what would happen after I left and went back to work. If I were writing in my journal, I'd know exactly how to end this.

Once Sarina's car had left the driveway and disappeared down the long road that led from my mother's house, I decided to start writing the article again to see if that would help me get out of my head. Inside, I grabbed my laptop and placed it on the small desk in my bedroom. I went to find my notebook next, and I realized I still didn't know where it was. I hadn't reached for my notebook, my journal or my laptop in days. It was unlike me. So much of my life right now was unlike me.

I looked through my bedroom, the desk drawers, even the closet, before I went downstairs and rummaged through the kitchen and living room. It was nowhere. I sighed. I'd have to work by memory. I went back up to the bedroom and sat at my desk. I watched the screen come to life and clicked on the browser I had left open. So many tabs were always open on my screen.

The last thing I had been looking at was Celine's story on the Marshall bus tragedy. I skimmed over it again quickly for the millionth time to give me a dose of inspiration. I found when I needed to do my best work, it helped for me to read really good writing.

Next, I clicked open my file and read over what I had written about Cullen. The story was okay, but none of it felt like it rang true. It wasn't the Cullen I knew now, it was the Cullen I'd known on the surface, back when I'd first met him.

This was the interesting thing about Cullen and what phase I was in right now. We already knew each other well, we were caught up in one another. He made me feel things I'd thought I could only feel when I made them up. The flip of my stomach, the way my body jolted at his touch, the way I was consumed by thoughts of him, the smell of his skin. And the way I was myself around him. Completely myself—not pretending to be perfect or the smartest in the room, or always in the know—and Cullen actually liked me that way. As far as I could tell, he liked me just the way I was. For so long I had been certain that opening myself up and being who I really was could only lead to being hurt. I'd hidden myself behind my writing, focused on what I wanted in my dreams rather than what I could have in real life, to keep myself safe. Untouchable.

Cullen had changed all of that.

I deleted the entire story and started over. This time, I closed my eyes and pictured him, pictured the moments we'd spent wandering through Old Port, the things he'd told me, the way his face looked when he was telling a story, and how the air crackled between us when we weren't speaking. Then I started writing again.

The words flowed out of me.

TWENTY-ONE

*I know it's still your vacation, so please don't answer until you're
ready.*

The words Celine wrote in her email sounded genuine, but I
knew her better than that. She wouldn't have emailed if she
didn't want to hear from me.

*Checking in on how the story is going... Please let me know at your
earliest convenience.*

I had been sitting at the desk in my old room and decided to
check in on work emails. That was my first mistake. Celine's
message caused me to temporarily stiffen. It was a mini red flag.
She was usually so busy that she didn't have time to ask me
about my work until I handed my story in. I wasn't sure what
this was all about, so I kept reading the email.

*Also, just a reminder that we have the Digital Publishing Awards
coming up on the 15th. Downtown. We're up for several awards, so
we're all expected to go.*

The fifteenth was in two and a half weeks. This was a stark reminder that my old life was waiting for me. Old Port had been for me what it was for most people: a place to escape to for a little while, not a place to live. And even though I'd suspected that whatever it was Cullen and I had was only a summer thing, I didn't want it to be. I didn't want to go back home—but I also couldn't stay in Old Port. I was stuck in between, flailing and unsure what to do.

As if she could sense I was reading her words right at that moment, Celine's number flashed across the screen on my phone. So much for "I know it's still your vacation...". I didn't want to pick up, but Celine had been good to me over the years. She usually offered me flexibility in my work life, so little things like this didn't bother me much.

"Hi, Celine," I answered.

"Hi." She cut right to the chase. "How's the story on Cullen Walsh going?"

"It's pretty good. I'm doing my best to up the human interest part."

"That's good. We're relying on this piece."

I frowned. "Relying on it to do what?" I understood from hearing Celine speak in past team meetings that we needed more readers, but I wasn't sure if that was what she was talking about, and if so, how she thought that would happen with an article on an author. This wasn't dramatic or big news. It was going to be a good read about a good person. To hear Celine was relying on it felt like a lot of pressure.

"We've talked about this before." Celine's voice was heavy, like she was tired.

"Only a little. I'm not sure what your expectations are?"

"We need more readers and more clicks online to demonstrate to our advertisers that we're a good business decision. They want to know that lots of eyes will be on their ads. We need big advertisers so we can keep doing what we're doing.

Especially if we want to win awards and be considered experts at what we do. The better we are, the more money and the better our reputation, the better our reputation, the more talent we can hire and the better our work gets. It's a virtuous circle."

"So how do I play into that? Or Cullen?"

She paused. A silence that made me wonder for a beat if she had heard me. "Your article needs to gain a lot of attention. It needs readers."

"But it's an article about an author. It's not breaking news. I plan to write as beautiful a piece as I can, but I'm a little confused here, Celine."

She sighed again. "We're banking on this one being of interest to a lot of people, but only if it's written really well. That's why I put you on the job. I respect your work."

"Thank you," I said. The back of my neck prickled at the compliment. I wasn't used to Celine saying that sort of thing to me. She wasn't unfriendly or unkind, but she was efficient, straight to the point. She said nice things when the occasion arose, but not often.

"Anyway, I won't bother you again while you're off. When are you back?"

Goosebumps sprang up on the back of my arms. I rubbed at them with my free hand and was hit with a realization: I didn't want to go back home. I didn't want to leave Cullen. Even Old Port was becoming more comfortable, easier to exist in. But I didn't have a choice.

"I'll be back on Monday," I said.

"Talk to you then." The call clicked off.

I put my phone on the desk and glanced back at my laptop. I touched a key so the screen would hum to life again. My words were in front of me. Words that had to somehow impress Celine, attract a lot of readers and do Cullen justice.

No pressure.

. . .

Later that evening, Cullen came over. It was our last Saturday night together before I had to leave. My mother went into the next town over for a movie to give us space, even though I'd said she didn't have to. When Cullen asked how I wanted to spend our night, he arched an eyebrow at me and made me laugh. But instead of hopping into bed, like we had been doing so often lately, I only wanted time to enjoy his presence. To talk until it was late into the night. To hold his hand and feel the warmth of him beneath my fingertips. Spending a quiet evening with him seemed like perfection, but I couldn't help but think about how many quiet evenings we could have if we both lived in the same place, imagine how well this would work out if Cullen and I were close to one another all the time.

We decided to grab takeout and bring it back. When we got out of the car at home, he went toward the house ahead of me— all broad shoulders and back, strong legs and tanned skin. My nerves fired all at once. I didn't want this to end, but I didn't see how it could keep going. We would have to have the conversation about who was visiting who, and when. Would he even want to come to Boston?

Inside, I placed the plastic bags filled with steaming hot containers of pad Thai and jasmine rice on the counter. Cullen looked through cupboards for plates and bowls. He pulled open a drawer and studied it for a moment while I pulled a container of spring rolls out of the bag.

"Hey, does your mother have any candles?"

"Candles?" I asked. "For what?"

Cullen let out a low chuckle. He came close to me and squeezed my shoulders. "For dinner. I thought maybe a candlelit... Actually, never mind. It's kind of silly."

His cheeks reddened. My skin tingled when I realized what he was asking. He wanted to make our takeout dinner special for us. It hit me that this was the kind of person he was. Somehow, Cullen had ended up in my life, and I wanted him to stay there. I didn't want to go home and only see him once in a while.

"That's a great idea. I love it." I kissed the smooth part of his cheek just below his eye. "I think the candles are in one of those drawers." I pointed to the entranceway of the kitchen, where the junk drawer was. The one that held phone chargers and loose pieces of paper and an old watch that didn't work any longer. All the things you save for some reason because you find it impossible to let go.

Cullen shot me a smile. I went back to setting out the food and grabbed a few spoons and forks to dish it out with.

"Is this yours? It has your name on the front." I looked up from the cutlery. He picked something out of the drawer and held it up. A black speckled cover. A white box squarely on the front where I had written my name.

My journal.

"There's two of them." He picked up my work notebook next.

He's holding my journal. With all my incredibly personal daydreams about men inside of it. Lots of men. And all the things I had written about him. My muscles tightened and my underarms went damp.

I dropped the utensils onto the counter and shot towards him. "That's mine." I snatched them out of his hands and put them under my arm protectively, as if he would no longer think of them if they were partially hidden.

Cullen flinched slightly. His forehead crinkled. "Are you okay? What's up?"

"Nothing. They're mine. They're just notebooks."

"Okay..." He kept his eyes on me. "I wasn't going to look inside. I'm not sure I understand your reaction."

"Can we just forget it?"

"Sure, but..."

"Stop. Please." I didn't want to explain, but I also couldn't help but be overly sensitive. My journal was deeply personal. It had been a private part of my life, and it was too hard for anyone else to understand from the outside looking in. "I don't want to talk about it." I could hear a harshness to my tone, yet I wasn't able to control it. I was in protective mode—like an animal on the defensive. I didn't want to lash out, but I had never been this close to having my vulnerability exposed before.

Cullen froze, his eyes on me. "Okay."

Silence followed. The air in the kitchen was tense. I looked at the containers on the counter.

"Do you want to take this to the living room?" Cullen said quietly. His head was bowed; he was staring at the countertop, expressionless.

Damn it. I had ruined it. The whole evening. It was stiff and awkward now. I had done this. My mind started spinning. First it was a small, uncomfortable argument, and then the fights would become more frequent. One moment, your pad Thai went cold while you argued, and the next thing you knew, your whole relationship was chilly. It was my fault. I had done this before—I had forced Daniel out by not being relaxed and easygoing about how we spent our time—and now I was doing it again. I was making it awkward. It wouldn't be long before Cullen would be telling me he wanted to leave, that it was over between us. My mind flashed to my mother, and the look on her face after one of the many times she had been crying. Her puffy, swollen eyes and her red lips. It had been right after my father had told her he wanted out. I couldn't do that. I couldn't live through it again. I wouldn't let it happen to me over and over.

"I'm actually not all that hungry."

"What?" Cullen raised his head and looked at me with wide eyes. "You're not?"

"I'm not feeling all that well. Maybe I should go to bed," I said numbly.

His mouth fell open. "What is this? I'm confused. Are you mad at me?"

I couldn't look at him. Not directly in his eyes. "I just need a moment." It was easier to lie than to tell him the truth. I could see the writing on the wall and we weren't going to last. How could we? There was too much stacked against us already—the distance, our schedules. Me.

"If... you're sure." His voice was so quiet it nearly broke my resolve. Nearly.

I nodded. Out of my peripheral vision I saw Cullen run a hand through his hair. I snuck a glance at his face and his expression had changed again. His mouth was turned down, but his eyes were soft. Wounded.

I wanted to tell him I was sorry, to tell him to stay so we could sit on the couch next to one another, our bodies touching while we talked late into the night, but I didn't see any way this would work, and I also wanted to protect myself. They always left. There was always a reason. If my past had told me anything, it was that this was the best way to stay safe.

I didn't say anything when he turned and left the kitchen, or when I heard the front door open and then close again. Instead, I waited until I couldn't hear anything except for the low hum of the refrigerator, the electric buzz of the lights above me.

Then I closed my eyes and allowed myself to cry.

TWENTY-TWO

On Sunday morning, I knew what I had to do. I packed up hastily to leave early rather than risk seeing Cullen again. It was too painful. I would send him a text, but I couldn't see him. I thanked my mother for everything, kissed her on the cheek and said I'd be back soon, even though I wasn't sure when I'd return. Then, once I was in the car, I typed out a quick text to Cullen.

> Really sorry, but had to leave early

That was it. It was all I could say. For the entire car ride home, thoughts exploded in my head like fireworks. I went over what had happened with Cullen. It had been such a minor thing, but it wasn't the incident itself that worried me. It was the potential. It was a sign of things to come. I cried as I drove—big, heaving sobs—because I was certain I wasn't enough. Love wasn't enough. Something would tear us apart like it always did. Even if it had only been a small disagreement this time, I knew there would be more problems, more issues, later on. I knew that opening myself up to someone would only turn south and go bad, the way it had for me in the past, and the way it had for my mother and father.

If I was being honest with myself, I also cried because it hurt to push him away. It felt so wrong. I wanted Cullen in my life, but I didn't want the inevitable pain. Removing myself and getting space first so my feelings wouldn't be crushed later was the only thing I could do. I had to take care of myself.

The truth was sobering; I hadn't had a relationship with anyone other than Daniel for years. I only had one good friend. My own father hadn't stayed in my life in a meaningful way. I couldn't understand what it was exactly about me that made the people in my life not like me long term, but I knew it was there. I was the common denominator. It was me people couldn't stay friends with, or in love with, or who they didn't want to be around. It was a terrible realization, crushing and painful, and it sent me into a spiralling state of depression.

Back at home, I sat on my couch staring at nothing. The television was off. My phone was turned upside down on the table in front of me. My body ached and my head felt like it might float away. I wanted nothing. I didn't want to go for a walk or watch TV. I couldn't bring myself to do anything productive, and I certainly didn't want to be around anyone. Cullen had texted me several times and even called, but I couldn't pick up. I wasn't ready to talk; as much as I wanted to hear his voice again, I doubted I could without crying. I sent him a short text saying I needed a bit of time to focus on work. No further explanation.

It was moments like this, when my feelings were the strongest, and when I was at my most vulnerable, that I needed to write. I needed to get the words out onto a page because it helped me process whatever was whirling around in my brain and my heart like a hurricane. Writing had always helped me sort out what I was feeling and it gave me an outlet so I didn't

implode. I got up and went to my bag, where I found my journal. Then I went back to the couch, sat cross-legged and opened
it. I skimmed through my stories again. They seemed silly now.
They were so full of hope.

My phone rang, startling me. I flipped it over and saw my
mother's name on the screen. I knew she meant well and loved
me, but I didn't want to talk right now. I couldn't pretend I was
okay and she would be able to tell. She would hear it in my
voice, and then I'd have to go into detail about what had
happened, and I didn't want to. I couldn't. I let the phone go to
voicemail.

After a while, I dragged myself to my bedroom. I left my
phone in the living room and went to bed, where I pulled the
covers up around my head. I had to get my mind to stop running
so I could sleep. I needed sleep now. Maybe everything would
seem better in the morning.

The next day, I woke earlier than usual. I could tell by the
dimness in my room. I leaned over to grab my phone and found
no text messages. Cullen had given up. Everything within me
wanted to stay in bed, but I had to get up and get ready for
work. It was Monday, which meant back to reality. I wasn't
scheduled to go into the office, but I had to manage my inbox,
work on some of my smaller stories. Anyway, it was better to be
busy. If I did nothing, I would never stop thinking about him. I
got up and went to take a shower, but realizing the bathroom
needed cleaning, I pulled out my spray bottle of vinegar and
water and scrubbed the sink and toilet to within an inch of their
lives. Then I changed into a pair of running shorts and a T-shirt
and went for a run before my day started. I was only gone for
fifteen minutes before I was wheezing and hoarse. I couldn't
run because my brain wouldn't let me relax. I went over and
over what I had said to Cullen, the look on his face.

Back at home, I had a quick shower, got dressed and located my notebook and my laptop. Maybe it would help if I went to the coffee shop to work. It was loud there, and I could get a latte and take a seat and still be by myself without feeling so alone. My journal was sitting on the coffee table in the living room next to my keys. I grabbed it and left.

As I'd suspected, the coffee shop was bustling with energy, crowded with people. This helped, sort of. I sat at my table and dove into work. I would have to eventually finish my article on Cullen, but I avoided it for now. Celine hadn't asked for it again, so I focused on my inbox instead. I had to go through the piles of messages I'd received while off and, after an hour spent wading through emails, I reached inbox zero. No small feat. I relaxed back into my chair and watched people for a minute. They came in droves, in and out, grabbing expensive coffee concoctions and talking to friends and coworkers. Late in the morning, Adam, my former crush who'd yelled at the barista, came into the shop. He went over to the counter and smiled and spoke quietly. When he turned, his eyes met mine. I immediately looked away, embarrassed to be caught staring. Even without looking, I could sense him coming closer.

"Hey. Uh—hi. Do you come here often?"

I almost choked on my drink. What a guy. "Does that actually work?" I wasn't in the mood, and I didn't want to bother with men who were rude to baristas. How embarrassing that I had written about him in my journal.

"Does what work?"

"That's a bit of an outdated line," I said dully.

"Sorry. It's not meant to be a line. It's an honest question. You look familiar."

I shrugged. "I usually stop here on my way to work."

"Thought so. Is there any chance you happened to be here when I was being a spectacular asshole one day?"

I arched an eyebrow. "I recall seeing you talk to a barista in a—certain way."

He winced, as if in pain. "Yeah. I recognized you."

I glanced up at him, unsure what else he expected from me.

"Anyway, not that it's excusable, but I was having a terrible day. The worst. I felt awful after and I came back and apologized to her later. I was way offside."

I wasn't sure why he was telling me this, but it piqued my curiosity. "That's good of you."

"I thought you should know."

Now I was no longer only mildly curious. "Why?"

He glanced down at his hands and then back up again, as if he were caught off guard. "Oh. Um, I guess I see you in here often and you seem so friendly. I, uh—I was hoping to maybe chat with you one day. But I had a feeling nobody in their right mind would want me to talk to them after what happened."

"It's nice that you apologized," I said again.

There was an awkward silence that stretched out between us for a beat.

"I didn't plan this very well," he said. "I have no follow-up conversation starters." He laughed and I felt myself softening. I laughed lightly, too.

The barista called out Adam's order. He glanced over his shoulder and then turned back to me. "I should grab my coffee. It was nice to see you—" He paused and watched me.

"Meg," I offered. "Nice to see you, too."

He flashed me a big smile, showing off his perfect teeth again. "Meg. I'm Adam. And I hope I see you here again soon."

I couldn't help but offer a tiny smile back at that. It had been an awful twenty-four hours and it felt good to hear something kind. I watched him grab his coffee and wave at me before he left, then turned my gaze back to the table where my coffee sat. Next to it was my journal. I sighed. Maybe it was easier to keep all my hopes and dreams within these pages. It was where people could be whoever I wanted them to be and nothing hurt. It was safe. It kept me from getting my hopes up and having them dashed when reality set in. And reality always set in. Real life was too hard, and it hurt too much.

I opened my journal and flipped to a new page. Then I started to write.

TWENTY-THREE

"I'm here. I have wine and takeout and I'm not leaving until you talk to him." Sarina stood on the other side of my open doorway, both hands full with bags. When I had called her and told her that I thought things were over with Cullen, she'd instructed me to hang tight because she was coming right over.

"Come in," I said, moving to one side. "And tell me what you really think I should do." I blew out in an exaggerated huff.

She laughed at that. Sarina was no-nonsense and didn't have time for anything but doing. If you had a problem, she thought you should work to solve it, not wallow. Problem was, I was still in the wallowing phase.

"You know I adore you," Sarina said. "But all of this could be cleared up by calling him."

"I haven't been ready. And besides, it's probably too late. I've ruined it. And I'm not going to beg—I have some dignity."

"You do?" Sarina teased.

"Ha, ha," I deadpanned.

She pulled a bottle of wine out of a bag and went to the drawer where I kept my opener. We were so close, she knew every inch of my house like it was her own. She was comfortable here, and I was the same at her house. She opened the bottle, poured a glass of red and handed it to me.

"You said you needed time, and he gave it to you. You've both had some space. Now he's worth fighting for."

My head tipped to one side. "How do you know that?"

"It's the way you've spoken about him to me. He's different. You're different. I can tell he makes you happy."

She was right about that. Cullen was as good as I could have imagined. But it was too complicated now.

"Listen," Sarina continued. "Something odd is up here. You said he found your journal, you got weird about it, overreacted, and you haven't spoken since?"

"I wouldn't say I overreacted."

"Meg, I love you, but you chased him off the first chance you got. There was barely the start of a crack in the foundation and you bailed. You ran away."

I bit at the inside of my lip. I didn't like what she said, but I knew it was true. "You know that things don't work out for me. Anyway, even if I hadn't done this, his life is there in Old Port and mine is here in Boston. It doesn't work to do long distance when you're both busy with work—he'll be busy travelling on book tours."

"You haven't even tried."

"I've seen how hard it is to make a relationship work. Having distance between us just puts up another barrier we have to try and overcome. It starts with the best of intentions, but he stays up until all hours to write and I have a day job. He likes the quiet life of Old Port and if I'm there long-term, I'll be constantly reminded of my unhappiness as a child. Before long, he'll be too tired to come see me in the city and I'll resent always having to go back to a place filled with bad memories."

"But you started to warm to Old Port again while you were there. You were happy, remember? And the alternative is not being together. Missing out on a really good thing. How is that better than working at this?"

I took a sip of my wine, then put the glass down while I thought about it. "I don't know."

The truth was, I didn't want to put myself out there only to be hurt and damaged. I had done that before, and I had seen it happen to others. Why do that to myself again? Things were safer when I didn't let myself get hurt.

On the other hand, it was Cullen. I already missed everything about him.

Sarina stared at me, her brow furrowed as if she knew what I was thinking. "Meg. You can't live a pretend life." She gestured to my journal on the counter beside us.

My face went flush with heat. "I know that."

"I told you I love you, but that also means I need to tell you the truth, plain and simple and with no sugar coating. Reality sucks. It's true. But living your life is the only way to experience the really incredible things. You won't find happiness within the safety of your big city where you're anonymous and not getting to know anybody. You won't find it within your writing about perfect people and things. You'll find it when you're putting yourself out there, living and experiencing everything, along with all the ups and downs of life."

I frowned, but eventually nodded to show her I was listening. It was a lot to think about. Part of me knew she was right. Another part of me wanted to protect myself by staying stuck in my old, safe way.

"The food is getting cold," I said as I gestured at the bags.

Sarina ignored me and came closer, until she was right in front of me, her arms stretched out as she held onto my shoulders. "Promise me you'll think about this. Don't throw everything away because it's easier."

I looked down at the floor. Eventually I nodded. "Okay. I'll think about it. I promise."

Sarina seemed satisfied with this. She smiled at me and gave me a quick hug. "Okay, now let's eat and watch trashy reality television like we used to until I have to get back home."

I laughed. It was exactly what I wanted to do. "Hey," I said, picking up my plate and gesturing at the wine bottle. "Where's your glass?"

"I'm good with water tonight." Sarina's face went pink. She cast her eyes down and then across the room.

My body went still. It couldn't mean what I thought it meant. No. That would be too incredible. "You're not having wine?"

She shook her head.

"Sarina. Why aren't you having wine?" I put my glass down, but otherwise remained unmoving, as if I would break the spell or ruin the moment just by breathing.

"Something happened. It worked." Tears had materialized in her eyes. Her voice shook when she spoke.

Full-body chills cascaded over every inch of my skin. "It worked?"

She nodded. "I'm pregnant."

"No! You are? You're pregnant? Sarina, oh my god!" My stomach leaped and flipped and then I jumped in place, too, slapping my hands together. I ran towards her and wrapped her into my arms, both of us crying and laughing at the same time until we were a blubbering mess.

"This is so fantastic," I cried. "I can't believe we spent the whole evening talking about me when you had this news! I'm so thrilled for you. You deserve all the happiness in your life."

Sarina leaned in and rested her head on mine. "Thank you," she said, sniffling and smiling. "And so do you."

TWENTY-FOUR

After a few days of thinking about everything Sarina had said, and after several texts from her gently reminding me to get off my butt and do something, I finally worked up the nerve to call Cullen. Time without him had made me realize how great it had been when we were together. I woke up thinking about him each day. I missed his body, the sound of his voice, the feel of his hand in mine. Gradually, my fears about what was going to happen between us dissipated. I didn't want to fight this or resist him. I dialed his number with shaking fingers and waited.

He picked up. "Hello?"

"Hi." I should have been more prepared. I didn't have a plan for what to say, and didn't know if I should start off with "I'm sorry" or wait to see how angry he was with me for running away.

"Are you okay?" Cullen's voice was so gentle, I immediately felt the familiar sting of tears behind my eyes.

"Yes. Are you?"

He let out a small breath. "I've missed you. I miss you."

Relief flooded my veins. It surprised me, just how much I

wanted this. "Me too," I said. "I'm sorry. I don't know what's wrong with me." My voice broke.

"Hey—please don't say that. Nothing's wrong with you. This is all new. We're figuring each other out."

My body relaxed. All the tension drained from me like air from a balloon.

"How's work?" he asked.

"Busy. But I haven't been back to the office yet, so re-entry after vacation has been a little easier. What have you been up to?"

"I started writing some notes for my next book. I had some ideas and I'm just seeing where they lead at this point." He sounded normal. He wasn't angry. Maybe we could pretend I hadn't freaked out.

"That's great. I'm so happy for you."

"You coming back this weekend?" Cullen asked tentatively.

"I'd like to. If you'd like me to?" It sounded desperate. I wished I hadn't said it, but he answered immediately.

"Of course I do. I can't wait." His voice was low and throaty.

Something thrummed inside me. Everything might be fine. We talked for a few more minutes about plans and then said goodbye and hung up. I tried to focus on work, but to no avail. I imagined being with him again, wrapped in his arms in his bed, holding hands while we walked through town, watching the sunset together. I had lucked out when I'd met him, and my fears had almost allowed me to risk it all. I had the kind of thing I wrote about in my journal, the stuff romantic movies were made of—and I'd almost run away.

The next day was Friday, and after I emailed Celine to tell her the article would be ready early next week, I finished with the rest of my work, packed my bag as quickly as I could and made myself a tea to take in the car. I was taking a final look around my house to make sure everything was clean and tidy for when I got back home again, when my phone rang.

"Hey, you," Cullen said. His voice was low, but missing something. It lacked his usual warmth.

"Hey. I was just walking out the door. I can't wait to see you."

"That's what I was calling about."

My stomach dropped. He wasn't saying those words in a good way, I could sense it.

"I have to be out of town this weekend. It's a last-minute thing."

"You do? Where are you going?" I tried to keep my voice steady, but a heaviness settled into my bones.

"I've got to do some promotion for my next book. My publisher wants me to get back out there and stay on top of everyone's mind in the lead up to book two."

"But you've only just started writing it." It would be months and months before it was even close to ready to come out. Why did they need him now?

"I know. It's a long game. They want me to keep everyone interested by talking about book two now. But it's just for this weekend."

"Where?"

"There's a book festival in Portland."

"Oh." I tried to say something else, something positive or light, but I couldn't think of anything. I hoped I could hide the disappointment in my voice. This wasn't how I'd pictured the weekend, our first weekend back together after our first fight. I wished he had asked me to join him in Portland.

"I'm really sorry. It's going to be a whirlwind. I'll be super busy all weekend long. But it's kind of a big deal for me," he said. "Although, I really don't want to leave you. I wanted to be with you this weekend. I miss touching you."

My stomach flipped at his words. A tiny bud of hope could

blossom again. I gave my head a small shake. "Of course it's a big deal. It sounds great. I'm happy for you, and everyone will be so excited to hear about your next book."

He breathed out loud enough for me to hear it through the phone line. "I can't wait to come back to you."

A jolt went through my insides at the low, rough tone to his voice. I could picture myself close to him, touching the button on his jeans, hooking my finger through his belt loop. I could almost feel his arms around me, his body on top of mine, next to me, his skin pressed against mine. We would be together again, but I would have to be patient.

"I can't wait either," I said. "Take pictures and call me when you get back?"

"I will."

We hung up and I put my phone into my pocket. I looked around at my empty house. The lights were off, and it was closed up in anticipation of nobody being there. I stood by the door for a minute longer and then pulled my phone back out of my pocket.

I dialed and waited. When my mother answered, I held my breath only for a beat before I spoke.

"Can I come spend the weekend with you?"

Before long, I was back in Old Port. The drive had been easy, with only a little weekend traffic to stall me. I got to my mom's house and grabbed my bag from the passenger seat before getting out of the car. The air was the first thing I noticed. It was so fresh; it smelled like salt and rain. The low thrum of the waves in the distance immediately lulled me into a calm state.

I let myself into my mother's house after a quick knock on the door. From the kitchen, I could hear the clinking of dishes being moved around, the mumbling of voices. I smiled. One of them was very distinct.

"Meg!" Rosie came toward me and folded me into her body.

When I'd called earlier, my mother had told me Rosie was visiting again. I'd tried to back out of my request to come stay, but my mother had insisted. She'd even got Rosie on the phone to tell me I had to come. They both wanted to see me and promised I was in no way interrupting anything. It had been a last-minute thing with Rosie, sort of like it had been with me. Now, here in the kitchen wrapped in Rosie's arms, I was glad I'd decided to come. I needed this.

Rosie eventually but reluctantly pulled away from me and asked how I was.

"I'm good. Everything's fine." I leaned over to give my mother a kiss on the cheek.

"So how did we get so lucky to have your company all to ourselves this weekend?" Rosie asked.

"I didn't feel like being in the city alone."

My mother nodded. "I'm glad you're here. Wine?" She held up a bottle of my favorite pinot grigio.

"Sure, that would be great."

She smiled at me, looking genuinely happy to have me here. Why had I resisted coming back for so many years?

The night was casual and easy. We had a glass of wine out on the porch while we snacked on chips. Later, my mother and Rosie made us spaghetti and homemade meatballs for dinner, and even though it was nothing fancy, it was one of the best meals I'd had in a while. Somehow my mother had the ability to make even the simplest of food taste better.

We talked until the sun went down. Rosie told us about her life back home in Maine. She ran a bed and breakfast there with her partner and was always busy, but now was looking to slow down. When she spoke, I could see the exhaustion in her eyes. And yet, as she looked from me to my mother, an energy radiated from her. Her dark eyes brightened.

"It's so good for me to be here. Thank you for having me."

My mother reached out and rubbed the side of Rosie's arm. "I love having you visit." She turned to me. "And you. This is my lucky day."

I smiled back at her.

"So, when are you going to tell us more about him?" Rosie asked, leaning forward in her seat.

"Rosie," my mother said. A gentle warning.

"It's fine," I insisted, waving a hand at her. "I'm not sure what there is to tell yet. It's all happened so quickly, and we're still getting to know one another."

"Have you started with the basics?"

I turned to Rosie. "What do you mean?"

"Have you told him how you feel about him?"

"Not really." I looked out at the horizon instead of directly at her.

"What? Why not?"

"Rosie," my mother repeated. This time she directed a semi-stern look at her friend.

I lifted my hand again to indicate it was okay. Rosie only meant well. I knew her well enough to understand her questioning wasn't prying; she was curious because she cared.

"I'm not sure."

That wasn't true. I did know why I hadn't been brave enough to lay it all out on the line. The fight, the resistance to being honest and saying how I feel. It was my barrier. What if Cullen said he wanted this to work, but then quickly realized how hard it was going to be? What if long distance was too complicated and it made him miserable? All my life I had been prepared for keeping things close to my chest. It was safer. If nobody knew what I really, secretly longed for, I wouldn't be embarrassed when it all fell apart. And it would probably fall apart at some point. If my parents couldn't last, I couldn't see how I was going to make it. I had no clue how to have an adult, loving relationship.

"I know it can be really hard to be vulnerable with someone," Rosie said. "But if you don't risk it, you don't reap the rewards."

It was as if Rosie could read my mind. I only shrugged in response. I adored Rosie, but I didn't want to tell her and my mom my most private insecurities at that moment. I wanted to enjoy the evening.

"Things have a way of working out," my mother said.

Rosie directed her gaze at me. "They do. But sometimes you have to work for them, too. I just want you to feel good, Meg. You deserve it."

"Thank you." I wanted to feel good, too. And I wanted to let myself believe that Cullen could somehow be a big part of that.

TWENTY-FIVE

The weekend went by quickly, and I enjoyed all of it. Rosie, Mom and I spent most of our time talking and eating. We sipped coffee in the morning and had scrambled eggs and buttered toast for breakfast. In the afternoons, we had sandwiches and chips and cold salads, and by evening, Rosie and Mom whipped up something delicious to dine on—fresh bakery bread, a platter of crudités and meats and cheese. We ended up on the porch after dinner with a glass of white wine or a mug of tea while we watched the sun dip lower and lower in the sky.

It was relaxing to do things like this, and it had been wonderful to spend time with my mother and Rosie, but I missed Cullen. I wondered how the book festival was going. He hadn't texted, and I realized he was probably extremely busy. I wished we could chat. I wished I had a bigger part in his life, because he was consuming all of mine at the moment.

Later, once I had packed my things, kissed my mother and Rosie goodbye and thanked them profusely for such a lovely weekend, I went out to my car. I couldn't help but notice Cullen's house. The driveway was empty, which seemed sad to me. He felt so close, but he wasn't. I gave my head a shake. Our lives didn't fit with one another. His life worked in Old Port because he didn't have to commute or be in meetings for most of his day. It was just him and his writing. And when he wasn't writing, he was busy on book tours or some other kind of promotional event. My life was in the city—two hours away. Sure, the drive wasn't far, but it wasn't close enough for the life I imagined for myself.

I got into my car and drove home, trying to ignore the pit in my stomach and the ache in my chest whenever I thought of how hard this would be between us. How could we move forward if we weren't doing it together?

At home, I unpacked my few things, went to the grocery store and back, and was in my familiar spot—on the couch with mindless television on in the background—when my phone rang.

"Hey. I've missed you." Cullen's voice had its typical low, throaty tone. A shiver ran through my body in response.

"I miss you, too. A lot. How's the book tour?"

"It's been..." He sighed. "A lot of time in front of a big audience and media. It should be good for sales."

"That's great." I tried to lift my voice to show him I meant it. I did. I was happy for him. It seemed like it was important to take the wins when you could with the book industry. His kind of success wasn't typical, and it didn't always last. This was important.

"I know, but it sucked not to be with you. I'm really sorry about this weekend."

"Don't be sorry. It's work." I settled back into the couch and made myself comfortable. "Are you home yet?"

"Almost. I'm at the airport waiting for my flight. Do you have time to talk?"

"Sure." I was playing it somewhat cool, but I was thrilled to have his attention for a while, to hear his voice. Talking to him made me happier than I had been all week.

"Good. I'm glad. I like this."

"Like what?" I asked.

"This. Talking to you. Any time I get with you at all."

I smiled to myself. I liked it, too.

"Can you come visit this week?" he asked.

My smile fell. I had work to do. It was only a two-hour drive, but that wasn't a quick visit. If I stayed late and didn't want a four-hour round trip, I would have to stay over, and work from his place the next day. Were we there already? We didn't know how we each worked. We hadn't been in close quarters with each other unless we were having sex or hanging around, eating and drinking, watching movies or taking walks. Working was different.

"Work is going to be pretty busy this week. Can you come visit me?"

I heard him blow a breath out. "I'd love to, but I'm just getting home. I've got to get settled again and I promised my editor I'd send them some pages. I'm kind of swamped as well."

"Oh." I knew I wasn't good at hiding the disappointment in my voice.

"I'm sorry. What about next weekend? Could you come then?"

I could. And I didn't mind. Although, it didn't escape me that it was me coming to him, rather than the other way around. I also wouldn't mind if we had a chance to spend the weekend in the city together.

"Why don't you come stay with me? I can show you around the city; we can go out to eat at some of my favorite restaurants." It could be so perfect. I could take him to the bookshop down the street from me. We could grab coffees and browse the aisles, then have lunch at the bagel place next door. My pulse quickened, thinking about how great it could be.

"I'm not sure. It's hard for me to leave here. When I do, I find I get out of my groove with my work."

My shoulders fell. "But I would be there, interrupting you. Is it really that different if you come here?"

"I know it's hard to understand. It's hard for me to explain, but I just need to stay here. At least until my first draft is done. It's all-consuming. I'm sorry."

That word again. He kept saying it. I didn't want to hear it. He didn't need to be sorry, I just wanted all of this to be easier.

"Okay."

"Meg," he said. "I miss you. I want to feel your body again. I want to be close to you."

It was all I wanted, too. I wanted his hands on my waist, or running through my hair when we kissed. I wanted to nestle myself into the groove of his warm body. If it had to be in Old Port, it had to be there.

"I can visit. I'll leave after work on Friday. Does that work?"

"Yes. Absolutely. I can't wait." He let out another low breath. "Thank you."

I smiled into the phone. I couldn't wait either.

TWENTY-SIX

Later, I sat at my desk and opened my laptop. I checked my email and was reminded that I still hadn't quite finished the article. Again. I opened my last draft and reread my words. They were good. Of course, Cullen made it easier. I'd written about his book, his success, his quiet life. I had only touched on his family briefly. I'd focused on what made him who he was and how he had brought that into his book. It was why his book was so huge, I was sure. He was easy to like. His warmth, his intelligence, his understanding of people, it all came through on the pages. Yet, something felt missing.

I stayed at my desk until I finished the article. Hours of scrutinizing every word choice, every sentence. I studied what I had written, I absorbed it as if I was one of our readers. Then I tweaked, revised and swapped out words and sentences and whole paragraphs until I was satisfied. When I was done, I checked the clock and saw it was later than I had intended on staying up. I stretched in my chair, leaning backwards, my arms high up in the air above me. Something was nagging at me, but I didn't know what. It was an unfinished kind of feeling, even though I was done. I hoped Cullen would like what I'd written. I'd find out soon, anyway.

Although this type of writing for the paper was nothing like the type of writing I did for myself, it felt closer to my journal than anything I had ever written before. I'd used beautiful, descriptive language. I'd poured my heart out onto the page, where it was safe. Only, the difference was that I would never let anyone read my journal and what I put into it. With this article, my vulnerability would be on display when it was published. My skin tingled uncomfortably.

To take my mind momentarily off my work, I did all the things I had to do before starting another week, like my laundry, and tidying the house. After I was done, I surveyed my empty, echoey surroundings. I stood in the middle of my tiny kitchen and listened. Nothing but the distant rush of passing cars coming through the open windows. Was it always this quiet?

I missed the gentle crashing of the waves. I worked out how early I could leave the following Friday for Old Port. The entire week would be me just going through the motions until I could get to Cullen again. Until I could be with him, on his porch at dusk, walking hand in hand on the beach.

When I went to bed that night, my dreams were of the ocean.

The next day was a scheduled day to go into the office. I arrived early and took a seat at my desk, coffee in hand, ready to scan the words in my article once more. I could have spent forever wondering if what I'd written was strong enough, or I could just send it. I attached it to a short email for Celine and hit send. Then I glanced at my phone as the screen flashed with a message from Cullen.

I smiled to myself. I would never tire of reading Cullen's words. Even a simple message like this one.

> Hey. Miss you. It felt wrong to not hear the waves today

> Miss you too. You're my first thought when I wake up every morning

My body buzzed with anticipation. I was still thinking about what to message back to him when he sent another one:

> All I think about is you… And me and you… And us in my bed

I flushed, and replied:

> Me too. See you in a few days

Cullen answered almost instantly:

> Can't be away from you much longer than that

This time, my face felt like it might crack from the size of my smile.

After lunch, Celine called me into her office. I sat across from her, palms clammy and damp. Feedback on my writing never got easier. Ever.

"It's very good. You're a great writer, but you know that," Celine said.

I breathed out a little. "Thank you. Any changes?"

"Well, yes. Of course there are some changes. There always are. I've made notes with some thoughts. You can read them over later, but the main thing I'd like to see more of is the part about his sister."

"His sister?"

"I'd like you to dive in further. Has he not told you what happened?" She sat rigid, watching me intently.

I shook my head. "He said she died in an accident a few years ago, but I get the sense that he doesn't want to talk about it."

"Well, it's got potential to draw readers. Sad stories always do—you know that, too. People can't get enough of tragedy, it seems."

My back went stiff. That was something Cullen wasn't going to want to focus on—he'd made that very clear—and I didn't blame him. This was supposed to be about his book and his life as an author. Besides, this felt flat-out wrong. It felt desperate. We weren't that kind of news.

"I'm not so sure..." I said, tucking a strand of hair behind my ear.

"This is a human interest story for the Lifestyle section, Meg. It's not a book review. I'm asking you to dive into the part of the story that is human. His loss." She stood up from her desk. "I'm your editor and this is your job." Then she walked out of her office before I could answer, leaving me alone and stunned. Even though Celine was indeed my boss, and I knew she was a no-nonsense kind of woman, I couldn't recall the last time she'd spoken so sharply with me. She had always had an edge. I understood that was her way. What I didn't understand was her interest in being sensationalistic with this. That wasn't like her. Or at least, I didn't think it was.

I went back to my desk and tried to distract myself by looking through my emails again. I had already received a few junk messages I could delete immediately, several pitches from people I didn't know, and a handful of emails from coworkers. I clicked on the feedback Celine had sent and reviewed her notes.

Dive in further. Need more answers, more detail about his sister here.

I couldn't manage dealing with this in that moment. I knew I had some time to spend on revisions, and I hoped it might be enough for me to figure out how to handle this.

I finished out the rest of my long first day back in the office and trudged home. When I got inside, I pulled off my work clothes and threw on loose pyjama pants and an even looser T-shirt. I decided on a bagel topped with a slice of cheese for dinner—I couldn't muster up the energy for anything else—and flopped onto the couch.

My phone pinged. A text from Cullen.

How was your first day back?

Long and awful

I'm sorry. Wish I could be there to make you feel better

He sent me a winky emoji. I smiled in spite of myself. A wave of unease washed over me when I thought about what Celine had asked me to do. Things were starting to get better between me and Cullen after I had tried to push him away. The last thing in the world I wanted to do was betray his trust. And if I told him about what Celine was asking now, it would ruin the mood of the weekend before I even got back to Old Port.

Old Port and being with Cullen were the only things getting me through this week. I couldn't wait to feel his arms around me, to sit on the porch and sip coffee together, to feel the warm salt air on my skin, to talk and talk and then stay in bed for as long as we possibly could. My shoulders loosened at just the thought of it. I pressed my fingers to my closed eyelids and sighed. When I opened them up again, I replied to Cullen.

I'll be there soon. Can't wait

Bringing my work issues with me to Old Port would only cause more strife between us. I had messed up with Cullen once, I wasn't going to again.

TWENTY-SEVEN

By some miracle, the rest of the work week went by in a flash. I made some of the small changes Celine had asked for to Cullen's article, but kept avoiding the rest. Celine hadn't asked for it back and I couldn't remember when she'd said it would go to print. I knew I'd have to double check, but I could do that some other time. For now, all I wanted to do was get back to Cullen. It had been so long.

When I reached Old Port, it was like I was seeing it anew. I had been so used to avoiding this place because all it did was bring back bad memories. It had felt stark and cold until recently. Now, the summer evening was light enough for me to see everything clearly. The water looked as blue as cobalt, the sand along the shore was smooth. My mother's house appeared in the distance. I glanced at Cullen's next to it. It was cute and homey, with grey siding and a red front door. There were lush green shrubs and flowers surrounding it, blooming. My shoulders loosened. This was exactly where I wanted to be. I wasn't sure why I had been so insistent that I didn't like it here.

I pulled into Cullen's driveway and got out of the car just in time to hear the front door creak, followed by the sound of wood slapping closed on the door frame. Cullen appeared. His hair was a tad messy, as if he had been running his hands through it —probably while writing, deep in concentration. He had on a black T-shirt that showed off his tanned, tattooed arms. God, those arms. It struck me now how much I had missed the feel of them.

"Hey," he called, smiling.

When I got close to him, he pulled me into him, nuzzling my cheek with his nose. I turned to him and he cupped the side of my face with his palm before he kissed me, long and sweet and tender.

"Glad you're here," he said when we pulled away.

"Me too."

He took my bag from me and my hand in his before turning in the direction of his house. "Come on. I've made dinner already."

"What are we having?" I followed him to the doorway, where I was met with an array of incredible smells. I couldn't quite tell what it was, but it was unbelievable.

"I made your favorites." Cullen placed my bag on the ground and pulled me gently towards the kitchen. There were two pots bubbling on the stove and fresh bread sitting on top of a wire cooling rack.

"Did you bake bread?"

"I did," he said. "And I made homemade sauce. It tastes so much better when it's fresh."

"When did you have time for this? Aren't you writing?"

He shrugged. "Some things are more important than writing."

"Even when you're on a deadline?"

"Even when I'm on a deadline," he said. "Taking the time to show you how much I want to make you happy will always matter to me. I like going the extra mile for you."

Heat rushed through my body. I moved closer to him and folded myself into the grooves of his body while he stirred the pot of sauce.

"It's ready. Let's eat." He grinned at me. I reached up and kissed him, thinking about how I'd like to hold the memory of his lips forever.

After dinner, we went outside for a walk down by the water. The moon was perfectly round and bright in the dark sky, and the air around us was still warm. It was the kind of summer night I adored, when the breeze came off the ocean and I could walk barefoot and feel cool sand between my toes. The best part was the soothing rhythm of the ocean. When I was younger, if I closed my eyes and really focused on it, my body would go calm and then still. A lightness would take over me, like I had endorphins swirling in my insides. There was something magical about the water. I closed my eyes again. I hadn't done this in ages.

Cullen took my hand. I opened my eyes, but he gestured at me. "No, it's okay. Close your eyes. I've got you."

I walked a few steps, listening. The rush in my ears could have been attributed to the waves, or it could have been the perfection of this night. I suspected it was mostly because of Cullen and the way his hand felt, slipped into mine.

I opened my eyes to look at him. His hair was shining under the moon, lit up like fireflies.

"This is the kind of night I want to go on forever," I said. I hoped I didn't sound too cheesy. It had come to mind and I'd said it without any further thought.

Cullen was silent for a moment. "Do you ever think about what happens when your article is done and the summer is over?"

I frowned. The article. I hadn't told him it was finished—at least the first draft. I didn't want to think about it at all anymore. It had led me to Cullen and that had made me so happy. Now it had the potential to cause a big issue. "Not really." It wasn't the right thing to say, I knew immediately after I said it.

His jaw flexed before he glanced down at his feet. "How come?"

"I don't know. I worry about thinking too far in the future. I love being with you, but I also know that it's hard to make a relationship work when you don't live in the same place." There was more to it than that, but I didn't say it.

He was silent.

"What do you think?" I asked.

He ran a hand through his hair. "I don't want to lose what we have."

My heart sped up. "I don't either."

"Have you ever done a long-distance relationship? They can work."

"I've never had to do long distance because I've never had a meaningful relationship longer than a few months." The words came out more pathetic than I meant for them to sound. It was as if I wanted to give him a reason to think this wasn't going to work. But I didn't. I knew this now. I wanted this to work so much.

"Well, I feel sorry for everyone else who could have potentially been your partner, especially that ass of an ex. They lost out. Big time."

I laughed. I appreciated that he was lightening the mood.

He tugged on my hand to get me to stop walking.

"Meg."

I turned to look at him.

"I really want to try. With us."

"I know. I do, too."

"I mean it."

"I know," I said.

"I love you."

I had opened my mouth to repeat the words *I know* again, but stopped. In the middle of the beach, right next to the ocean, where I had always felt my most calm, Cullen told me he loved me. I couldn't have written it better. In fact, this was much, much better than any of the stories in my journal.

Back at his house, we went into the kitchen to make tea. I knew by the feel of his hand in mine on the way there that I wouldn't be able to wait for the water to boil, but I filled the kettle anyway. He stood behind me and leaned into my body, pressing his lips to my neck.

I stopped filling and turned around. He took the kettle from my hands and put it on the counter next to him. His face had such a serious expression, I wanted to reach up and touch his lips, run my fingers over his jawline.

He leaned into me and kissed me, his hands on my back, slowly moving up and down, sending shivers over every inch of me. I couldn't remember the last time a kiss had been this long and felt this good. I let out a soft moan.

"I love you like this," he said quickly, in between kisses.

"Like what?" I was almost breathless.

"Standing in the middle of the room, next to me, touching me."

Heat radiated from the top of my head all the way down. "Me too."

We stayed there, wrapped up in one another, his hands everywhere and lips pressed into mine, until I felt delirious. Then he pulled me gently to his room and onto the bed, where our clothes couldn't come off fast enough.

I loved the feel of his smooth skin on mine. I loved every moment of this—the way my body responded to his touch, the way my mind went blank, focused only on right now, this very moment and the way it felt to know Cullen was with me. Nothing else made sense, nothing else entered my consciousness, but Cullen. Now. Here.

He stopped kissing me for a second and looked at me again with a serious expression.

"What?" I said.

"Meg." His voice came out low and hoarse.

"Yes?"

He didn't answer. Instead, he leaned in again and pressed his lips to my neck, to my collarbone, while his hand ran over my hip, along the outside of my thigh. Desire ripped through me. I closed my eyes and allowed myself to be touched, to be discovered, until I couldn't think any longer at all.

The next morning, I sat on Cullen's porch, stretched out, sipping a coffee. Even though I was sitting, I was still floating, lost in memories from last night. It was as if the entire evening had been a scene from a movie. The way the moon had been shining in a clear sky, the way the waves had gently lapped onto the shore, Cullen and I alone, together, wrapped up in one another. And his words.

I love you.

I hadn't said it back, for some reason. I'd wanted to because I had never felt like this with someone before, but it hadn't come out. He had been quiet when we were walking on the beach afterwards and it had made me wonder if I'd hurt him by not saying it back, but by the time we got back to his house, we had connected in a way that I had never connected with someone before. Not with Daniel, or anyone else from my past. I smiled at the memory. In the kitchen, and then upstairs, under his covers, slow and gentle, communicating with one another in whispers and quiet murmurs while we moved. A complete dream and I was living it. How did I get so lucky?

"Good morning." Cullen came through the back door and out onto the porch. He took a seat next to me and placed his hand on my thigh. "How'd you sleep?"

"Great." I gestured to the ocean. "It lulled me right off to dreamland."

He laughed. "I thought I had something to do with how exhausted you were."

"That, too," I agreed, grinning.

"Speaking of exhaustion, I need a coffee. Do you want a refill?" He pointed to my cup.

"Sure." I sat upright and handed Cullen my mug. Then I leaned over towards my laptop. I brought it everywhere with me because that was what Cullen did, too. He was always walking from room to room with his. Habits of a writer, I figured. Before long, I'd started doing it, too.

I waited for my screen to hum to life and saw my words about Cullen in front of me. I frowned and minimized the article. I didn't want it to potentially ruin this weekend. Not after the perfection of last night.

A moment later, Cullen came back out onto the porch balancing two mugs of steaming coffee. He handed me one and sat next to me on the couch again.

"Thank you." I sipped and closed my eyes. He made the best coffee.

"What's that?" Cullen asked.

I turned to look at him. He was glancing at the screen of my laptop.

"What do you mean?" My work email was open, but only to my inbox. There was a long list of names of senders with subject lines. I didn't understand what he was getting at.

"You work with Celine St. Clair." It wasn't quite a question. His voice was heavy.

I tilted my head at his odd reaction. "Yes?"

He placed his cup of coffee on the table in front of us and

frowned deeply. I thought I noticed his body stiffen for a second.

"Do you know her?" I asked.

He ran a hand through his hair and went to the edge of the porch, where he kept his gaze directed out at the water. Why wasn't he looking at me? There was something I didn't recognize in his face. An uncomfortableness I couldn't put my finger on.

"No. Not personally."

I swung my feet to the ground and stood up, moving closer to where he was, leaning against the railing.

"It's her work," he said. "She seems like a sensationalist."

My mouth dropped open. "You've read her writing?"

"Some of it." He turned to me. "Is that why you were reading that old article of hers?"

"I was reading it because I admire her writing. I don't think she's a sensationalist. I think she's really good at what she does."

Cullen shrugged and was quiet for a moment before he said, "I didn't know you worked with her."

"I didn't think to tell you," I answered.

He shook his head. "No, of course not. Anyway, forget it. I'm sorry." He ran his hand over mine. Relief flooded through me.

"What's our plan for today?" he asked, changing the subject.

I smiled. "You're looking at it." I held my arms out wide, gesturing to my pyjamas. "I don't feel like getting out of these."

"I might know how to change your mind." He moved closer, pulling me toward him. I touched the back of his neck, and he leaned in until his perfect lips were on mine again. When he pulled away, he took my coffee cup from my hand and placed it on the table by the chairs.

"I'm not sure I was done with that," I teased.

"Let's go find something else to do. Coffee later."

"And food?" I asked.

He laughed. "Yeah, we'll need to replenish our energy."

I let him take me by the hand and lead me back to his bedroom.

TWENTY-EIGHT

After going back to bed for a while, we got up and Cullen made us pancakes and more coffee. We sat on the porch, watching families on the beach—kids making sandcastles, one little girl burying her father's legs under an impressively detailed mermaid tail of sand. Then we showered and dressed and went into town to stock up on groceries. I found that I loved walking through the grocery store with him, pushing the cart and watching him place things inside it, like we did this every week. I could imagine a routine with him. I could imagine doing every daily task together, and none of it feeling mundane. I tried not to think about how this was only our weekend reality.

"I've got to look for olive oil. Can you grab me some milk?" Cullen asked.

"Sure." Again, I liked the casual comfort of the question, like this was what we did when we went grocery shopping.

In the dairy aisle, I saw a familiar face.

"Meg, hi!" Gwen smiled at me, a brilliant smile, like we were old friends.

"Hey—nice to see you."

"Are you still writing that article? I thought you were only in town for a couple of days, but I keep running into you."

"What can I say? I keep getting pulled back."

Gwen leaned in closer and lowered her voice. "By Cullen? I saw you two at the barbecue together."

My face warmed, and she must have noticed.

"It is him! I knew it," she said. She nudged my arm. "Good for you. He is so handsome and such a kind person. I've had a very hard time understanding how he's stayed single."

"I know," I agreed.

"Well, I'm glad you two found each other. Old Port is a great place for romance." Her eyes widened suggestively.

My smile faltered for a beat when I thought of my mother and father, but I recovered quickly.

"It is lovely here," I admitted.

Cullen joined us. "Hi, Gwen," he said.

Gwen's smile got even brighter. She pushed a piece of hair behind her ear. "Hey you." Was she flirting? I smiled to myself. "I won't keep you two, I'm sure you have better things to do than spend hours grocery shopping." She raised her eyebrows, and I had to bite back a laugh.

Cullen smiled kindly at her. "It's good to see you. Hope you're having another barbecue before the end of summer?"

"Only if you promise you'll be there." She waved her hand at us as she turned to leave. I watched her walk away, a little surprised at the conversation we'd just had.

"You certainly have an admirer in her." I nodded in Gwen's direction.

"And do I have one in you?"

I snaked my arm around his waist. "Do you even have to ask?"

He leaned in and brushed his lips over my ear. My body melted. This was how it felt to be your very best self, I imagined. Everything felt right and good. I hadn't been this happy in so long, it felt like a luxury.

After a day that was as close to perfect as possible, I slept deeply in Cullen's bed. When I woke the next morning, I was alone. Cullen's side of the bed was empty. I got up, pulled on one of his hoodies and went downstairs. He was at his desk, head bent in concentration. I went to him and ran a hand over his shoulders. He hummed lightly. Such a sweet sound.

"I'm going to let you work," I said.

"No, it's okay. I can stop." His heart wasn't in what he was saying. He wanted to write. I understood.

"I'm going to see my mom. I haven't stopped by yet. You keep going and I'll be back in a bit." I leaned over and kissed the side of his head.

At my mother's house, I knocked once on the side door and then went through the kitchen. "Hello?"

"I'm in here!" Her voice came from the direction of the living room. She was on the couch, next to an open window, a mug of tea in hand. Her eyes were closed. It brought me back to how I used to see her. This was her calm, happy place.

I didn't want to disturb her. I pressed my shoulder up against the door frame at the entrance to the living room and watched her instead, a tiny smile on my face.

"I can hear you." Mom opened one eye. She smiled and then opened the other. "Glad you're here. What's going on? You look different."

Damn, she was good.

"Does this have to do with Cullen? I'm guessing since you've been visiting but haven't been here, you two are good now?" she asked.

"It's good," I agreed.

"But?"

She was incredibly adept at reading me. I didn't have to say a word for her to know what was rolling around in my head and my heart. I pushed myself off the wall I was leaning on and went to sit on the couch across from her, folding my legs underneath me.

"It's close to perfect, and I feel so good with him, but I don't know if it can last."

"Why not?" She put down her mug and turned to face me.

"He has a life here. I have a life in Boston. We only see one another on weekends."

"Oh."

"What does that mean?" I asked.

She frowned, briefly, before continuing. "It means I think you might be inventing problems."

My back went rigid. "Why would I do that?"

"Because you feel safer pushing people away. I don't know why, but I can see it in you. It happened with Daniel. It happened before that."

I didn't know what to say to that. It hadn't happened with Daniel. I wasn't the one who had given up. I glanced out the window at the water.

"I don't mean to upset you."

"You didn't," I said. A lie. "Anyway, I didn't push Daniel away, he left me. Someone always leaves me."

A gentle look crossed her face. "Meg." There was so much compassion in her voice, tears pricked at the back of my eyes. I blinked to stop them.

"I like Cullen a lot and he likes me, but my life isn't here. I have to get back to the city and my house and work."

"You're alone there."

I nodded. "I'm used to that. Besides, I have my job. I'm good at it."

"I know you are," my mother said. "You should be proud."

I smiled weakly.

"So, what's going to happen with you and Cullen then?"

I shrugged.

"Haven't you two talked about it?" Her voice was somber.

"Not really. I don't know what to say. I guess we try the long-distance thing and figure out if it'll work as we go." I brushed a piece of hair off my face and avoided making direct eye contact.

"Sometimes figuring life out as you go is all you can really do."

I looked up and my mother's face wore the same reassuring, calming expression she'd always had, despite what life had thrown at her.

"Maybe I should go back and talk to him."

"Yes, maybe you should," she agreed.

I pushed myself off the couch and leaned in to give my mother a hug, then I went to the doorway, where I slid my feet into my flip-flops and walked across the gravel-filled pathway to Cullen's house.

He came into the hallway by the door and stood in front of me with damp hair and his face pink, like he'd just gotten out of the shower. He looked so good. He always did. My resolve weakened at the same time as my knees did. I didn't want to have any kind of serious conversation. I didn't want any of this to be interrupted or ruined.

"Hey." A slow grin developed across his gorgeous face. I took a step forward and he leaned in to kiss me.

I pulled away. "How'd your writing go?"

"Okay, but I got stuck and needed a break. Sometimes I do my best thinking in the shower." He turned and went toward the kitchen. "I'm making coffee. Want some?"

"Of course." I followed him and stood by the doorway of the kitchen before I let out a small sigh. Might as well jump right in. "So, I know you said you wanted this to work—us to work."

"I do. Very much." Cullen stopped fiddling with the coffee maker and put the carafe down. He looked at me. "Do you?"

"Yes," I said quickly. "Yes, of course. I'm adjusting to the idea of distance." I couldn't explain the other part. That I worried about it being too hard because most relationships are too hard.

He put water into the coffee maker, filled it with grinds and clicked it on. "Meg, we can visit each other. I can come there some weekends, you can come here. We can even pop by during the week. This is completely doable. It isn't that far."

"I know. But it's also not... being together."

I didn't say that I wanted this to work out the way I would have written it in my journal. That we should be together almost all the time. There would be late nights over takeout and wine in the middle of the week just because we could. We would linger in bed in the mornings. I would feel his warm skin next to me when I woke up. That was what I wanted.

But that wasn't reality. Reality was one of us driving for four hours each weekend and getting by on phone calls during the week. I thought about the harsh reality my parents had had to face. My father had decided his life with my mother wasn't enough for him, and they hadn't even had distance to contend with.

"I want any amount of together I can get." Cullen moved closer to me and touched the side of my jaw, running his thumb over to my lip. I pointed my face up to him.

He was so close, I leaned in and pressed myself to him so I could feel his skin on my forehead and the warmth of his body through his shirt. He pressed his lips to mine and stayed there, lingering over a long kiss.

When he pulled away, he looked down at me. "We'll make it work. I promise."

In that moment, I could believe him. I nodded.

"Do you want to stay over tonight?"

I did, but it was Sunday, and I had to go into the office tomorrow. "I should get going in a few hours."

He nodded, and then he wrapped me up in his arms for another hug. "Let's make the most of our time, then."

I allowed myself to melt into his body. I even allowed myself to believe this would all be okay.

TWENTY-NINE

At work the next day, I had planned to get settled, answer emails, go to my morning meeting and finally decide how I was going to handle the article. I had made some revisions, but I hadn't figured out what to do about Celine's request to bring in more of Cullen's sister. She wouldn't accept any delays much longer.

In the boardroom where we had our usual update meetings, I turned my phone upside down on the table in front of me. Celine was looking directly at me, which meant I needed to be present.

"Meg, how are the changes to your piece going? I'd like to get it ready to go to print this week."

My stomach twisted. "Almost ready."

"I know it's not finalized, but once those changes are made, we're thinking of entering it into next year's Digital Publishing Awards Best Article Feature. It's past the deadline for now, but I think you'd have a great shot at it next year." She smiled at me. A rare thing from Celine who was usually so serious.

My chest expanded. This was big. I nodded and tried to smile back, unable to say much more than a mumbled thank you. It felt incredible to be recognized for my writing. It was all I'd ever wanted. I spent hours and hours writing for myself and yes, they were silly made-up romances, but they were also practice. I worked on perfecting sentence structure and word choice, even if it was only for my own eyes. I wanted to be good at it. To be recognized by Celine, who I'd admired ever since I first read her piece on the Marshall bus tragedy, felt like I was finally coming into my own. But at what price? I thought of Cullen. The way he'd looked when we spoke about his sister. How guarded he was about his family.

The meeting continued with a mention of other nominations, a quick recap on what everyone was working on and then, once it was over, we all got up and left. I took my phone and my notebook and went down the elevator to stand out front of the building, where I could get a little privacy. I called Cullen.

"Hey."

"Hey you," Cullen said.

"How's the writing going?" I asked.

He hesitated for a few moments before his voice came across the line again. "It's been hard. I'm stuck. Nothing very good is coming out of me and onto the page right now." He sounded so defeated, I wanted to be there next to him, to fold my body into his and wrap my arms around his waist.

"I wish I could help you," I said.

"I think I write better when you're here with me. You're my muse." He laughed lightly. "I know you were just here, but do you think you could come back?"

"I think so." I wanted to. I could almost already feel his body in every cell of mine. It was like a guttural, innate feeling. It was more than just desire. It was deeper. Like a need. Like I could only exist with him in my life.

"Next weekend?"

I shifted weight on my legs and folded one arm under the other. "Sure. I'd love that."

Cullen breathed out.

"I know you're always coming here. I'll make it up to you. I'll come visit you, too, as soon as I make some progress on this draft of the book. I really just want to be with you," he said.

Warmth simmered beneath my skin. "Me too." I turned around and faced the building, looking inside the large glass windows to the lobby. "I have some good news."

"What's that?"

"My boss loves the article about you and your book. It might be entered into the Digital Publishing Awards for next year. They're a big deal among journalists. I'm already picturing my business card now—*Award-winning journalist, Meg Adamson.*" I smiled at my reflection in the window.

"That's amazing. Congrats, Meg."

"I just have to make a small change." I hesitated, closed my eyes and then opened them back up. "I've been asked to bring in more about your sister."

Silence followed. I waited a moment and then pulled my phone away from my ear to look at the screen to see if I was still connected. It was.

"Cullen?"

He cleared his throat. "My sister? Why?"

I lifted my chin. "People can relate when they hear someone has gone through something hard. There might be readers who have gone through something similar and it might help them."

There was a brief pause, almost an awkward silence, before he cleared his throat again and spoke. "No."

"No?" My head jerked back at the finality of his word choice.

"I don't want to bring her into it."

"I would be so sensitive. You know me. I would never—"

"I said no." His voice was sharp, but when he spoke again, it was gentle. "Sorry. Listen. I've had... I'm having some second thoughts."

Goosebumps sprang up on the back of my arms. Second thoughts? What kind of second thoughts could he be having? About us? "What do you mean?"

"I'm not comfortable with personal stuff about my family. I really don't want it to be in there."

"At all?" My chest twisted. I couldn't understand what he was saying. Logically, my brain heard the words and knew what they meant, but I was unable to make sense of them. If we took out his family, it would take out so much of the human side. All that would be left was a book report, as Celine had put it.

"I don't want my family in the story," he repeated.

"But I'm really proud of the way I've done it. I thought you would like the way I wrote about you." There was so much vulnerability in those words, I was almost embarrassed to speak them out loud.

"You're a great writer, Meg. You know I think that. But it's too much—and now Celine wants more of my sister? I'm not comfortable."

I frowned. The way he mentioned Celine's name was odd.

"I really don't want it out there for the public," he said.

My mouth dropped open. "It's press—for your book. You said you need that."

"And now I'm saying I don't want press if it comes with scrutiny into my family." His tone was only the tiniest bit more serious, but it didn't go unnoticed by me. It sent my stomach twisting.

"I don't understand."

"Please don't put those parts in. Don't put any of my family in."

Coldness rushed to my core and spread out through my limbs. "I'm not the editor. That's not how it works."

"There has to be something you can do."

"Cullen, Celine likes the piece. The award nomination—" I was fumbling over my words now. If I didn't deliver, I'd be stuck in my job writing boring pieces, never growing into the writer I wanted to be.

Something seemed to shift in him. His voice grew deeper, thicker. It was almost desperate. "I don't care who likes it. I don't want it to be published with my family in it. I need you to do something to stop it. Please."

For the second time, I flinched. "Cullen, this is my job..." I started.

Something made a noise in the background on his end of the call. "I have to go. I'm sorry. I just—I can't. I have to go." His words were choked.

The line went silent. I stood in the middle of the busy sidewalk, my heart in my throat.

I stumbled into the office and went to my desk, where I sat trying to understand what had just happened. I was upset with Cullen for asking me to change the article completely, confused by his reaction. But I was also worried. He had sounded so hurt. I had never heard him that way. It wasn't the Cullen I'd gotten to know over the past month.

Part of me wanted to protect myself from the pain I could sense coming. But a larger part of me remembered that my mother and Sarina, even Cullen himself, had told me I should fight for this. I had never been happier, so why shouldn't I? I needed to push past these issues and see if we could make it work.

I wanted to call him back, but first I needed to do something.

I shifted in my desk chair and eyed Celine's office from where I sat. I could see her bent over her large oak desk, her brow furrowed in concentration. She fiddled with a delicate silver necklace around her neck.

It likely wasn't the best time for me to interrupt Celine, but I had to. I stood and went to her glass-walled office door, wiping my hands on my jeans before knocking.

She glanced up and waved me in. "Yes?"

"I wanted to talk to you about my article." My throat tightened.

"Again? Why's that?" Celine looked at me over the top of her reading glasses. She wasn't smiling.

"I don't think it's quite ready. I would like a bit of time to make some more tweaks. And I talked to Cullen. He doesn't want anything about his sister in there."

Her frown grew deeper. She took her glasses off. "That's not his call to make."

"I don't feel comfortable doing it," I said. "He doesn't want it, and I want to respect that."

Celine let out a long sigh. "I can't deal with this right now. I'm knee-deep in budget issues. You must have a horseshoe or something around your neck. Joanne just asked me to slide another story in for this week that's more timely. We don't have space for yours in the schedule for another few weeks, so you can have more time."

Joanne was Celine's boss. I had never felt so grateful for her in my life. Tension escaped my body.

"His sister needs to be in there, though. Now, is there anything else?" Celine stared at me. The warmth I was starting to get used to from her had disappeared. Stress came easily to people in higher positions around here, so I assumed that was where this was coming from. I'd handle the problem of including Cullen's sister in the story later.

"Thank you." I turned to leave her office.

"Don't thank me, thank Joanne." She paused. "And for God's sake, do your job, Meg."

I stopped in my tracks and turned back around, my arms dangling at my sides. "Sorry—pardon me?" I must have misheard her.

"I mean, the article's about him, and I know you've gotten close to him. Maybe it's getting in the way of your work?"

I hadn't misheard. What was she implying?

"It isn't getting in the way, but how do you know who I'm close to?"

"It's in the way you write. You're slipping a little. Showing your hand. Now, if you don't mind, I've got urgent things to get back to." Celine put her glasses on and looked at her computer screen. The conversation was over.

I guess I didn't move fast enough because she looked at me pointedly. I fumbled with the door handle and left in a daze. Back at my desk, I tried to ignore the quiver in the base of my stomach. I didn't like the way Celine had implied something about Cullen and I—even if it was true. I was good at my job, I was a professional. Now I felt like I needed to reread my article over again to see if I had slipped, as she'd said. Something hot and tight swirled inside my chest. No. There was no way. I'd done a good job. It wasn't my fault Cullen didn't like the direction I had to go in, and that Celine thought I was unprofessional.

I let out a shaky breath and stared at my laptop screen. My head was muddled. The rest of the day was going to be long and impossible to focus. I pulled out my phone and sent a short text to Cullen.

The article's been delayed

That was true, at least.

Shortly after, he replied.

Thank you

I thought about what to say back, but saw the bubble of dots pop up, indicating he was typing something more.

I have to leave again

My stomach dropped. The timing was bad. I wasn't sure where we stood, and now he had to leave.

Book promotion?

I typed back while disappointment coursed through me.

Yes

How long?

Two weeks. A long one this time

I slumped down in my chair. This wasn't what I wanted to hear. At all.

That sucks

I know

When the bubble and dots didn't appear again, I put my phone away.

THIRTY

The night of the Digital Publishing Awards was three days later. I had only heard from Cullen once in that time. He'd texted me back with *Good!* when I'd asked him how things were going. He was busy, I knew it, but I had still hoped for more. The silence was hard and I wasn't used to the short answers. At least he had used an exclamation mark. I supposed that was a positive sign.

That night, I did my best to push Cullen to the back of my mind. I put on a soft black dress that stopped just above my knees. It was form fitting and showed off my legs, which I thought were my best feature. I curled my hair and then watched a makeup tutorial on my phone and ended up pretty satisfied with the results.

The awards were being held in a swanky hotel, in a large room decorated with white and navy linens and shiny table settings. Everything was glamorous and gorgeous. I felt vastly out of place, but was comforted by the appearance of a few of my coworkers. Ahmad waved at me from the bar when I walked in. He mouthed the word "Nice" and nodded his approval at my look. I grinned at him and my shoulders relaxed.

Celine stood by a table, frowning at her phone. She was alone, so I decided to approach her.

"Celine. How are you?"

She looked up. "Hey, Meg. I'm good, thanks. How are you?"

"I'm good."

"This could be you next year," she said, smiling. Was she making small talk? It felt stilted after our last exchange.

I nodded and smiled back, but didn't say anything. It was a big deal to be nominated. On the other hand, all I could think about was Cullen.

"Did you just get here? You should grab yourself a drink. It'll be a while before they start announcing." Celine held her glass up in salute to me. This relaxed version of Celine was nice. I guessed she'd forgotten that she had told me I was slipping.

"Thanks, I'll do that." I left her and made my way over to the bar. The line wasn't enormous, but it was busy. Everyone had the same idea.

I ordered a glass of wine and stood at a high-top table. The air around me crackled with energy. This was a big event, one that was highly recognized by people in the industry. I'd always thought I wanted to be here, nominated for an award, getting my name out there. Now that I was here, and I had the potential to be nominated, I felt almost... nothing. I didn't care as much as I should have that my name might be on one of those categories next year. Something about the news had been lost for me. I'd got into it when I was right out of school, and I'd learned a lot at the start of my career, but lately, it had felt like a job. I was churning out articles, and I was doing good work. Yet I couldn't deny that I wanted something more. I wanted to feel more about my work.

Ahmad approached the high-top table with a ginger ale in his hand.

"Hey." He raised his glass to me. "Nice to see you outside of work."

"Nice to see you, too. And congratulations on your nomination." I clinked my glass to his.

Ahmad was a bright spot at work for me. He was older, I thought probably in his late fifties. He had started young and had been in this business for so long, had been through various titles and roles at newspapers and still did excellent work, day in and day out.

"How do you do it?" I asked.

He laughed. "Do what?"

"Everything you do." Ahmad was an editor, but he had started as a writer. He was excellent at everything, and he had never lost his passion for it. That amazed me.

"You're so great at all of it. I wish I was like you."

His eyes widened while he was mid-sip. When he put his glass down, he smiled kindly. "Meg, you're great at what you do. I mean it. Sometimes it seems like you don't even know it."

I thought of Celine. *You're slipping. Showing your hand.*

"I'm not sure everyone agrees."

Ahmad shrugged. "You can't worry about what everyone else thinks. I learned that a long time ago. Someone out there will always be mad or have something negative to say about what you write. The important thing is getting the facts straight and telling a strong, honest story. But that can only happen if you're happy with what you do." He studied me. "Are you happy with what you do?"

Tears pricked at the back of my eyes. "I don't know." I took a sip of my wine to hide my reaction. He must have noticed because he patted my hand.

"Listen, I'm creeping closer and closer to retirement age and if I've learned anything in all those years, it's that you spend a long, long time working in life. A lot of people don't love their job, I get that. You're lucky if you really love what you're paid for. But you have to at least be happy with what you do. It has to make you feel some kind of achievement. If you do good work, you should feel good about it. If you don't feel something positive about it, maybe it's time to reassess."

"But what should I do?"

Ahmad took a sip of his ginger ale, placed it on the table and shrugged. "If I knew that I'd be making millions as a consultant. I can't tell you what to do, but I can see that you're not as happy as you deserve to be."

A rush of gratitude swept over me at Ahmad's kindness. "I think you're right."

He nodded.

"How do you know me so well?"

"I've been conducting interviews my whole career. I'm an expert at reading people."

"You *are*."

Ahmad winked. "Let's go find our table. I hear they're serving wagyu beef nachos as part of the meal. And it's halal. Can you imagine? We used to get dry meat and potatoes at these kinds of things. Now we're being fed fancy foods that I would never eat otherwise. I don't want to miss out."

I laughed at the excitement in his voice. "Let's go."

Later, when the categories were being announced, they called the names of the nominees and I tried to imagine hearing the announcer's voice call out my name, but it didn't give me that feeling Ahmad had talked about.

Afterwards, the rest of the evening went quickly—and then I was home, on my couch, in my pyjamas.

I wanted to call Cullen. I wanted to ask him about his day, listen to his voice, and try to figure out what was going on in his mind. But I also wanted to understand what was happening with me. Why did I feel so unsatisfied? And what was I going to do to fix it?

THIRTY-ONE

On the Friday after the awards, nobody was expected to go into the office. I got up and went for a run to clear my head. It was short, yet gruelling; my body felt leaden during the entire jog, but it did the trick for my mind. Back at home, I answered some emails, worked on a few stories and tidied my house. When I checked my phone, I couldn't help but notice the blank screen. I hadn't heard from Cullen yet. His schedule was hectic, but still. My stomach flipped uncomfortably. I wish we hadn't left things so—unlike us. He wouldn't be back for another week and a few days. It was a long time to leave things unsaid.

By early evening, I realized this was the first Friday in a month that I had spent in the city instead of driving back to Old Port. Summer weekend traffic aside, it left an empty feeling inside me, and I was hit with the realization that Old Port had grown on me. Maybe my brain was rewiring the old association from childhood and was finally seeing it for what it was—a beautiful, serene spot, with sand and sun, where my mother lived. And where I'd had so much happiness lately.

I didn't have enough food in the house to make a decent dinner, so I went for a walk to pick up a Cobb salad from one of my favorite little bagel and salad places nearby. The fact that I still hadn't heard from Cullen ran through the back of my mind while I meandered along the streets. I tried to focus on the here and now: it was a Friday night in mid-August in the city. I loved warm nights like this, and how quiet the city became in the summer. People left to go on vacation, especially on weekends, leaving a slow, still feeling in the streets and in the air. I reminded myself that Cullen was on a book tour, and his schedule was packed. He must be exhausted, running from event to event. It wasn't only up to him to text me. I slid my phone from my pocket and texted.

Hey

He didn't reply right away, so I put it back into my pocket. After I got home and had my salad while watching a trashy reality television show, I picked up my phone again and looked at the last message I sent him. No response. But there was tiny, grey type under my text.

READ

I swear, read receipts were the single worst invention after social media. Knowing he had looked at my message but had decided not to answer caused my overthinking superpower to go into overdrive.

I took a deep breath. He was busy. This was fine.

The next morning, I rolled over in bed and reached for my phone only to find the screen blank. This wasn't like Cullen. It was Saturday, he must have some time to talk.

I dialed his number and waited. When it went to his voice-mail, I froze. I didn't know what to say, so I hung up, knowing he'd see I called and would get back to me when he could. I didn't want to look desperate, but when I hadn't heard back from Cullen by that evening, my body deflated. I could text or call him again, but it felt like I'd be chasing him. My mother hadn't chased when my father had left, and I wasn't going to either. I told myself I had too much pride for that.

Instead of letting myself obsess over something out of my control, I retreated into my words over the next week. I focused on work. Celine hadn't asked for Cullen's article back yet, and I was thankful for the fact. I didn't know what to do about it, which meant avoidance was my only option at the moment. So I zeroed in on all my other assignments. No matter what I was writing, I wrote it with everything I had within me. I sat at my desk with my hair up in a loose bun, favorite hoodie and sweatpants on, and I made certain every time I handed something in to Celine that it was my best work, so she could never accuse me of "slipping" again.

On the days I went into the office, I did the same, only without the sweats. And when I went home at night, I wrote in my journal. Writing was the only time I felt like myself. At work, my writing was structured and backed up by facts, but at home, it was anything I wanted it to be. It wasn't real life, it was better.

Only this time, instead of writing short vignettes about men I thought were attractive, I started to plot out something bigger. I wrote it down as it came to me—a shy woman who meets a successful yet reclusive man. I set them in summer. On the ocean. They fell for each other fast and hard and seemed perfect together. I wrote about their meet cute, their long conversations and the moments that helped them grow closer. The words came quickly to me, and before I knew it, I was doing nothing but writing in my free time. I would come home from work, put on my pyjama pants, head straight to my desk or flop onto the couch to write in my journal. It gave me a much-needed reprieve from the confusing feelings swirling through me like a hurricane. I told myself it didn't matter that I hadn't heard from Cullen yet. He would get back to me when he got back to me.

When Friday rolled around again, I thought of Old Port. I convinced myself to text Cullen again—just one more time.

> Are you okay??

By this point, I just wanted to know he hadn't ended up in a ditch somewhere. When that tiny, painful word "Read" popped up under my message again, my stomach flipped. He was fine.

> Sorry

I stared at his response, trying to analyze it. Why was it so short? What was the intent behind it? There had been so many times I had read text messages wrong or had sent them and had been read wrong myself. I didn't want to give this meaning that wasn't there. I needed to relax and calm down.

There was only one place I could do that.

THIRTY-TWO

I needed a good dose of mothering, and, thankfully, she answered my call. In fact, my mother very easily convinced me to come stay with her for the weekend. Immediately, my shoulders relaxed, and my mind started to calm. This would be perfect.

As soon as I showed up at her door, she held her arms open and folded me into them. "Come here." She must have sensed that a hug from my mother, even as an adult, was exactly what I needed. "I've made dinner. Let's go eat."

It was close to seven on Friday night, the sun was just starting to dim, and my mother had laid out a great spread for the two of us. It was a beautiful evening. I tried not to glance at Cullen's house through the window, but it was difficult. Maybe this hadn't been the smartest decision I'd ever made.

I breathed out. As much as I didn't want to read into whatever was happening, I couldn't help it. Things had been so good and now there was nothing but distance. I had opened up to him, allowed myself to believe in the possibility of being in love —only to feel like I was heading down the track I'd always known would come. It was too good with Cullen. It couldn't work. Those kinds of romances were for the movies. They weren't real.

Mom and I sat out on the porch, our favorite spot to be, and I tried to let the breeze coming off the ocean relax me. I had to admit that the salt air was soothing. Funny how this place used to be somewhere I could never imagine coming back to, and now its familiarity calmed me when I was here. Despite the fact that it reminded me very much of Cullen, it also brought me happiness to be here with my mother. She was relentlessly present for me when I needed her. It struck me that for my entire life, I had ever so slightly pushed her away, nudge by nudge. We'd fought when I was a teenager. As an adult, I'd chosen not to visit her much before this summer—I couldn't believe now that I had planned to visit Old Port and not even tell her that first time I came here. My cheeks burned with shame when I thought of it. At least I called her often, but I had always held her at arm's length, and I didn't really know why. Yet, despite all of that, she'd showed up for me. Over and over.

I studied her face now. The soft lines around her eyes, her thinning eyebrows, sprinkled with grey, the creases around her mouth.

"What is it?" She looked at me with a hint of a smile.

"Thank you."

"For what?"

"For always taking care of me, and for being here for me now." The words came out choked.

She tilted her head. "I always will be, pumpkin seed."

I laughed and swiped at my sniffling nose. She hadn't called me by my childhood nickname in ages.

"Why pumpkin seed? Why not just pumpkin?"

"A seed is capable of developing and growing into a plant. I always knew you'd do many incredible things in your life as you went. And I was right."

"I'm not so sure about that."

"You're not done growing yet." She leaned over in her seat and patted my leg.

My chest expanded. I wasn't sure I deserved so much love. Whatever happened between Cullen and I, however I felt about my job, at least I knew I had my mother. It helped to know I wasn't completely alone. I never had been.

She held my gaze for a moment and then smiled, rubbed my leg once more and stood up. "I'm going to tidy this up." She picked up our empty plates off the coffee table. "Can you do me a favor and run out to the grocery store? We ran out of milk and we'll need it tomorrow morning for coffee."

"Sure." I stood and stretched. I watched the waves for a moment longer, feeling my body loosen, my limbs go light. I breathed out and then went to find my keys and wallet.

Inside the grocery store, I went towards the refrigerated section near the back. At home in Boston, it felt like there were eighteen different types of milk you could choose from. Here, there were three. I could have been losing it, but damn it, that milk seemed like a metaphor. Life was simple here in Old Port. It was slower and quiet. It was the kind of place that didn't give you too much to overthink. You had your three choices of milk and you were happy with them. I thought of the last time I had been here—grocery shopping with Cullen like we were a proper, regular couple.

I grabbed the milk my mother always bought and turned to leave. As if I had summoned him, Cullen appeared at the end of an aisle. He stood casually, a bag of chips in his hand. My forehead immediately tightened in confusion and shock. What was going on? Why was he here?

"Cullen?"

His head snapped up and his eyes widened. Something about the way he was standing there nonchalantly, while I had spent the last few days stressed out and unhappy and obsessively thinking about him, caused a hot swirling inside me. He hadn't been in touch for days, not really, but here he was, getting chips?

"Meg? What are you doing here?"

"What am *I* doing? What are *you* doing here?" I didn't understand. Why? Why would he be here and not tell me he was home? He wasn't supposed to be back for another few days.

His mouth hung open, but he didn't answer.

"How long have you been back?" I asked.

His voice came out low. "A couple of days." He looked over my shoulder rather than right at me.

A rushing flooded my ears. "You didn't message me back. Were you ever going to answer me? Or call me?"

"Meg..."

I shook my head. I didn't want to know. I couldn't. This was awful. It was exactly what I thought it was. Tiny dots appeared, blurring my vision.

"I thought we were happy." My voice broke and I hated myself for it, but I went on. "We had something really special, but then you just stopped talking to me. You didn't answer my texts. Who does that? And here you are—you've got home and you weren't going to tell me? How could you decide it was just... over?"

My hands shook. I couldn't believe how much I spat out at him. How loud had I been? I glanced around to see if anyone was watching. When I turned back to Cullen, his face was pained, his brow furrowed and his cheeks pink.

I wondered what his reaction meant, if he was sorry or just embarrassed by my outburst. Everything was too muddled and confusing. I gave him a moment, a chance to respond, but when he said nothing, my stomach sank. I had to leave now, while I still had some dignity.

"I—I have to go. Please leave me alone." I turned on my heel and went to the front of the store to pay as quickly as possible. When I got back into my car, I turned my key with shaking hands.

I sped back to my mother's house and told her I was exhausted from the week and was heading up to bed. Despite everything inside of me telling me not to do it, I checked my phone for a missed call or text from Cullen. Nothing.

A painful tightness gripped my throat. I was cracked open and raw. I'd thought everything we had was real. I'd thought this time, things would be different. Cullen was nothing like Daniel and he wasn't like my father. He was better than anyone I had imagined. With him, I'd thought I had everything I ever wanted, but I had turned out to be wrong. There could be no rational explanation for why he'd stopped texting me completely and why he'd come home and hadn't told me. Or why he wasn't trying to reach out to me now.

It hurt so much, I worried I might not be able to catch my breath. My bag sat on the bed. I knew what was in there. My journal. Writing in it had always been my safe place. For so many years, I hadn't risked the pain that came with reality, I'd protected myself and had been okay. But ever since I'd put myself out there with Cullen, I had been hurt, and now I was alone. Again.

I picked up my journal and found a pen. I sat on top of my bed and started to write. When my emotions were heightened, when I felt things so deeply that my hands shook, it was the best time to get it all down. I made up scenarios and daydreams where I was the one someone chose, where I wasn't unlovable and where I didn't end up alone.

This time, I left Cullen out of it.

THIRTY-THREE

Back in Boston, I started to spiral, and I couldn't stop it.

On Monday, and for the rest of the week, I opted to work from home rather than try to put on a brave face in the office. Celine didn't push it because of my recent output. I was churning out good articles quickly; she probably didn't want to stop the momentum.

I tried not to focus on the mess of my real life, but it was impossible. I'd had it all, everything I had been writing about for years, and then lost it. I'd been myself with Cullen, I'd shown him who I was, and he'd rejected me. My heart was still wide open, in need of being shut down, closed up. But I didn't know how.

My mother called often. She asked me to come visit her again. She must have noticed something was up, but I gave her several excuses. I had a deadline. I was meeting up with Sarina. I needed to spend the next weekend doing a deep clean of my house. After a while, the calls stopped.

Almost a week later, on a Sunday afternoon, there was a knock at my front door.

I swung it open and almost choked when I tried to speak. "Dad?"

My father's eyes widened. "Meg," he said.

I looked down at myself. I was in ratty old striped pyjama pants and a giant, baggy tie-dyed T-shirt that didn't match. My hair was greasy because I hadn't washed it in a week. Since I was working from home most of the time, I didn't see the point. I was barely leaving my house, switching from work writing to writing my story in my journal, only stopping to find some scraps of food and use the bathroom.

"What are you doing here?" He looked older than the last time I'd seen him. His short hair was almost exclusively white now, with only hints of greyish black left, although his eyebrows remained black and wild and bushy. His thick mustache was neatly trimmed in contrast to his brows. I hadn't seen him or spoken to him in ages. He was busy living his life, and I had long ago grown tired of trying to pin him down, trying to get his attention. I didn't need a constant reminder that he had a better life somewhere else, without me in it. I remained where I was, taking up space in my doorway.

"Can I come in?" His voice was gentle. I hesitated, but then moved to the side to let him past. I didn't want this. Not right now, when I was in a flow state with my writing. What on earth could he possibly be here for?

"Why are you in the city?" I asked.

"Your mother called me." He gave me a long look, one that indicated that it had been a hard phone call for her to make. She must have been worried. She didn't speak to my father unless she had to.

"Why?"

"She's worried about you, Meg." His deep voice softened even more.

I flinched. "What does she have to worry about?"

This time, he tilted his head and looked down at my outfit and around my house. It was a huge mess. There was an old comforter strewn across the couch, a pair of socks on the floor, a pizza box on the kitchen counter. I was also a mess. I had been so laser-focused on my writing, I hadn't had time for anything else.

"Haven't you been going to work?"

"I work from home," I said. "Anyway, you didn't answer my question. What is she worried about?"

He gave me a long look before speaking. "She said you've been visiting Old Port. You've stayed with her a few times?"

I nodded.

"But something—or someone—upset you last time?"

I folded my arms across my chest. "It's complicated."

"Is it about a boy?"

"Dad. I'm not a teenager, I'm thirty-five years old." Since he'd left all that time ago, he'd never known much about what was going on in my life. Aside from calls on my birthday, and short texts here and there, he barely ever contacted me. He didn't know anything, and I wasn't about to tell him now.

"Can I sit down?"

I sighed and gestured to the couch. We sat.

"I'm sorry for showing up like this, but your mother is worried about you. She loves you so much. I love you, too."

The sound I made was louder than I meant it to be. A pained expression crossed his face.

"I haven't been a good father or a good husband, I know that. But this isn't about me. It's about you. Your mother said she thinks something happened. You met the neighbor living next to her and you were happy—and now you're not."

That about summed it up.

"Do you want to talk about it?"

"There's not much to say. I got close to him, he didn't like something about me, he stopped talking to me. He left. Classic.

I'm used to it happening." I tried to hide the break in my voice, but my father must have detected it. He reached out and placed his large, warm hand on top of mine.

"You are perfect just as you are."

I huffed out a rough laugh and then sniffed.

"You are. You're an amazing young woman. You're smart, you're driven, you are so talented at writing."

I sensed a "but" coming, so I tried to beat him to the punch. "But?"

He shook his head. "No but. You are wonderful, and if others don't realize it, it's their issue, not yours. You can't be someone you're not, and I would never want you to try. Neither would your mother. Or Sarina. The people who love you most love you just the way you are."

"How would you even know who I am?" I said. "We barely speak." I was suddenly furious. What right did he have to tell me stuff like this?

He lowered his head and looked down at his hands. "I know you. I also know I'm not perfect. Far from it." He looked back up. "I'm not always the man I want to be. I make mistakes. But that's because I'm not in hiding—I'm living my life. Life is one huge trial and error, where you choose some things and they end up being right, and then you choose others and they end up being mistakes. You take the good with the bad, because it's better than not living at all."

"What is that supposed to mean?" I could hear the sharpness in my voice. "You think I'm not living?"

"I think your coping strategy is to hide. You avoid the hard stuff, and you become reclusive. Like now."

My lips pressed together into a tight line. It was hot in here. Or maybe the heat was because I was uncomfortable. He had me pinned down—he was right, and I didn't like it.

"I don't like the alternative solution," I said.

"Which is what?"

"Which is knocking on Cullen's door and asking if we can try and make it work and being rejected. I can only take so much."

My father reached out for me again. This time I moved back an inch. It was enough for him to notice and his shoulders to fall. I didn't want to feel bad that I had caused that reaction in him, but I did.

"You don't know that you'll be rejected," he said. "You're assuming. Is it really better to never try and not know if you could have made it work? From what your mother said, it seemed like you had a lot of happiness in your life."

I crossed my legs and then uncrossed them. The idea of being vulnerable in front of someone made me twitch. I had been before, and it had never ended up the way I wanted it. It left me broken. But on the other hand, he was right. I'd had a lot of happiness in my life when I was with Cullen. He'd made me feel better than I ever had—even in my stories.

"I don't know," I said eventually. I still had to think about this.

My father stayed seated, partially leaning forward in his seat, studying me. Eventually, he said, "Can I go get us some dinner? Maybe some takeout from that pizza place we both like?"

It had been ages since we had shared a pizza. I didn't think he still knew what I liked and didn't like. I studied him back: the lines around his mouth, his heavily creased eyelids, his cleft chin. There was a familiarity to him that time and history couldn't completely erase. He was still my dad.

"Sure," I said.

I could at least have dinner with him.

He came back with pizza and garlic bread. We sat and ate and talked about lighter topics. It was mostly Dad filling me in on what had been going on in his life, or him asking me about things in mine. I told him about my work. He said he had read my recent articles and thought they were fantastic. My chest swelled the slightest bit when he said that. I guess you never get over wanting your parents' approval.

I found I enjoyed the evening despite myself. Dad was interested in me, but didn't pry. He was sensitive with his advice. He spoke kindly about Mom. Eventually, I took a deep breath and asked what I had been wondering about for most of my life, but had been too nervous to come right out and ask.

"How could you fall out of love with her?"

A flash of pain crossed my father's face. He was quiet for such a long pause, I filled the silence with more rambling.

"I mean, you don't have to tell me all the details. I guess I don't understand. You had everything, and you've said yourself that she's wonderful. She is. You and Mom both exemplified love. I don't understand how you could leave that all behind."

"I think it was bad timing." His voice was so quiet. "I didn't know what I had until it was gone. I made a choice, now I live with it, and I've moved on. But I like to look back on the situation and think about the good I did have, not focus on what I don't have anymore."

"You told me love was enough." The night had been going well, but now my heart sped up, my pulse quickened. I was annoyed with him for having lied to me as a kid.

"Sometimes love *is* enough." He put his pizza down and looked into my eyes. "But you'll never know if you don't put yourself out there. For a long time, your mother and I had the most beautiful life together. We had you. You can't get much better than that. I wish we had been able to make it last longer, but I have no regrets. I have so many good memories."

I looked down at my knees from my seated position on the couch. When I raised my head, he was smiling at me, the most tender expression I had ever seen on his face. My body flooded with warmth. I didn't want to be angry at him anymore, but there was so much history. I smiled back and hoped he couldn't detect the sadness or the truth behind it. A truth I struggled to forget.

Sometimes, no matter how hard you try, love just isn't enough.

THIRTY-FOUR

"I've gotten used to you coming to visit. I miss you." My mother's voice over the phone was smooth and comforting. It was like she knew how much I was hurting without even seeing me. A mother's intuition.

"I've missed you, too." I was in bed. It was late Sunday night, after my father had left. I'd had trouble sleeping. "What are you doing up so late?"

"I never go to bed early in the summer," she said. "I want to soak up all the warmth in the air while I can."

I smiled a weak smile to myself. I loved nighttime air in the summer, too. When the sky was dark, but it was warm enough to stay in a T-shirt and shorts. It had a dreamlike quality to it. I'd never wanted to go to bed early in the summers when I was a kid either.

"Do you think you'll come back for another visit?" she asked.

I paused for a long beat before answering. I wasn't sure I could do that. It would be too painful, and now summer was ending. "I don't know."

"Too hard?"

I felt a lump in my throat. "Think so," I said.

"I get that. I just don't like to think of you going back to being alone."

The tenderness in her voice made my eyes water.

"Can I come to you?" she asked.

"I'd like that."

"Good. Okay. I'll call you when I'm heading to you. Tomorrow."

It was Labor Day the next day, and I had nothing else planned.

"Sounds great," I said. Then I added, "Thank you."

I clicked off the phone after saying goodbye and stared up at the ceiling. There was a tiny brownish stain in the right corner. Water must have seeped in through the roof. Another thing to put on my to-do list. Life felt like a long list of things I should do each day. Get up. Go for a run. Shower. Clean up. Work. Make a healthy dinner. Do my skincare routine. Get a good night's sleep.

I had trouble determining the point of it all. Would I do this forever and ever on repeat until death? Was this it? When I'd been with Cullen, there had been unbridled joy intermixed with the daily things you have to do as an adult. But then reality had got in the way. The reality was, something wasn't right between us, and he'd wanted out. It was over.

The next day, my mother showed up at my door with a bucket full of cleaning supplies in one arm and a basket of baked goods from Old Port in the other.

"It's Labor Day. Let's get to work." She held up the bucket and smiled at me. I had never been so happy to see her.

"Come in." I gestured for her to follow me inside and then held my arms up for a hug. I shrank my body until it could be wrapped up by her thin frame. No matter how old I got, or how long it had been since I'd had a full-body hug from my mother, this would always feel like home.

She helped me do a deep clean of my house and then stayed for a visit for the day. After I showered and double washed my hair, we went for a walk and then went back to my house for mugs of hot tea. We talked about Cullen and what had happened. I decided I had done what I could, and the rest was up to him. I didn't understand it, but if he didn't want to talk anymore, if it was over, I wasn't going to beg.

"I don't understand your resistance to being happy," my mother said to me.

Even though I was taken aback by her blunt words, I didn't pause before answering. "I'm not resisting. I'm being realistic. I know love isn't enough. You and Dad loved each other, and he ruined it. You had love, it didn't last. It didn't work for me and Daniel or anyone else before him, either. And now with me and Cullen, it feels like there are constant signs that it's not working. He's stopped calling or texting. So, it's over. He rejected me—not the other way around. I guess I shouldn't be surprised. Why would this be any different to the others?"

"But love *was* enough for us for a while for me and your father. For eighteen years, love was enough. We had a good marriage while it lasted, and we had you. I was happy. It didn't end because he didn't love me enough. It ended because I told him I wanted out."

I felt like I had been slapped. This was a new piece of information, one I hadn't ever heard before. Why hadn't my father told me this when he was here? I adjusted my spot on the couch, trying to process. "Why did you tell him that?"

"We had grown apart. The things we wanted from life had changed. He wanted to work all the time so he could travel and afford expensive things, and I wanted a quiet life in Old Port. I didn't want to be a workaholic. I wanted to be with my family. Eventually, we decided to go our separate ways. I just started the conversation about it."

"But he left you for another woman. He cheated on you."

"He did not cheat on me." My mom's head jerked back. "What gave you that idea? Have you thought that all these years?"

I nodded. Of course I had. That was the story. Wasn't it?

"Oh, Meg. No. He didn't cheat. He moved on quickly, but it wasn't cheating."

Now that I thought of it, she had never actually used any terms about infidelity when describing the end of their marriage. It struck me like lightning that I'd had my story wrong all along. I had made an assumption somewhere along the way and I had believed it wholeheartedly.

"What happened?" I asked.

"We grew apart, but it took forever for us to actually separate our lives." My mother shifted in her seat but kept her gaze squarely on me while she spoke. "We had to figure out our financial situation, which was a mess, before we could actually move out and not live with one another anymore. Besides, we both wanted to be with you. It took a while for us to figure that out, too. And while we were figuring everything out, he found someone else. It was over between us, but we were still living together. It was messy." She shook her head.

I let that sink in, unsure how I felt about learning this now, as an adult.

"I still don't see how my relationship would be any different," I told her. "Cullen lives there, I live here in the city. We aren't together all the time, and that's just one issue." I held up my hand and touched my fingers, one by one, to indicate the problems. "He gave up so easily. He's ghosted me. That's the clearest sign you can give a person."

"A sign of what? You aren't completely sure what happened there. There might be some kind of explanation that makes sense, but it's like you're not open to giving this a chance. Meg, think about it. How happy are you in this city? How happy are you with your work and your day-to-day life? If you tell me you're good with how things are, that's wonderful. All I want is for you to be happy, but I can't make your decisions for you. You have to decide what it is that makes you satisfied. If it's your life in the city and the job you have, that's great. But if it's not, how do you know it might not be a quieter life with Cullen?"

"I'm not about to give up my career. Come on, Mom. You taught me better than that."

"That's not what I'm saying. You're a damn good writer. Why can't you write from Old Port? Or anywhere?"

"I haven't really thought about it," I said. "Anyway, Old Port has always reminded me of what happened between you and Dad. Our lives felt cold and tense there."

"I'm sorry about that. I really am. I wish we could have uncoupled in a way that didn't leave behind any scars."

"Not you using the term 'uncoupled.'" I let out a quiet chuckle.

She inched closer to me on the couch. "At the end of the day, I still believe that love can be enough. If you want it, if you try hard enough, you can make almost anything work. If you think about what you want from life, what is it?"

It took me a while, but it shouldn't have. "I want to write, and be happy, and feel loved and valued."

"That's what we all want. To have a purpose and to feel valued. You deserve it. You can have it."

"But I can't. He made a decision. And I can't imagine going back to Old Port. Uprooting my life..."

"Can't you? Are you sure? You still don't know what happened. I have a hard time believing he's just done and over it," she said. "And when it comes to Old Port, you like the quiet life, too. You're just like me. You've always loved being near the water, and feeling sand under your feet, and the way the bakery smells first thing in the morning. When Cullen took you around on a tour of the town, did you hate it? Did you picture yourself getting out of there as quickly as possible?"

No. Not at all. I opened my mouth, but didn't know what to say. She kept talking.

"Did you feel worse than you feel right now? At any point when you've been in Old Port, or with Cullen, were you as unhappy as you are right now?"

"Okay, okay." She had a valid point, and she knew how to drive it home. She always had.

My mind worked it over. I had been so certain that I could never live up to the expectations I had set for my life, for what I wanted out of a relationship. I was so certain that nobody was safe, and every relationship was destined to end. Life was too hard. I had seen it with my own eyes. But that was before I'd known Cullen. Before I could imagine a life without waking up to him. Without him and me sipping coffee on the porch early in the morning and having a glass of wine together at night. Before I realized that any amount of time having something wonderful was better than a lifetime of so-so. Had I decided it was over before giving him any chance to explain or talk through it?

"I think you might be right," I said.

"I know I'm right." She crossed her arms over her chest in a huffy kind of way.

I laughed. "What now?" There was still a corner of my mind that believed Cullen might be done with us. He might be tired of me after the way I'd stormed out of the grocery store. I might be too late.

"I would start by giving him a call." She looked at her watch. "And I have to get back home."

"You're not staying over?"

"No, I just came for a few hours. You don't need your mother to stay overnight. You're a strong and incredible person. People are lucky to have you in their lives. Cullen will know that, if he's half as smart as I think he is."

I nodded. At the door, she leaned in and hugged me. "Give him a call," she said. "I love you."

I gave her a kiss on the cheek instead of answering. I wasn't about to tell her I wasn't completely convinced yet.

An hour later, Sarina called and asked me what the chances were that I had time to meet up with her for dinner.

"School starts tomorrow. I could use one last night out with my friend before I get wrapped up in the schoolyard politics."

I breathed out. "Sounds perfect."

We agreed on a place and time, then I ran a brush through my hair and looked at myself in the mirror. It had been a day—actually, a week—from hell, but I was presentable. You couldn't tell I'd had my life recently crushed. Maybe I was getting better at bouncing back.

"I love you, but you look terrible," Sarina told me when I arrived at the restaurant.

"Please. Feel free to let me know what you *really* think." I gave her a quick hug. She didn't mean it the way it sounded. I knew this by now, but I ran a hand through my hair anyway.

"I told you I love you first," she said as she took her seat. "And it's not your hair or your clothes or your skin. It's something in your face and your body language. Is this about Cullen?"

"How can you tell?"

"When I saw you in Old Port, you looked happier than I've seen in a long time. Now you don't."

I nodded. "You're right. I think it's over." I didn't want to go into detail. It was too painful. Sarina, thankfully, didn't press.

"He was clearly good for you."

"I know." I looked down at my water glass. What else could I say? He was good for me, but then he stopped calling and I don't know what it means and I didn't try to figure it out? It sounded so pathetic.

"Anyway, how are you feeling?" I asked. Her skin was glowing and dewy, and her hair was thick and shining. Pregnancy appeared to agree with her.

"I'm feeling good this time around. No morning sickness or anything," she told me. "But don't change the subject, please. You deserve to have happiness. We went over this." Sarina's voice was serious. It touched me, but I could only nod instead of trying to speak.

She was silent for a while. Then she changed the subject. "I was on the train the other day, and I was listening to this smutty new audiobook. I thought my earphones were connected to my device…"

I looked up at her. A waiter came and asked us for our order. While he was writing down what we wanted, Sarina grinned at me, eyes wide, and mouthed the words: *The earphones were not connected.*

I laughed, loud and deep. Thank goodness for Sarina. She brought levity to my life exactly when I needed it. I wanted to tell her everything, but now wasn't the right time. I was still too raw. Instead, I handed my menu to the waiter, thanked him and then turned back to Sarina.

"Classic you."

"I know. By the way, how were the awards? You haven't said much since."

I took a breath in. My blood pressure was lowering. "Our paper didn't win, but there was good food. And my coworker gave me some great life advice."

"That was nice of him." She reached for her water. "You know what I think should be next for you?"

"What?"

"Writing smutty books like the ones I'm reading. You're a great writer. I bet you could do sex well."

I laughed again, but I pushed the thought to the back of my mind. "Thank you. I think I might put 'could do sex well' on my resume."

Later, back at home after dinner, I felt a little lighter. A day with my mother and an evening with my best friend had been exactly what I'd needed. The more I thought about it, the more I began to believe that they were right. I deserved to be happy. Why couldn't I have everything I wanted? Why couldn't I write from anywhere, and try to find out what had happened with Cullen, and try to make it work and give Old Port another chance? I had made such a firm decision and had been so closed off. I'd spent most of my life believing that I couldn't have happiness, or didn't deserve love. But why not?

It had taken an entire summer of me resisting, and now I could finally see what had been in front of me this whole time. Cullen. He had consistently been patient, calm, loving. It didn't add up that he'd changed on a dime.

Did it?

The sky outside was dark. The day was over. Summer was over. I had to get back to work early the next morning, and I still had to figure out what to do about the article. This moment right now wasn't the time for big decisions. Instead, I changed into my pyjamas, washed my face and brushed my teeth. As I crawled into bed, I looked up. The stain on the ceiling in the corner of my bedroom was still there, but it looked smaller. It could have been the light, or maybe it was the way I was looking at it.

THIRTY-FIVE

At the office the next morning, I set my bag down on my desk and looked at my phone. I hadn't texted or called Cullen yet. A tendril of doubt curled around my spine when I saw the empty screen staring back at me. He hadn't called or texted either. My mother was convinced there was some kind of explanation for all of this, but the truth was, it worried me that I still hadn't heard from him.

I put the phone away and finally focused on his article again. I wanted to do the right thing for him, even if we weren't talking yet. I planned to put my heart and soul into ensuring the article contained just a gentle mention of his family and a small, sensitive commemoration to his sister, while still being about him. I wanted it to be delicately balanced and have nothing sensational, none of the parts Celine wanted, and only what I thought Cullen wanted. I wasn't sure this would go over well with Celine, but I couldn't focus on that. I had to focus on the now.

I had been so close to finished with it before, but it needed this final revision. A better one. I spent the entire workday at my office on it, and when six o'clock rolled around, I went home, changed into comfortable clothes and kept on writing and revising.

When I was done, I was proud of it. It felt more honest. It might have been much quieter than Celine wanted, but I thought it had turned out beautifully. It was nuanced and subtle, but it also told the hard stuff: how it had felt for Cullen after his sister's death, how she had influenced his books. I thought it was one of the best pieces I'd ever written for the Lifestyle section, but it wasn't a piece that would go viral. It was better than that—almost like art. It was also a risk; Cullen had said he didn't want any mention of his family. But I hoped when he read it, he would see how sensitive it was, how truthful, and how loving.

As if Celine could sense I was finishing it, an email from her appeared in my inbox. I looked at the clock and shook my head. It was just past ten o'clock. The woman never stopped working. I clicked on her email and read:

Please send me your article on Cullen Walsh by the morning.

Regards, Celine

Before I did that, I had to get Cullen's okay with it. I dialed his number nervously and waited, but it went to voicemail. I left a message asking him to give me a call and hung up, hoping he would get back to me soon. After an hour, and no phone call back, my body drooped with exhaustion. I had no other choice but to send Celine the article without Cullen's eyes on it.

In bed, I tossed and turned for who knows how long. I stared at the ceiling as if I would find an answer to my anxiety there. A whirl of nausea went through my stomach as I thought of all the worst possible outcomes. What if Cullen hated it? What if I'd been too personal and told too much of his family life? He'd probably never want to work things out with me after this. He wouldn't forgive me and that would be the end of us. I couldn't stop these kinds of thoughts from running through my head, over and over, until I finally, mercifully, drifted off into a fitful sleep.

The following morning, I went to work, my head groggy and my eyes sore. After consuming a very large coffee, and after an hour of answering emails and touching up some other articles, I glanced at Celine's office. Her door was closed. I went over and knocked.

"Come in," she called.

It was still early in the morning, but Celine looked like she had been there for a few hours already. A planner and a notebook were open on her desk, along with an empty coffee cup. Her glass of water only had a little left in it. Her head was down; she was jotting something in her planner.

I stood in front of her and cleared my throat.

"What can I help you with?" She looked up at me and smiled faintly.

I had been on pins and needles about my article all night. I needed to know what she thought.

"My article?"

Celine's smile faltered, and in response, my stomach dropped.

"Yes, thank you for sending that over," she said.

"You had a chance to read it then?"

"I did." Celine nodded.

"And?"

"If I'm being honest, I preferred the first version of the article better."

My skin went cold. I tried not to allow my face to react. "What part of it?" I asked.

"The whole thing." She sat back in her chair. "I'm sorry. I know that's probably not what you want to hear, but the first version was much more readable. It'll draw attention and gain reader interest. The one you sent me last night is very beautiful, but it's not newsy. It's quiet. It's more suited to a magazine. Although, that said, neither version has enough of what I asked for." She looked down at her desk again and wrote something in her planner. She was already done with me and this exchange.

"But the article is good. I did what you asked, but in my own way." Desperation reverberated through my body. I felt everything I'd worked so hard on slipping away. Even if I had my doubts about how Cullen would react, I knew this version was at least more respectful of him and his family than the one Celine wanted. I knew I could never write that version.

Celine tilted her head. The space between her eyebrows creased and then uncreased. I had an overwhelming sense that she felt sorry for me.

"You know by now what gets read. Sensational stories. Stories about when someone dies and how it happened. Politics. Love. Scandal. Things that are trending. You know all this. Your own stories like this have gone viral."

"Then why did you ask me to write about Cullen and his book? Why try to make it something it's not? The first version I sent you is a good story about a successful author and his book. It's honest and people might enjoy it. But this one"—I pointed to her laptop—"this one is storytelling. It's beautiful and human and I'm proud of it."

"You should be," Celine said, shifting in her chair to sit more upright. "It's great storytelling. But it's not the kind of story we need. We need to sell so that advertisers want to keep giving us money. You haven't added enough about his past. His tragic past—not an artsy story that only touches on his sister. The details, Meg. It's all about the details. Tragic stories are like car crashes. We all want to know more, even though we know we shouldn't be prying. I've gone back to your original piece and added some notes to give it that edge."

My mouth dropped open. "Celine. You can't be serious."

"I have someone to report to. It's *my* job on the line if we don't increase our revenue. You're an excellent writer. I knew you could do a good job of it and it wouldn't just be some hack clickbait type of an article. If we had some other massively trending story that would gain us loads of new readers, I would have assigned you that and we wouldn't need to do this. But we don't."

"I can't betray him," I told her. "He doesn't want to tell that story." She knew this.

"Meg, we've invested too much time on this already and we need to make it work. You can add those details—or I will." She held up her hands as if she were surrendering.

"I—I don't understand. Do you mean I *have* to write it the way you want it?"

Celine sighed. "I can't force you to write it, obviously. But I am your editor. And we need to run it, so it's your choice."

I nodded, even though I was numb. Celine's words were heavy. Loaded. If I didn't do what she asked, it would affect my job and which stories I got to write in the future. I would be stuck writing articles that didn't interest me. I might even be let go.

On the other hand, if I added in the details Celine wanted, I'd betray Cullen's trust. He would never forgive me for telling a story publicly that he didn't want told. His book was fair game; his personal life was not. I knew that. But I also knew it wasn't so easy to choose between my career—my livelihood—and the person I had been falling in love with. It should have been easy, but it wasn't.

"You know, I thought you were tougher than most women," Celine said.

My face must have been blank. I couldn't process any meaning behind that, so I stared at her. "What?"

"Don't get all upset about me saying that. I mean it as a compliment. I didn't think some man could make you crumble."

"I'm not crumbling, and I'm not sure I know what you mean."

"Cullen Walsh. Just because you're not together—or whatever it was you had—doesn't mean you have to fall apart. There are plenty more men out there."

My throat closed. What did she know about me and Cullen? And how dare she offer me dating advice? Talk about overstepping. Celine had no right. Wait. What *did* she know about me and Cullen? I hadn't told her anything. She'd suspected we were "close", but I hadn't confirmed it. I hadn't given any details, and I certainly hadn't told her we were no longer together.

"What do you know about that?" My voice was quiet but steady.

Her smile dropped from her face. "Just that you're not together." She turned and glanced back at the screen of her laptop.

"How?"

She let out one of her signature sighs. "Listen. I'll only tell you this because I care about you. I know that's hard for you to believe, but I do," she said. "I called him."

I gave my head a quick shake and then touched my forehead. "I don't understand. Do you know him?"

Celine gestured to the chair in front of her desk. "Maybe you should sit down."

I pulled it out and sat, my mind a messy jumble. I couldn't connect the dots.

"How do you know him?" I repeated. I needed to know what was going on, immediately.

"I met him when I was writing a story."

I frowned. This made no sense. "On his book?"

She shook her head. "No. On his family."

"What story?" I tilted my head.

A stiff expression crossed her face. "Marshall."

My heart sped up—quick, short palpitations that made it hard for me to breathe normally.

Celine pinched the bridge of her nose. "His sister died in that crash. She was the team's physiotherapist. She had been travelling with them to their game."

A stark coldness washed over me, from the top of my head down into the soles of my feet, like a glass of water had been poured over my head and tumbled down my body. How awful. I wanted to be with Cullen, to wrap my arms around him.

Celine continued. "I was only trying to tell the stories of those people. It was such an awful accident. Their families deserved to have their loved ones remembered in a meaningful way, not as just another statistic in some cold account."

"I remember." My voice was hoarse. "I thought you did a beautiful job."

She smiled weakly at me. "When I met Cullen and his family, his parents were confused. I'd thought the reason they agreed to meet with me was because they wanted to have their daughter's story told and wanted her to be remembered, for people to know her. But the more I talked to them, the more hesitant they became. And the more hesitant they were, the more protective Cullen was. He said I was getting too personal. It was too painful and I should leave them alone. His parents had wanted me there at first, though. I wasn't ambulance-chasing. They said it was okay."

I ran my hand over my forehead, trying to take it all in, to absorb what she was saying so I could later process it.

"Eventually, he told me to leave and not come back, so that's what I did."

"And? What about the story? What happened?"

"Well, you saw the end result. It was damn good." Celine crossed her arms over her chest.

Cullen's reaction to Celine flashed through my mind. His tight expression and the way he said her name.

"But—I still don't understand."

Celine frowned. She ran her fingertips over her mouth. "Cullen's parents didn't want her to be in the story at all, but I included her anyway."

"Why?"

"You read it," Celine said. "It was a terrible tragedy, but people wanted to know. Readers wanted to know all the details. People will pretend they're better than that, and that it's the media who is awful and sensationalistic, but when it comes down to it, they always want the details. I gave them the full story."

My mouth fell open. "And you haven't spoken to him since?"

"No. I tried." She shrugged. "He's never returned my calls. His parents stopped answering them, too. He was so angry. I've had angry subjects before, but this was the only time I've had such a strong, visceral reaction to me. I know he's private and didn't want her story out there, or attention on his parents, but I was trying to do good. I know it really hurt him."

A thought dawned on me. "Why did you ask me to cover him and his book for the news?"

Celine diverted her eyes away from me and looked across the room.

"Celine?"

She sighed. "I thought if we did a great piece on him, he'd get over his anger and maybe speak to me again."

"But why does that matter to you?"

"It's hard to explain," she said.

My stomach dropped. It felt like we were getting into some kind of territory I didn't want to know about. "Was there something between you two?"

"No." She drew her head back. "No, of course not. It's just that I was so proud of my article, and I thought I had done a good job. It was my best work. It bothered me that a family member of one of the subjects was so angry. I wanted to try and fix it or make it right."

"But then why did you push me to include all that detail about his sister? Isn't that exactly what you did to him in the first place?"

"Plans change. I *wanted* to make it right, but then I had all of the pressure on me to increase our views and sales at the paper, which is why I asked you to up the intrigue of the piece." She frowned. "I had good intentions initially. I know I can come across unfeeling, but I'm sensitive, too. I can care about people." Her shoulders were high and tight around her ears.

I did know that Celine could be caring. I had seen it in her. When Ahmad's mother had died of breast cancer, Celine had used her own money, not the company's dime, to send him flowers and to donate to cancer research in his mother's name. And when Elise had come back to work after her brother's death and told us what it had been like to be with him when he took his last breath, Celine's eyes had gone red and glassy as she'd welled up. She had a soft side.

"Why didn't you just tell me you wanted me to write about his sister?" I asked.

"I left it to you to find the story about him because I know that's what you're good at."

"So you thought that if I wrote a good piece on him, your guilt could be wiped clean?"

Celine's head jerked in surprise at my words. She opened her mouth to say something, but I stopped her. I needed answers and clarity. "Wait. Why did he answer your phone call this time?"

"He seems concerned about you. I had a feeling he'd answer me if he knew it had to do with you. So I texted him first and told him I had something important to tell him about you."

My breath hitched. "What did you tell him?"

Celine looked away.

"Celine?" I said. "What did you tell him?"

She looked back at me, her mouth turned down. "I told him he was jeopardizing your career."

My stomach dropped. The room went hot and stuffy, and my throat was dry. "What? Why?"

"Because I could see it happening." She lifted her chin. "I told him that if he was going to meddle with your work and with how I asked you to tell the story, he was going to put you at risk here. And then I told him he should give you some space to do your job."

My vision narrowed. This wasn't possible. How on earth could someone do something like that? A trickle of sweat ran down the middle of my back, along my spine. I stood on weak legs.

"How could you do that to me?" My brain felt like it wasn't functioning. I couldn't process. I had to get out of there.

"I was looking out for you," she said with an air of incredulity. "It's your work. This is your career. I would think you'd take it more seriously than some summer fling you're having."

Summer fling? She had no idea. My mind flashed to Cullen. He hadn't answered any of my texts. He'd stopped talking to me. I'd thought it was because of me. I'd thought I was the problem, once again. Things started clicking together.

"That is so wrong. On so many levels," I said.

I managed to stumble out of Celine's office. I grabbed the few things from my desk—my laptop, my notebooks—and left the building immediately.

I had no clue what to do next, but I knew I had to leave. I had to be alone.

THIRTY-SIX

I almost felt sorry for anyone in my general vicinity. I trudged along the street with my head pointed down, but I knew my red eyes and the tears rolling down my cheeks were on full display. It was impossible not to draw attention to yourself when you were crying in public.

I couldn't think straight—Celine's betrayal hurt so much. It wasn't just that she was my boss, who I'd trusted, and a role model I'd looked up to—it was because she had ruined the only good relationship I had ever had. Everything fell into place: the silence from Cullen, the way he'd reacted when I'd mentioned Celine. He had been hurting in a way I could never imagine, and Celine must have brought it all back. I'd brought it to the surface for him. I'd been a reminder of how painful it was to lose his sister.

Yet, despite all of that, he had still been in it. He'd wanted us to work. Until Celine told him to back off. A hot rage circled through my blood.

I ran the last several weeks through my mind and tried to catch my breath. Cullen. I could picture the way half his mouth went up in a smile, the way he nudged his glasses up onto his nose when he was thinking. I could visualize every beautiful and wonderful part of him that made him who he was. And he had wanted this, he'd wanted me. But he'd thought I was going to lose my job.

When I finally got home, I went straight to the bathroom to wash my streaky, messy face. I threw my hair into a bun and crawled under the covers of my bed, even though it wasn't close to bedtime. I thought about the last time I had been with Cullen, the life I'd had with him over the summer.

I grabbed my phone from my nightstand and tried typing out a text to him, but I didn't know where to start. I typed and erased it a few times until I ended up with:

> I talked to Celine today. She told me what she said to you

I pressed send.

My phone rang in response immediately. I almost dropped it, but recovered in time to see Cullen's name flash across the screen.

"Hi." My pulse sped up, my insides a tangle of happiness and nerves. I wondered how he felt. Maybe Celine had just been a catalyst for what was inevitable. Maybe all of this was too hard.

"Hey. What did she say? How much did she explain?"

"Most of it," I said.

"Can I come see you? In person? I don't want to do this over the phone."

The muscles in my arms went quivery. "Did you say come see me? Like, in the city?"

"Yes."

I stood and walked into my living room and kitchen area. I pushed a pad of paper that had been sitting on my counter, lining it up flush against the wall. "Okay, sure. When?"

"I'm in my car. If you send me your address, I can be there in just under two hours."

My eyes darted around the room. The place was tidy enough. I looked like a mess, but I wanted him here. I wanted him to see me. "Alright. I'll text you."

Cullen let out a sigh that I could hear over the phone line. "See you soon." His voice was low and loaded.

After an hour and a half had gone by, the house was even tidier than it had been before, I had fixed my hair and got dressed, and I was sitting on my couch, trying not to overthink. I kept tapping on the screen of my phone to see what time it was, or to see if I had missed a text from him. Eventually, there was a knock at my front door. When I pulled it open, Cullen stood on the other side, his head slightly bowed, his broad shoulders accentuated by the grey T-shirt he wore. His hair was slightly messy, and his defined jaw was covered in light stubble. When he looked up at me, there was a hint of shadow under his eyes, like he hadn't been sleeping well. And yet, my breath still caught in my throat at how good he looked, at how much I had missed seeing his dark eyes, his tanned forearms, his half smile.

"Hi." He ran a hand through his hair.

"Hi." I smiled.

After a moment of standing there, watching each other, unsure what to say, Cullen gestured behind me. "Can I come in?"

I turned and let him follow me inside. Why was I so awkward around him suddenly? This was new.

We stood in the open-concept kitchen and living room, and I put my arms out like I was offering him a spectacular view. "This is my place."

"It's nice. I like it." He nodded appreciatively.

"It does the job," I said. "Do you want to sit? Can I get you a drink or something?"

He must have sensed my nervousness because he came closer to me and put a hand on my hip. I touched his forearm, as if it were by instinct, as if I could keep him here, holding me, instead of talking about heavy things.

"I'll take water," he said, his voice low and a little hoarse. "Then let's sit."

I got both of us a glass of water and sat next to him on my couch.

He let out a long breath. "How much did Celine tell you?"

"She explained about your sister." I wanted to reach out and put my hand on his, but I stayed in place. "I'm so sorry."

"Thank you." He took a shaky breath. "When we lost her, I was devastated. I didn't know it could hurt that much. That entire tragedy—all those young boys. All those families... And my sister." His voice broke. "When the press came around, it overwhelmed my parents. They decided they wanted to grieve privately, so I got protective. I didn't want anyone calling my parents and asking them to comment on the accident, but the reporters just kept calling. It was terrible. Mom and Dad wanted to be left alone. They didn't want her story told."

"I can understand that," I said. I studied him. It felt like he'd left something unsaid. "What did you want?"

Cullen's jaw flexed. His eyes went glassy. "I wanted something different. I wanted the world to know how incredible my sister was. But not in a sensational way. Not in a way that exploited innocent victims for sales." A pained expression crossed his face that made my stomach drop. I wanted to hold him so much, but I could tell he wasn't done. He was silent for a while and then he spoke again. "I didn't get a chance to say goodbye to her."

"Cullen," I whispered. "I'm so sorry."

He put his hand up and rubbed the back of his neck. "I

hadn't spoken to her in a week at least. And the last time we did speak, I was short with her. I was on a deadline and I was stressed, so the last exchange we had was me being an ass. That's how I'll forever be remembered by her."

"I'm so sorry. This must be devastating, but she was your sister. You had a good relationship. She would know that wasn't typical. She would know you loved her."

He was silent a long time. "I hope so," he said.

"Did you ever read what Celine wrote?" I had to be delicate and careful with this.

He frowned. "I did."

"I thought it was a really powerful story," I said. "It was such good writing."

Cullen was silent. I waited for him to say something. After a moment, his body softened back into the couch a little.

"It was a good piece, but it also wasn't what I wanted. She didn't get Jen right. It should have been perfect, and personal, and only someone who loved her could do that. Instead, the lasting memory of her came from a stranger who wouldn't leave my parents alone. I asked Celine not to write about Jen out of respect for them, but she did anyway. Anything for the story."

I was silent, considering this. It came to me after a moment. "You've already written about your experience of loss in *The Ninth Village*—what if now you write about her? About Jen?"

He looked over at me, his eyes still glassy. "I've written many things since then, but I couldn't write about her."

"When I'm hurting the most, or feeling the most vulnerable, the only thing that's helped me to process those emotions is to write." I watched him for any sort of reaction, a sign I should stop. I changed the topic. "I rewrote my article about you."

"You did?"

"I changed it." I sat up straighter. "There's a little more of a focus on what your sister meant to you and your writing, but I was careful. From the way you speak about her, I think I got it right. I think I made it meaningful and important. It's what I've always wanted to do with my writing."

He leaned forward, closer to me. "I bet it's beautiful. When is it going to run?"

My stomach dropped. Why had I even brought this up? "I don't think it will. Celine wants to run the original article, only she wants more detail. She wants it to be more personal. It's what she's wanted all along, but I didn't want to write it that way." I left out the part about how she'd wanted me to capitalize on his grief and family tragedy. He must have known. His forehead creased, a frown crossing over his face.

"So now what?" he asked.

"I don't know."

I had thought about every scenario I could imagine. If I didn't write the article Celine wanted, would I be happy enough with my career? I knew the answer was no. I needed to be creative and be given opportunities to write good things. I couldn't make a life out of city hall meeting stories or tips on gardening. But I would never hurt Cullen. I couldn't break his heart.

Cullen was silent a long time. "You have to do what's right for you."

"What's right for me is what's right for you." I took a deep breath. "I could never hurt you. I care about you too much. Way more than a job."

He looked into my eyes, like he hung on my words. "This whole time I thought I was helping you by giving you space. I thought it was for the best, but I missed you so much. I hated every minute I wasn't with you."

"I figured you'd decided it was too hard. That something had got in the way, like it always does for me."

He shook his head. His voice was gentle when he spoke. "I'm sorry I made you feel that way. I should have listened to my instincts."

He placed his hand next to mine and the edges of our fingers grazed one another. A mix of electricity and desire reverberated through me, the way it always did when he touched me. I moved closer and nestled into his body. I didn't think about it first; for once, I simply acted on what my body wanted. I put my head on his shoulder and moved as close as I could to him. Cullen wrapped an arm around me and let out a low sigh. He relaxed even more into the couch.

"I've never been more myself than when I'm with you," he said.

I let that settle and sink in and warm my insides. We sat for a long time. I had no idea how long, but it felt like ages of easy silence before he put a hand on my leg, his fingers settled just on the edge of my inner thigh. I had missed this. I had missed him.

He tilted his face down to look at me. "I'm sorry about everything. I really want to be with you. It's all I want."

His words set off a thrum in my chest, like it was hard to catch my breath. "Me too."

He moved his fingers slowly, trailing back and forth over my leg in a rhythm. I turned my body toward his and he looked down at me before putting his mouth on the side of my face, just by my ear. I closed my eyes and allowed the sensation to move through me, over me.

"I want to make this work, Meg. Having you in my life makes everything better and I can't imagine life without you."

My breath hitched. I never in a million years thought someone would say those kinds of words to me with so much honesty in their voice. And certainly not someone as incredible as Cullen. I had been convinced our relationship was destined to fall apart, but he wanted this as much as I did. He was showing me over and over.

"I want to be with you, too," I said. "I'm just so used to being—"

He moved even closer to me and placed one hand on the small of my back. "You're the one, Meg. You could never, ever *not* be the one for me."

My entire body felt flushed.

"How is this going to work?" he asked. "Maybe I should move to the city."

I chuckled. "No, you don't have to uproot your life for me."

"I will." His face was serious.

That wasn't what I wanted. I didn't realize it until I'd almost lost it. I shook my head.

"No. The city is great, but it's not where I imagine myself long-term. I think I'm ready to try life in Old Port. I could... if it was with you."

"What about work?"

I shrugged. "I'll figure that out." I had time to work out what I wanted. I had always been careful and cautious. Maybe now was the time to do something exciting and out loud. For real.

"I thought you didn't like the memories Old Port brought back," Cullen said.

"I had it in my head that it was an awful place, but when I went back and spent time there—when I was with my mom and her friends and with you, I realized I had painted it with the wrong brush. I needed to give it another chance."

"Kind of like us?" He smiled and leaned in to me. "You're okay with giving us another chance?"

"It would be the biggest mistake of my life not to."

I meant it. I meant it so much.

THIRTY-SEVEN

The weekend couldn't come fast enough. When Friday arrived, I finished work—having successfully avoided Celine for the majority of it—went home to throw a few things into a bag and got into the car, ready to make the drive back to Old Port to see Cullen. Traffic was lighter than usual now that summer was over, but it still felt like it took forever to get there. Oddly enough, it also felt like coming home. Even though I hadn't thought of Old Port as home in ages, Cullen made me want to come here and be a part of his world. My tires crunched over the gravel of his driveway as I pulled in and parked. He must have heard my car from inside, because he appeared at his front door and leaned against the doorframe. He had on a navy-blue hoodie today, and a pair of shorts. He stood smiling, relaxed, his face tanned.

I turned off the car and stepped out. He caught my eye and his smile grew bigger. My chest fluttered. He pushed himself off the doorframe and came towards me.

"Hi," he said when he reached me. He wrapped his arms around my waist. I wanted to fold my body into his, but I didn't want to look away from his face. His gorgeous, thoughtful eyes beneath his thick brows. The way his mouth turned up at one side. The feelings I had for him when I was in his presence were full and deep and strong. Like the pull of the ocean. They hadn't gone away when we'd had our misunderstanding, or when we weren't speaking. It was easy to picture this working with him, because I wanted nothing else but to be around him. I never wanted this to change.

"Come inside," he said. His voice was low.

I nodded; he covered my mouth with his. His hands rose to my back, skimming my body lightly at first and then with more intensity. His touch made every nerve ending I had electric. I couldn't get inside his house fast enough.

"I want to feel you," I said.

Cullen's eyebrows shot up.

My face immediately went warm. It wasn't like me to talk like this. I didn't need to be embarrassed though, because Cullen smiled down at me, his eyes locked onto mine. He took me by the hand and gently pulled me towards his house. I left my things in my car and followed him. I would follow him anywhere in that moment.

The next morning, when I woke, I sat up slowly and tried to get out of bed as quietly as I could so I wouldn't wake him.

"Where are you off to?" Cullen mumbled from behind me.

I turned from where I sat on the edge of the bed. "Sorry. I was trying to let you sleep. I'm awake. I can't fall back asleep once it happens."

"That's one of many more things I hope to learn about you." He rolled over and smiled at me.

"When?"

"When we're living together?" It was a question, not a statement. He was treading carefully, but the idea thrilled me.

"You look like you're still tired," I said. "Go back to sleep. I'm going to get some coffee." I patted his leg.

He rolled back over and mumbled, "Save me some."

I grabbed his hoodie from a chair and left his room, pulling the sweatshirt on over my pyjamas. I hesitated only for a brief second about knocking on my mother's door in this state. She would immediately know why I looked like this and what I had been doing. The thought of having coffee outside on the porch with my mother won over the cringey feeling I would get from her knowing looks.

At her door, I raised my hand, poised to knock, when it flung open.

"I saw your car over there last night," she said, smiling. "I made coffee. I was hoping you'd pop in this morning."

"You know me well." I smiled back at her and lifted my arms to her for a hug. She wrapped me in hers and let out a sigh.

"I know you well," she repeated. "Now, let's go out to the porch."

After we had our coffees in hand, I followed her to sit outside. The ocean was louder than usual, due to the slight uptick in wind. The air was warm, though. And the way it brushed over me made me feel good in my skin.

"What's going on with you two?" my mother asked. "I mean, besides the obvious." She gestured at my pyjamas and Cullen's hoodie.

I choked on my coffee, giving her a good-natured look of warning. My sex life was always going to be off limits for conversation.

"I don't know, but I'm happy," I said.

My mother nodded and sipped her coffee. She wrapped the mug in her hands and placed it on her lap. "I'm glad."

"I really think my writing has improved. Celine doesn't want to run what I wrote, but I'm proud of it." I turned toward my mother.

She gave me a look this time. "I wasn't talking about you being happy with your writing."

"I know."

"I've seen you in all states of happiness, but nothing like the way I've seen you this summer. It's like you're a new you."

"I'm not," I said. "I'm the same me."

Only, I knew that wasn't true. Cullen had changed me completely.

The only problem was, there was no life for me in Old Port outside of Cullen. No jobs meant no income. Once again, reality could put a damper on everything. I decided to forget about it for the time being and focus on being with Cullen. For two days I could pretend nothing else was happening and that all that mattered was him and I.

Saturday was bliss. Cullen made lunch for me while I read on the porch. We rode our bikes into town and window-shopped, then went for a late dinner. We walked around hand in hand. On Sunday we slept in late. It was exactly what I needed.

When I got up, I went to sit on the porch, my laptop open, trying to organize my thoughts in an email to Celine. I told her I was coming into the office the next morning. There was something I had to tell her, but it had to be in person.

The scent of fresh coffee floated out and interrupted my thoughts just as Cullen's screen door opened. He pushed it with one shoulder, two coffee cups in his hands.

"Good morning." He handed me one of the cups, filled to the brim.

I smiled up at him. "Thank you. I didn't want to make any noise and wake you, but this is exactly what I need right now."

"You can do whatever you want to around here. I want you to feel at home."

"I do feel at home." I meant it. I felt a sudden lift, as if my limbs were tingling with happiness. I wondered if it showed in my face.

"I'm glad." Cullen took a seat next to me on the porch. I moved my laptop to the coffee table in front of us.

He took a sip of his coffee and winced a little when the hot liquid met his mouth. I had such an urge to reach out and touch his perfect lips. While he gazed out at the horizon in front of us, I studied his profile. His jaw was square, his nose gently sloped. His hair was messed up from sleep. He looked both disheveled and ridiculously handsome.

"What do you want in a few years?" Cullen asked, seemingly out of nowhere.

"What do you mean? Like what's my five-year plan?"

"Yeah, sort of. Like where you'll be, what things you want, how you'll get them."

"I don't know if I'm much of a planner in that way."

Cullen turned, and half of his mouth went up in a smile. "You're not a planner? I see you making notes in your notebooks all the time. You write everything down. That's a planner tendency if I've ever seen one."

"It is? How do you figure?"

"Do you fly by the seat of your pants on decisions? Or do you like to carefully consider all the pros and cons before you make any plans?"

I looked up into the sky. A slight frown must have crossed my face.

"I don't mean it in a bad way," Cullen said. "I think it's nice how you know what you want and you make plans to get it."

I shrugged. "I guess I like to avoid any potential disappointment." Or heartbreak. "If I can organize most things and plan it out, I think I'm less likely to be hurt."

Cullen nodded. "Makes sense."

"But I don't have a solid five-year plan. Do you?"

Cullen seemed to consider this. He kept his gaze out on the

ocean and was silent for a while. Then he reached for my hand and slipped his fingers under my palm.

"I have an idea of what I want."

My heart sped up. I smiled at him. He stared at me for a beat longer than was comfortable. I squirmed a little. "What? What are you staring at?" I laughed.

"You're beautiful."

This was what I wanted and needed. To be with Cullen and hear these kinds of words. I felt so grateful to be here, right now, in this moment.

"You are, too," I said.

Cullen laughed. From the other room, my phone dinged.

"You're wonderful, but you have to turn your ringer down. Your text messages are so loud. I could hear them from the bedroom this morning."

"Where did I leave it?" I must have put my phone down somewhere. I hadn't realized it wasn't beside me.

"Kitchen," Cullen said.

"Be right back." I took my laptop off my knees and placed it on the table in front of us.

Inside, I found my phone on the kitchen counter and glanced at the screen. Several social media notifications and a text from my mother.

> Coffee's on. When are you coming over?

She had added three winky faces to the end of the message. Hilarious.

I typed back:

> I don't know...

Almost immediately, the three dots appeared, indicating she was typing.

> Don't worry about it. I'm teasing you. Have fun.
> Come say hi if you can before you leave. Xo

I smiled at my phone and closed my text messages. I clicked on my social media apps and then closed them almost as quickly as I had opened them. I didn't want to scroll through my feed mindlessly the way I usually did. I wanted to get back to Cullen.

When I went back out through the screen door and onto the porch, Cullen was turned, his back to me, his head bent. He was looking at something. I inched forward and got a glimpse over his shoulder.

My laptop and journal were open in front of him. He turned his head around when he heard me. "Hey. You left this open, but I didn't read it. I can tell it's personal."

My gaze went down to my journal. A heat immediately engulfed my body. I was dizzy with embarrassment. "How much did you see?"

"Nothing. I didn't read it."

I went over to him and picked up the journal.

"But, Meg—I think it's great that you're always writing. You have stories to tell. I've never seen someone write so much all the time. Why don't you explore it?"

"Explore what?"

"Writing books."

Sarina's words popped into my head. I hadn't given them any serious thought at the time. "I don't know." I shrugged. "My friend Sarina told me she thought I'd be good at writing sexy smut." I laughed to cover my embarrassment.

"I can give you some material if you wanted to write sexy stuff." He stood and came over to me, eyes widened dramatically. He wrapped his arms around my waist and I leaned into him.

"You can't be serious."

"I am," he said. "I think you should try it. Only if you want to, of course. It seems like you love it." He nudged his chin at my journal.

I could have been embarrassed again, but I wasn't. I realized I was at ease with myself. I glanced at Cullen and he looked back at me with bright eyes.

"I'll think about it. It's a good idea," I said, and I meant it.

Later, I walked into the ocean. I let the water swirl around my calves, and then, further in, up to my thighs. Eventually I lowered myself and dove under. I allowed the coolness of the water to glide over my face, through my hair. Then I flipped over to my back and let the lull of the moving water carry me. When I got out of the water, endorphins vibrated through me. I was overcome with such strong feelings for this place rushing back, as if they hadn't ever been gone, but had been momentarily hidden or forgotten. I went inside to towel off, but I hoped the tingling of my skin would linger.

Cullen's words percolated in the back of my head for the rest of the day and during most of the drive home that night. I had nothing to lose—maybe I could write a novel, even if I did it only for myself. It didn't have to mean something or end up published. When I wrote anything creative, it had always been my best outlet for emotion and expression. This didn't have to change.

At home, I unpacked my things, opened the windows and sat down at my desk. It was late, I should have probably gone to bed, but instead I opened my laptop to a new, blank document. I pulled my journal out and set it beside me. I had pages and pages of stories already written. All I had to do was weave them together with a central character and plot. I knew it wouldn't be easy, but I had been practicing for years.

I wrote for an hour, only stopping when I was too tired to keep my eyes open. When I went to bed that night, my dreams were of love stories.

THIRTY-EIGHT

The next morning, I made coffee and opened my laptop to check my email while I woke up. Celine had sent one at an ungodly hour this morning. She truly had no boundaries. I clicked on it and read.

I need your story on Cullen. First thing tomorrow. No more extensions.

A sick feeling settled into my stomach. I closed the email, went to the file that had both versions of my article in it and reread them. They were both good. The one Celine wanted—with Cullen's personal life, and details of his sister and the family heartbreak—would certainly get more readers if I added all the changes she'd demanded. It had the things people loved to read about—tragedy, death, love. The other version was so much quieter. But I still loved it. I loved everything about the way it had come to be. But Celine had made it clear to me that I couldn't have everything.

I sighed and closed my laptop. My concentration was

broken; I couldn't keep writing. Instead, I tidied my house, made myself breakfast, reread my journal. For years I had been retreating to my journal, where my stories felt safe. My writing had become my refuge. It was only after meeting Cullen that I had even begun to see that being vulnerable and open with someone could be better than anything I could make up.

I got into work early the next day. I had a coffee in one hand, hoping the caffeine might be able to still the slight shaking. I wasn't doubting any of my decisions, but I was nervous.

Celine was already there. I could see her through the glass walls of her office. She was slightly bent over her laptop, her tongue touching the edge of her lip in concentration. She worked so hard and she was good at her job. She was smart and successful and seemed like she had everything—as far as her career was concerned, at least. I suspected she'd forgotten what it was like for someone like me, who didn't. She'd asked me to choose between a job and my life. I wasn't confident she knew it wasn't an easy decision.

But I had made my mind up.

I clicked send on the email from my phone and walked up to her office door. She glanced up and I lifted my hand to wave. She frowned, but motioned for me to come in.

"Why are you here before everyone?" Celine asked.

"You mentioned needing my article first thing."

She nodded. "You've got it ready, then?"

"I just emailed it to you."

Celine turned to her desk and clicked a few times before she settled into reading. As I'd suspected, it wasn't long before she stopped and looked at me. "What is this?"

"It's the story I want to run," I said.

Celine touched her forehead. "Meg. We've been over this."

"I know we have, and I feel certain about this. I've never

been more sure in my life. This is the better article. It's well-written, it does Cullen and his family justice while also keeping the most important parts of their lives private. The other one you wanted is designed to be flashy and to get people reading, but it's not the story I want you to run."

"I hate to remind you of this, but you don't make the final decisions around here. I'm the editor. I'm the one with the experience. I know what's going to do well and I know what's going to help prove to our advertisers that we can get eyes on their ads. It's about money."

I shook my head. "It's not about money for me. You don't pay me enough to do that, and you couldn't if you tried. I'm not putting my name on an article I don't feel comfortable running."

"Your name is already on it. You wrote it and handed it in a while ago. You know this. I can run it." Her voice had become slightly more gentle. "It's really good. You should give yourself credit."

"It's not what I want. If you run it, consider this my official notice."

Celine's head jerked back slightly. Her eyes widened and she touched her throat with one hand.

"You can't be serious. This is the way the news works. You know this."

I shrugged. I had nothing else to say and I was done arguing. I took a deep breath in. "Goodbye." I turned and pulled the office door open with a shaking hand. I went to my desk to gather my things so I could leave before Celine had a chance to say anything else. As I hastily shoved whatever was in front of me into my bag, Ahmad came to the edge of my desk.

"I knew you'd figure things out." He winked at me and sipped his coffee.

"You're an expert on reading people." I smiled and reached out to place a hand on his arm. "Thank you."

He shook his head. "Not needed," he said. "I look forward to reading whatever comes next from you."

I was about to ask how he knew it would be something in writing, but he had already walked away.

Outside, on my way home, I typed out a message to Sarina.

I just quit my job

WHAT??? Are you okay?

Think so

My phone rang. Sarina's name flashed across my screen.

"What happened?" she asked.

"They want me to write in a way that's not okay with me. I don't feel good about it and they won't bend. So, I quit."

"Wow. Good for you. That takes a lot of courage."

A hint of a smile broke across my face. "Thanks." It would take a little adjustment, but I felt good about this. It was the right decision.

"So now what?" she asked.

"Now, I go home and figure out how to make money and have everything I want without compromising."

"Is that all? That should be easy," she deadpanned.

I laughed.

"Seriously, though, I'm happy for you. That took guts. If there's anything I can do to help, please let me know. Anything at all."

"I will." Thank goodness I had Sarina in my life. After we said our goodbyes, I walked in the direction of home.

On the way, I passed the coffee shop again. There was no reason for me to rush anywhere, so I stopped inside and grabbed another coffee before taking a seat. This time, I didn't pull out my journal and start writing. Instead, I sat back and watched people go by, rushing in and out of the shop. It wasn't long before a familiar face entered my line of sight.

"Meg?"

It was Adam. He'd remembered my name.

"Hi," I said, looking up at him. He was handsome. He had a friendly smile and warm, blue eyes. Interestingly enough, I felt nothing. Still, I smiled back at him.

"You haven't been around here much," he said.

"I've been out of town a lot."

"Oh? Anywhere interesting?"

"Yeah." When I didn't offer more of an answer he smiled politely and looked away, over at the counter. Maybe he knew I wasn't going to offer anything else, or maybe he wasn't looking for more. He could have simply been making small talk, and that was it. I didn't know, but I didn't care. It was nice to see a friendly face, but I had no interest in writing about him in my journal anymore. Suddenly, it was gone, like a wave washing over sand and disappearing onto the shore.

"Enjoy your day." He tipped his coffee cup at me and left.

I eventually made my way to my house. The pale grey walls reflected the morning light coming in through the windows. It was a cute, homey little place and I had liked it here. It had made me feel safe and comfortable. It had done its job. Now, I was ready for a change. I was ready to face the truth: it wasn't Old Port I had been avoiding all this time. It was what I'd thought it represented. I'd thought it had been a place where my family's world had fallen apart—and although it had once been that, it wasn't only that, and it didn't hold that power for me any longer. It was where I could see my future.

My story ran the following week. I was at Cullen's place when I first noticed it. I had picked up my phone while waiting for my morning coffee, scrolling through my various feeds. I noticed the headline first. Then my byline. Something in me couldn't bring myself to *not* look at the story. I needed to digest it first, so I could then prepare Cullen for it.

I braced myself as I scanned the first few sentences—and then I stopped. My pulse quickened. This wasn't the story I'd thought it would be. It was the one I'd wanted to run. The beautiful one. The one Cullen had wanted, too.

I read through the rest of it, the words familiar to me by now. When I finished, I sat and stared, mouth hanging open while I attempted to compose my thoughts.

"What's that?" Cullen appeared on the porch with two cups of coffee. He handed me one and nodded at my phone.

"It's the story."

He frowned, but only for a moment, as if he didn't want me to notice the change in his expression.

"It's the version I wanted," I said quickly.

Cullen's head moved back an inch. His forehead crinkled. "Really?"

I nodded.

"How?"

"I have no idea. I can't imagine Celine changed her mind."

He gazed over my shoulder. "Wow."

"I know."

He sat down and I put my phone away. We drank our coffee, a little quieter than usual, but I felt at ease. Somehow, it had worked out.

Later, when I emailed Celine, I left it to a couple of lines.

Saw the article. I don't know how that happened, but thank you.

I hadn't expected a reply, but when I got it, it was in true Celine fashion.

It wasn't my choice. Joanne saw both versions by accident and chose the one you wanted. She loved it. I still don't think it'll bring us the numbers we need.

Maybe sometimes things just had a way of working out for the best.

THIRTY-NINE

Over time, I settled into Old Port. My father wasn't ready to let go of my place in Boston, so he found renters. I moved most of my things in with Cullen. My mother was ecstatic that I would be her neighbor. Sarina was happy for me despite our distance, and she said it gave her an excuse to get away for a girls' weekend. I couldn't wait to spend more time with her in Old Port. In the meantime, I used my savings to get by until I figured out my career, and in my free time, I worked on my manuscript.

One afternoon, I sat in the living room on the couch and frowned at the screen of my laptop. Cullen had been walking by on his way to the kitchen.

"What's the face for? Are you stuck?"

"Yeah. Can you help?"

He came and sat next to me on the couch. I pointed my laptop towards him.

"These two characters. There's something not right."

Cullen scanned the page, his brow furrowed. "Have they had sex yet?"

"What? No, I haven't written a sex scene, if that's what you mean."

"You should."

I laughed. "Why?"

"Because you're good at writing and you're a romantic."

My face flamed. I was happy writing romance, but I hadn't yet been able to bring myself to write sex, despite Sarina's early insistence I should. I couldn't imagine someone reading my made-up sex scenes.

"Meg, you've got a steamy side. I know this by now." He raised his eyebrows at me and I laughed again. "I think you'd be great at writing it. And it could be fun. Remember that romance comes with benefits." He smiled at me before he nuzzled my neck with his mouth. He hadn't shaved in a couple of days and the roughness of his stubble grazing over my face made my skin tingle.

I considered what Cullen had said. This *was* fun. All of it. I was living and breathing the romance I'd always wanted, and I was writing it, too. The best of both worlds. I might as well make the most of it.

Eventually, I found my voice. I wrote and wrote until I had an entire manuscript. Then I set it aside for a while and searched for a new job, while enjoying every moment I had with Cullen and spending more and more time with my mother. It was as close to perfect as you could get.

I honestly didn't think about the *Globe* or my old job at all until Celine called out of the blue one afternoon. I was sitting on the porch, watching the sun rise while Cullen was still asleep in bed, when my phone rang.

"Joanne nominated you," Celine said in her blunt way. Even though I couldn't see her, I could picture her—sitting upright in her desk chair, frowning while she pinched the bridge of her nose.

"I'm sorry?" I asked.

"Your article on Cullen. Joanne nominated it for a Digital Publishing Award."

"Oh. That's—nice. Thank you for letting me know."

There was a long silence over the phone line. So long, I almost asked if she was still there. Then, Celine spoke again. This time, her tone was quieter, subdued.

"It was a great story. I think it deserves to win."

My mouth fell open. I wished I knew what to say, but I didn't. I remained silent until Celine spoke again.

"Please tell Cullen I'm sorry."

"Why?" I asked. It wasn't the right question, but it came out of my mouth before I could think about it.

Celine breathed out. "I've had a lot of time to reflect. I don't particularly like the way I handled this. I know I've got a tough exterior, but I care about people. I'm sorry I pushed for a story his family wasn't ready to tell. Again."

"Thank you. That's kind of you. I'll let him know." I hung up the phone and stared at it in my hand. People, I thought, never cease to surprise you.

"Who was that?" Cullen came outside, his hair a mess and creases from his pillow still carved into the side of his face. He stretched his arms above his head, revealing part of his tanned stomach.

"It was Celine. My article on you was nominated for an award."

"That's fantastic!" He swept me up into a hug. "I'm so happy for you. Congrats." He kissed me then sat beside me, taking my hand and squeezing it.

"And Celine wanted me to tell you she's sorry."

"Okay," he said. "That's a lot to take in first thing in the morning."

"I know. How do you feel about it?"

Cullen shrugged. "It's nice, but it doesn't change a lot. I'm here with you. I'm happier than I've ever been."

I leaned in closer to him. "I feel the same."

And I did. Finally, I had let him in, stopped hiding. And when I had, I'd ended up with so much.

It was better than I could have ever written.

FORTY

ONE YEAR LATER

My head was lowered, and my shoulders were hunched over my laptop. The chatter from the coffee drinkers around me didn't break my concentration. I was in the zone. Flow-state. It felt so good to be here at Peach Coffee, writing. Or I suppose I was in the editing phase. After spending a long time looking for an agent, I'd found one. And then, a publisher—a publisher my agent and I had found on our own, without Cullen pulling any strings for me. They loved my manuscript. Now I was editing it and getting it ready for publication. Like I was a real romance author or something.

The coffee shop was quieter than usual. It was fall and the summer tourists had all left town, but it was still warm enough for me to enjoy the patio, thankfully. I sat outside, shaded by a colorful umbrella. It wouldn't be long before they were closed up for the season. I had only experienced one winter in Old Port, and it had been mild. My mother had told me Old Port winters were typically very cold and grey, but somehow still managed to be romantic. I'd wondered if she'd said that just for me, or if it were the truth. It didn't matter. I was here now, living in Old Port and about to publish my first romance novel.

If you had told me that a year ago, I never would have believed it.

I scrolled back in the document until I got to the dedication and scanned what I had written.

For Cullen. You're the reason I can write romance so honestly.

And for Sarina. You're right. I do sex well.

A voice came from the far side of the patio. It was a familiar voice, deep and also smooth like honey, speaking to a waitress by the doors to the inside of the shop. Cullen. He stood there glancing around, eyes searching. When they connected with mine, they softened, became rounder. He smiled and raised a hand at me. Then he turned back to the waitress and said something to her, nodding and smiling.

He made his way to me, and when he approached the table, he stood over me.

"Meg."

"Hi?" I squinted one eye at the sun and smiled at him. "Do you want to sit?"

His body seemed to relax, his shoulders dropping, his arms loose at his side. "I didn't want to break your concentration."

I shook my head. "No, no. Come join me. I'm done." I was ready for a break anyway. This was one of the real, great benefits of living together. Cullen was in my world at any moment. In a flash, we were together.

He took the seat next to me instead of across from me. "What are you drinking?"

"A regular drip coffee—the best coffee around, though."

He raised his own takeaway cup of coffee at me. "Agree."

"So, what's the plan for today?" I asked. This was our life now. Casual, relaxed. I was getting by on the advance I had made on my book, and Cullen was still doing very well with his.

When his next book had come out, it had been as hugely successful as the one before it. He had made it. Again.

"I'm not sure. I thought maybe we could go to the bakery and get some of those cinnamon buns they make on Sundays."

I nodded in agreement. Cinnamon buns and quiet Sundays with Cullen. How had I gotten so lucky?

Cullen's phone buzzed. He looked at the screen and pursed his lips.

"Do you have to take that?" I asked.

He shook his head. "Nah. It can wait."

He reached for my hand and interlaced his fingers with mine. The feel of his smooth, warm skin sent a thrill through my arm. It had been over a year since we'd met, but the fluttering feeling was still there. I was consumed by Cullen. He brought the best out in me. I had managed to find love, and now I believed that it could work. I was living it.

"Should we go?" Cullen asked, with a smile.

I grinned back. "In a minute."

I was in no rush.

I'm so thankful *At the Ocean's Edge* found its way to you, and I hope you loved reading about Meg and Cullen. If you want to join other readers in hearing all about my new releases and bonus content, you can sign up for my newsletter:

www.stormpublishing.co/heather-dixon

If you could also spare a few moments to leave a review, that would be hugely appreciated. Even a short review can make all the difference in encouraging a reader to discover my books for the first time. Thank you so much!

Like Meg, I have always loved love—especially when expressed in books, movies, music and on the stage. There is something so enjoyable and satisfying about a well-told love story. A while ago, after I had been in a bit of a reading slump (I blame Covid for this), I picked up a book by an author named Annabel Monaghan. She had written the book *Nora Goes Off Script*, and I was instantly swept up in Nora's world. I didn't want to put it down even for a minute. It was a beautiful love story, with rich characters, and I especially loved that the protagonist was close to forty years old and had children. After I read it, I knew I wanted to write a love story. It was scary for me, because I had only written about love between mothers and daughters and sisters up until this point. But it was something I knew I wanted to try to do. I wanted to see if I could write one of those stories that you don't want to put down. A book that might remind you of that frenzied, falling-in-love stage of life. A book that entertains. A book you can escape with. I hope you found all of that and more with this book.

Thank you again, so much, for being part of this amazing journey into love and romance and storytelling with me. I hope you'll stay in touch—I have so many more stories to entertain you with.

Heather

www.heatherdixon.ca

ACKNOWLEDGEMENTS

Every year, after watching the Oscars, I lie in bed at night before I fall asleep, imagining what I would say in my acceptance speech if I won a writing award. Here's my chance to (hopefully) be witty and heartfelt and tell all of you how grateful I truly, truly am.

Thank you to my incredible, kind, encouraging, brilliant editor, Vicky Blunden. I consider myself very lucky to work with you and I'm so grateful for your guidance. Huge thanks to Oliver Rhodes and everyone at Storm Publishing who has had a hand in making this book come to life. You are helping me realize my dreams every single day.

A massive thank you to my wonderful agent, Carolyn Forde. I'm still in shock that I get to write those words. *My agent, Carolyn Forde.* I am so thrilled we found our way to one another and I'm extremely grateful that we get to work together. My gratitude also goes to everyone at the incredible Transatlantic Agency.

I have to thank all of the wonderful writing friends in my life, because I absolutely would not be doing this without all of you. Georgina Kelly, Lydia Laceby and Rosemary Twomey, thank you for reading early pages of everything I write and encouraging me endlessly. Jackie Khalilieh—our voice note conversations are better than podcasts. Thank you for listening to me, letting me vent, providing me with advice and encouragement. It means so very much. And thank you to Sydney Leigh for our long conversations and pep talks. I will always be by your side at fancy agency events as long as you'll have me! Thank you to everyone in the Toronto Area Women Authors group. I leave every get-together feeling energized and excited to write. And thank you to the SPs. (If you know, you know.)

Thank you to the incredible bookstagrammers I've met, for championing books and getting them into readers' hands. Thank you to my local library—one of my favourite places to be! And to Parampreet Khanuja for putting on the most incredible events for readers. A special thank you to Karma Brown for always being so kind and generous with your time. And a massive thank you to the readers. I wouldn't be here if you weren't willing to take a chance on me. Thank you, thank you, thank you.

To my family—my mom and dad, who I love very much. What can I say except thank you for basically everything. It all started with you!

And thank you to my most favourite humans on the face of the planet—my three daughters. I love that you think I'm kind of famous. And thank you for telling me that one day I'm going to be big, big time.

Finally, to Andrew. You are the one I model all of my loveable male characters with broad shoulders on. We may be long, long past the flirty, falling-in-love phase of life, but what we have is something so real and hard and wonderful and messy and perfect. I love you, and I love our love story. Thank you for being the strong and steady ice to my fire.